THE TRIPLE POINT OF WATER

The
Triple Point
of
Water

Fiona Dunscombe

Polygon

First published in Great Britain in 2007 by
Polygon, an imprint of Birlinn Ltd
West Newington House
10 Newington Road
Edinburgh
EH9 1QS

www.birlinn.co.uk

ISBN 10: 1 84967 000 8
ISBN 13: 978 1 84697 000 9

The publisher acknowledges subsidy from the

Scottish
Arts Council

towards the publication of this volume

British Library Cataloguing-in-Publication Data
A catalogue record for this book is available on request from the British Library.

Typeset by Palimpsest Book Production Limited, Grangemouth, Stirlingshire
Printed by Creative Print & Design, Ebbw Vale, Wales

To Father John with love and thanks

And there is me ... not knowing what a father is, what he should do, or even what a man is now. This speculation about fathers isn't only local: there is a profound relation between the sort of families that exist in a particular society – the family ideal, as it were – and the kind of political system that's possible.

Hanif Kureishi, *My Ear at His Heart*

PROLOGUE

Soho, London 1990

Saf's father is missing. The same could be said of my own, although I'm making no effort to find him. I'm sitting underneath the mirrors where we do our make-up, holding on tight to a broken wine glass.

'I couldn't see anything,' Saf says. 'At least . . . last time . . . there was a moon.'

Almost directly in front of me are Saf's feet. She sits with her legs crossed at the ankles. Her feet, encased in a pair of scarlet and silver sandals, rest elegantly on the chrome pedestal of the old office chair in which she sits. There's a make-up bench above my head so she and I can't see each other, but she speaks slowly, pausing between words, and I know from this that she's fixing her false eyelashes on. (False eyelashes are compulsory here, as are red lipstick, red nail varnish, and weighing the same as you did when you came in.)

I don't say anything and she carries on. 'This time he was just . . . a shape. I was scared to go close.'

Saf thinks her dad is homeless. Day or night, a few times a week she'll wander the streets peering into the faces of down-and-outs. She must have seen just about every tramp in London by now, but the tramp in St James Park is new. She hasn't seen his face yet.

She uncrosses her legs, swivels her chair sideways and steps down. I put the broken wine glass back on the floor as her sandals retreat to the far side of the room, where she retrieves her crown from the shelf.

Saf's solo act is called 'Miss United Kingdom' and she's on straight after the parade, which is where everyone else is now. I watch her as she adjusts her crown. Her body is very angular:

broad hips with protruding bones, long, rectangular thighs and square kneecaps. She looks better than Superwoman in the scarlet bikini and silver cape of the Miss United Kingdom costume.

She opens the dressing-room door and music from the stage comes thumping in. Then she turns around and looks back at me, bending slightly to see me better. 'Are you okay, Harri?' she says.

'Yeah, yeah, fine,' I say and wave my arm around a bit, noting the way it feels as though it doesn't belong to me. The music is muffled again as she closes the door.

I've worked in the Pageant for three years, and this is the first time I've sat in precisely this place. There's a feeling that the carpet isn't all that clean, especially if you haven't got any clothes on, and we mostly haven't. If I didn't work here I'd probably imagine the girls wearing dressing gowns backstage, but for the most part it's too hot, we're accustomed to being nude, and we can't be bothered to dress in between costumes.

I bite my top lip, forgetting that it's gritty with glitter. I had already put on full stage make-up when I came to sit here. I'm also wearing high-heeled, gold, T-bar sandals, and my gold 'harness', which is a pattern of thin gold straps outlining my breasts, fastened on with press-studs at the back of my neck and around my waist.

I told the others to tell Sean our stage manager that I'm ill. He'll dock my wages of course. At Vincent Veroni's Pageant of Venus we lose a 'bonus' of one hundred and twenty-five pounds for a night off sick, and smaller amounts for other misdemeanours. Last time I lost bonus money it was twenty quid for not wearing red nail varnish – my nails are bitten down and red nail varnish just makes them look a mess. Tracey, Vince Veroni's daughter and our choreographer, says the audience can't see that much detail: apparently they just get a vague impression of long red nails. Everyone laughed at that afterwards. Saf said, 'She's talking about *her* vague impression of things, the dope-head!'

'If we can see the creases on their faces, they can see the creases on our arses!' shouted Lynn.

'Yeah – you don't need a gynaecologist anymore – just ask 'em to file a report on the way out!'

Actually we see about the first five rows fairly clearly from the stage. We identify regulars from time to time. There's a couple who come in about once a week at the moment. At first we thought the guy, bearded and overweight, was bringing a different woman with him on each visit. Then we realised it was the same woman, in different wigs and outfits.

The Miner is another regular. He's got black rings under his eyes. Elaine says he looks like her dad after a day down the pit. The Miner's been coming for as long as anyone can remember. We like the Couple and the Miner because they look at our faces, at least when we're looking at them, and they smile sometimes. But now and then someone will spot a wanker.

Wankers are not allowed. Two or three times now since I've been here one or other of the girls has come off stage shouting 'Wanker!' and Sean will ask her where the man is. Sean has to phone front of house to tell them. If she's lucky the next girl on will see Brian, the front-of-house manager, shining his torch along rows of disconcerted faces.

Once Graham, our man on the spotlight, actually directed the beam at the man Lynn had spotted, a newspaper on his lap, hand moving quickly in the dark.

Looking at my own hands now I see they are rough and dry. Red nail varnish bleeds over the edge of each ragged nail onto skin. I pick up the broken glass again and cup the shattered edge in my left hand, applying pressure with my right, watching the skin turn white.

I remember standing on the polished wooden threshold of the sitting room at my parent's house, in a new blue velvet dress. I was eleven years old, all dressed up for a friend's birthday party, and pretty pleased with the way I looked.

'Dad!' I said.

Except for a pair of crossed legs Dad was invisible behind the *Daily Telegraph.*

'Dad!'

The paper crumpled in the middle and Dad appeared to one side of it. I smiled, there was a pause, and then, 'What big hands you've got! What big red hands!' He threw back his head and guffawed.

I used to feel ugly all over then; now it's mostly my hands and feet. The rest of me doesn't feel beautiful, but lots of other people seem to think it is. When I sleep with men they never take any notice of my hands and feet. Except Andy. Andy put my hands inside his so I felt like they belonged there. He called them 'precious little hands' once. It made me laugh with delight, because it was so outrageous, contradicting my father, and the factual evidence, all in one go.

I release my left hand from the grip of my right, and examine it. There are only indentations; I didn't even break the skin. The glass in my hand is cheaply thick like plastic, and I have to push down hard now to cut into my wrist. There's blood, but it's not deep enough. I carve at the skin again, but the glass is too blunt. So I turn it around to find the sharpest point.

I stab at and puncture an artery, just as the others walk back in from the parade. Olga is first and she swears in Polish, turning to push her way back through the arrangement of girls and gold ruffles in the doorway.

There is a dark fuzz like visual pins and needles creeping in around the edge of my sight. It soaks up everything I can see like blotting paper, until there's only black.

PART ONE

PART ONE

Nottinghamshire 1969

Listen! We are beginning our story! When we arrive at the end of it we shall, it is to be hoped, know more than we do now. There was once a magician! A wicked magician!! A most wicked magician!!! Great was his delight at having constructed a mirror possessing this peculiarity – that everything good and beautiful, when reflected in it, shrank up almost to nothing, whilst those things that were ugly and useless were magnified and made to appear ten times worse than before.

The loveliest landscapes reflected in this mirror looked like boiled spinach; and the handsomest persons appeared ugly, or as if standing on their heads; their features so distorted that their friends could never have recognised them. Moreover, if one of them had a freckle, he might be sure that it would seem to spread over the nose and mouth; and if a good or pious thought glanced across his mind a wrinkle was seen in the mirror.

I looked carefully at the picture of the Real Princess, asleep on top of twenty mattresses and twenty feather beds. At six years old I knew two big things about princesses: they had lovely tiny feet to fit into glass slippers and they would always know if they were sleeping on a pea.

The next story was 'Goldilocks and the Three Bears', but I renamed her Darkilocks when I was reading the story to myself. At school we had this story too, but it was better. My book said Darkilocks wasn't a very nice little girl, because she went into someone else's house without asking and used their things. But I never really believed she was bad. When I read the other Darkilocks book, the one at school, I knew I was right because it didn't say anything about her being bad, it just had the story.

I wondered where Darkilocks came from, and where she went. I thought she was trying to find a place for herself – she didn't know the house belonged to bears, or that she was a completely different kind of animal.

On the last page of the book was a picture of Darkilocks running away from the three bears' house. In my book she ran away when she saw the bears coming back, but in the school book the bears surprised her and chased her out of their house. It made me feel cross, the different endings. I wanted the truth. Were the bears good or bad? I stared at the pictures, looking for clues on their faces.

But I could no longer see the pictures clearly. There was too little light, despite it being only early afternoon. I looked up. A blurry darkness had descended on the kitchen. Through the window I could see the sky was black with clouds. There would be thunder and lightning soon.

Dad sat in a corner underneath his recently acquired reading light. He was bent forwards over one of the huge newspapers he was always reading. He held it open with a hand at each side, his elbows resting on the armrests of a big, blue, scooped-out armchair. He was long and thin, and in this position he looked a bit like a triangle with legs. I could see the top of his head where some hair was missing and his scalp shone in the light.

I took a few steps forward, until I was standing on his left. The material of my dress touched his arm and he frowned, glancing round quickly, then back to the paper again. I stood on tiptoe and reached over awkwardly to put my arms around his neck. My right hand made contact briefly with the skin above his collar, but he sat up abruptly, shaking me off.

I moved my hand to his upper arm, which felt surprisingly hard. He looked at it as if an insect had landed on him.

'Arabella. What do you think you're doing?' he demanded.

Some energy he let loose on me, something invisible and

intangible, but with all the sudden undeniable force of a strong wind, prevented me from saying that I was going to kiss him.

He shook the paper, then leaned back holding it up in front of him like a shield, rendering us invisible to each other.

Nottinghamshire 1972

How delightful it was to sit under those rose trees, which seemed
as if they never intended to leave off blossoming!

It was my turn to bang the gong that hung by the kitchen
door. This was an old brass thing Dad had got in a junk shop.
It had a felt-headed drumstick attached to it on a piece of string
and we used it to summon Dad for his meals.

Dad's passion was machinery. If he wasn't at work or reading
the paper he was usually in his workshop. An old brick barn
which stood at the far end of the field behind our house, his
workshop was a place full of bits of old cars and motorbikes, cans
of oil, and lots of unidentifiable tools and pieces of metal.

I stood on the back step and banged the gong ten times – any
more and Mum would come and take it off me. Then I went
and took my place on the bench seat at the kitchen table, where
I sat and waited hungrily with my younger brother, Teddy.

We listened to Dad's heavy tread as he arrived in the utility
room. He wore steel toe-capped boots when he was in his workshop, and now I knew he would be changing them for a pair of
black leather carpet slippers.

He made a lot of noise slapping his hands around vigorously
under the utility-room tap. A smell of oil and Swarfega, an interesting, green, jelly-like substance Dad used instead of soap, wafted
through the open doorway.

'I've replaced that main driving-pin, Eileen!' he shouted to
Mum.

Mum was busy rinsing off cooking pans in the kitchen sink
but she stopped when Dad entered the kitchen. He sat down at

13

the head of the table in an upright wooden chair with a high back and smooth, polished arms.

'I've sorted out the problem with the injector valve too.'

Mum said nothing, only gave him a little half smile, a response which conveyed acknowledgement, both of the fact he'd spoken, and that she had absolutely no idea what he was talking about. She finished dishing out the lunch, then sat at the other end of the long oak table in a chair of a lighter wood than his, with no arms.

Being understood or not didn't make any difference to Dad, who continued to enthuse about cylinder drain cocks, crankshaft rotation and connecting rods while we ate. This mechanical language was poetry to him, and his enthusiasm for his current project – rebuilding an old steam engine – took him into a realm where he was completely confident in his ability to interest anyone in his latest boiler inspection.

Struts and pistons with carrots; cogs and bearings with potatoes; I had long ago digested the basics concerning the engine, which Dad always referred to as 'our' engine, having convinced himself, or perhaps just trying to convince Mum, that he had embarked upon a worthy, family-oriented mission. I knew for example that our engine was a traction engine, a road locomotive of a type that had been used in the past for heavy haulage, carrying stuff that was too heavy or too big for the railways to transport. I knew that it had a compound engine, in which the steam is used twice, and belly tanks to hold water for long journeys. I wasn't mechanically minded, and in any case Dad's engineering eloquence was mostly reserved for Mum, but some of the information just went down with the food.

It was hot the day Dad's steam engine finally appeared, like a genie or a giant beanstalk in our back yard. I walked home from school in a mid-afternoon stillness that was difficult to move through. My bag was heavy and I was feeling uncomfortable in my polyester dress. There would be, I thought, nothing to do when I arrived. I walked slowly up the drive, catching and pulling at strands of weeping willow which over-hung it. I let one hand trail on the surface of the painted blue drainpipe as I rounded the corner of the house. Then I stopped and stared.

It stood in the middle of our yard with heat emanating from it, as if it had burned its way through the core of the earth to reach us: Dad's steam engine, shining black and brass, with red wheels higher than the top of the kitchen window.

Way above my head on the boiler barrel was a red nameplate with gold writing: THOR. Higher still the engine's black chimney seemed to touch the sky.

I stared and stared. It seemed to me that this proud giant stood in a blaze of light, magical light which spoke of its glory days, of one heart-stopping romance in the Industrial Revolution.

There was a hiss of steam and Dad appeared, almost leaping around the engine, telling us all about his plan to get steam up, find water stops, and drive to Rempstone rally single-handed.

Dad got up at four o'clock in the morning to light the fire in Thor's boiler. He had to wait several hours for the pressure to build up to full steam and he pottered around the engine checking and polishing. He'd bought an authentic Romany caravan to tow behind Thor and now he hitched it up to the back of the engine with a huge iron pin. My mother had already packed the caravan with food and bedding, but Dad filled a container with orange squash to drink on the journey. He put lots of salt tablets in it, telling us as he did so that this would help replenish his body's supply of salt, as he expected to sweat a lot shovelling coal.

It would take Thor two days to get to Rempstone, travelling at walking pace. When the pressure gauge showed steam up, Dad added a jaunty red neckerchief to his usual outfit of blue over-alls and set off. Mum, Teddy and I lined up by the front gate to see him go. We were going to meet him at the rally in a few days.

The engine filled our lane with no room to pass either side. As it moved forward it made a deafening, clanking noise and the iron wheels left deep indentations in the tarmac. It disappeared around a bend, but there was lots of loud chuffing, and we could see intermittent balls of smoke thrown high in the sky as Dad encountered the hill on the main road. When he reached the top he blew the whistle in triumph and when I heard it I felt like one of the Railway Children.

The rally was another country. Everything was so different to the way it was at home. On Friday night we slept in a cupboard in the gypsy caravan. The cupboard had a sliding wooden door and inside it smelled like seaweed. It was underneath Mum and Dad's bed which was high up off the ground. I awoke in the early hours to hear Mum and Dad giggling like schoolchildren as they returned from the beer tent and tried to clamber up. I felt I was on a great raft in uncharted waters, but I fell asleep sure in the knowledge it would take us to morning.

Loudspeakers woke us with piped classical music and the sound of brass marching bands. Outside the air smelled of sooty black magic. We stood in our pyjamas on the caravan steps and watched as steam wagons driven by young lads bounced over ruts in the grass, going too fast, Mum said.

We hurried to dress ourselves and then, carrying our loo roll, we made our way through the dewy grass, where engines stood in rows, simmering like kettles. Men flourishing oily rags climbed all over them or, dwarfed by giant wheels, stood talking quietly together, looking out across the fields with their arms folded.

The toilets were just wooden boxes straddling a deep ditch. The hole in the wooden seat was too big, and I perched precariously, peering down between my legs at the abyss below. The smell was terrible, and I worried that flies might land on my bottom.

When we had added our own loo paper to the pattern of white streamers several feet below us, we walked back past the white plastic tarpaulins and metal poles of the stall holders setting up. We skirted around the still sleeping fairground, eyeing it suspiciously, as if it were the deep dark woods of a fairytale. Fairground people were bad, and the fair was out of bounds to Teddy and me until Sunday, when Dad had promised to take us on the only rides he thought had enough skill or showmanship to them: the cakewalk, the galloping horses and the helter-skelter.

Back at the caravan Dad ran a little brass tap at the back of Thor, filling a red washing-up bowl with hot water. He set it down on the caravan steps and we fetched our toilet bags and washed our hands and faces.

We sat casually on the caravan steps to eat in a way that seemed like wild abandon to me as it contrasted so completely with meals together at home. Dad went around the back of the caravan to tip the dirty water away on the field. We watched as he reappeared and bent down by Thor with the empty bowl, half filling it again with a carefully measured amount of hot water. He added a quick squirt of Fairy Liquid from an unusually filthy white and green bottle and left the bowl on the grass at the bottom of the steps, ready for Mum to do the dishes.

Next, he hauled a huge plastic container out from underneath the caravan. It was full of cold water for teeth-cleaning, and too heavy for anyone except Dad to move.

'Come and clean your teeth,' he ordered, and we followed him to the back of the caravan.

Teddy and I brushed our teeth to a foam, smirking as we did so in anticipation of what came next. Then we spat white gobs of toothpaste onto the grass, exploding with nervous laughter at the outrageous impropriety of it, less because we were doing it in public than because we were doing it in front of Dad.

The next couple of hours were spent polishing and watching the pressure gauge. Dad fetched oily rags, one for Teddy and one for me. He lifted Teddy up onto Thor's belly tank where he could wipe the brass nameplate, and I scrubbed away at the lower parts of the huge red wheels. The reward for polishing was a ride round the ring, and for this Teddy and I sat in the coal bunker.

The massive engine moved slowly away from its parking slot in front of the caravan and we lifted our legs out of the way of Dad's coal shovel, listening for Thor's name and description to come over the loudspeakers.

Pressing against the rope surrounding the ring were crowds of people who didn't own engines. 'Enthusiasts,' Dad said; I could tell he was scornful of them. Perhaps he felt a bit like a king as we paraded around high above everything, men without engines hoisting little children up on their shoulders to see us better.

Now the air smelled of everything: hot dogs and onions, coal and potatoes, oil and brandy snaps. Thor jolted along, clacking and hissing, lurching from side to side as we sank down a little in those places where the ground was softer.

Above the heads of our audience, multi-coloured streamers flapped on poles placed around the perimeter of the ring. On grass the noise of Thor was no longer deafening and I could hear the celebratory sound of an organ, as well as a klaxon from one of the fairground rides.

Just ahead of me Thor's flywheel turned, pistons pumped, and the black tower of the chimney, which seemed a long way off in front, lead us around the ring. I turned to look behind us and saw a showman's engine with all its lights on. The driver and his mate had rosy faces. They grinned and one of them reached up and pulled the chain which blew the whistle. The sound, so loud and shrill, made me jump when it came, even though I'd been expecting it. I laughed, catching sight as I did so of excited faces at the ringside, strangers all smiling and waving. I turned back to see Dad leaning forward to blow Thor's whistle and then all of the other engines in the ring blew theirs, some more than once. I could imagine Bonfire Night and Christmas were about to arrive together.

I gripped the side of the coal bunker and looked up at Dad. His face was poker straight as usual, but his body language had changed, so he looked looser and more relaxed. His face glowing, he reached again for the chain that would release steam and make the whistle blow. Thor responded to Dad, our conductor, our majestic controller – the whistle shrilled and we thundered forwards.

A lot of people took photographs, and one photographer followed us back to our caravan. He said he was from the newspaper and he took several shots of Dad shovelling coal, as well as some of Teddy and me sitting in the coal bunker. Then he said, 'Can the little girl stand on the caravan steps for a minute?'

I looked at Dad, doubtful of his permission. But he was jumping around looking really pleased and agreed straightaway.

'Absolutely! Arabella, just go and stand over there.' Then, too impatient to watch me scramble down from the coal-bunker, he held his arms up. I jumped into them willingly. As he carried me over to the caravan I made the most of his rare and unexpected proximity, surreptitiously brushing my nose against the tips of his ears, breathing in deeply his perfume of oil and coal dust.

The photographer asked me to take my engine driver's cap off, which I was a bit sorry about because I felt like Casey Jones in it, and he took two more photos of me sitting on the caravan steps. Dad shook his hand and asked which paper the photos were for.

It was the local evening newspaper and Dad appeared with it the following evening as Mum was getting tea. There was a photo of me with a dirty face sitting in front of the caravan, and a headline that said, 'GYPSIES? NO!' The story called me an authentic-looking character, and said that Dad was a chartered accountant and steam-engine enthusiast. There was another picture with a line-up of engines but none of Thor, Dad or Ted.

Dad's face fell. 'They've absolutely no interest in steam engines whatsoever!' he said. 'All they want to do is cobble together some ridiculous story. The chap took some super pictures of Thor and they haven't even used them!' He folded the newspaper. 'Well, I don't know what I expected,' he said. 'The chap's name was *Smith*.'

I looked at Mum to see her reaction, wondering if she had known about the man's name before. Smiths, that is to say, people called Smith, were one of Dad's pet hates. Even worse were people who tried to disguise the fact they were called Smith with a double-barrelled family name like Bradley-Smith. Dad would laugh and point to those names wherever he came across them. 'We all know this is really a Smith,' he'd say. I wasn't allowed to play with Smiths because they were common, so the fact that Dad had been nice to the reporter at all was surprising.

'An ignorant Smith! Hah!' Dad stuck the newspaper in the bin for burning.

'Dad! I want to see it!' I said and Teddy joined in, 'Yes, Dad, we want to look at it for longer.'

'Oh, let them see it, Duncan,' said Mum who had looked over Dad's shoulder briefly, then gone back to preparing tea. Dad fished it back out of the bin, put it on the table and bent down to unlace his boots. Teddy and I unfolded the paper again and scrutinised my picture and the words underneath.

'What does "authentic" mean?' I asked.

'It means that you look as you're supposed to,' Mum said. Then we had to clear the table so she could put the food down on it.

I was sitting on some coal sacks in between Thor and the next-door engine when a lady called to me from the Romany caravan parked next to ours.

'Hello! Hello!' she said smiling and waving. She beckoned me over with a long orange arm, 'Come over here, I've got something for you.'

I got up and walked towards her pretty caravan a little hesitantly, thinking about the sugar-candy house in 'Hansel and Gretel'.

'That's it. Come on,' she said, like someone talking to a small animal. Then she turned and vanished back inside her caravan. I stood still, not sure if she had changed her mind, but she was back in a few seconds, brandishing two battered-looking books.

'Books,' she said as she gave them to me, looking pleased with herself. 'You can keep these if you want. Sit down there and read them.' She nodded towards her caravan steps.

I sat and looked at the books she'd given me. The first was *The Brownie Guide Handbook*, which I already had at home. I had tried very hard to be interested in it, but it was full of things like being a WW (Willing Worker). This meant cheerfully doing things you didn't want to do. Or you could be a GCU (Good Cleaner-upper), or both. There were things that sounded great like 'Ventures' and 'Challenges', but they all seemed to involve making aprons or dolls' clothes, cleaning and collecting things, and looking after old people. I opened the handbook anyway, to be polite.

The first line on the page on the left asked, 'Have you some good washerwomen in the pack?' My eyes fled to the first line on the page on the right: 'Are you remembering to be a good GCU and a WW?' Underneath there were pictures of happy Brownies leaping around cleaning things. I felt guilty. I should be happier. I should enjoy helping my mother. I shut the handbook and put it down on the step on which I was sitting.

The other book had a picture of Little Red Riding Hood on the cover. Above her head were the words 'Fairy Tales', written in gold. This was clearly too young for me. Didn't she have any Enid Blyton? I opened a page at random anyway. It was the start of a story: 'The Snow Queen' by Hans Christian Andersen. A tall, glittering queen in a white cape stared cold-eyed from the page. I was transfixed by the mixture of beauty and cruelty in her face.

The orange lady's voice came from behind me, 'Do you know that one?' I shook my head, surprised at finding a new fairytale. 'It's one of my favourites,' the woman said. 'Read it, go on, see what you think.'

So I sat and read about the wicked magician who made an evil mirror that broke into a million pieces. The fragments scattered and fell into people, and then they saw and felt things all wrong. I read about Kay the little boy who got a piece of mirror in his eye and another in his heart, how he left his best friend Gerda and was taken away by the Snow Queen. The Snow Queen kissed Kay and when she did that he sort of froze inside until he couldn't feel or remember anything anymore. He sat in the Snow Queen's palace for years doing a giant jigsaw puzzle made out of pieces of ice from a frozen lake. His friend Gerda went to look for him and she had lots of adventures on the way. She met a little robber-girl who was going to kill her but then helped her instead. When Gerda got to the ice palace Kay didn't know who she was, until Gerda kissed him. Then the icy splinters in his eye and his heart melted and he remembered, but he was all grown up at the end and so was Gerda.

The orange lady came back before I'd finished reading and she sat looking over my shoulder. It was such a good story, I was only vaguely aware that she was there. When I finished I felt as though I was still in the story, sitting with Kay in the palace of the Snow Queen, trying to make sense of the ice puzzle.

I looked up at the lady, who was watching me with her head on one side. 'When our dining-room mirror got broken, Mum said it was seven years of bad luck,' I said.

The lady nodded, then reached over and smoothed the pages of the book with her fingers. 'All the answers are in there. And all the questions.'

'What questions?'

'Every question you've ever asked or will ask. Ask something and see.'

My mind went blank. 'I can't think of anything.'

'Don't worry. It's hard when you're put on the spot. The best questions always come when you're on your own anyway.'

'Yes,' I said. I knew what she meant.

After lunch I went to see Auntie Irene in the huge modern caravan that belonged to her and Uncle Donald.

Irene and Donald were old friends of Mum and Dad, and Donald had an engine too. They had to park their caravan in the next field because it wasn't in keeping with caravans like ours. But Auntie Irene said she didn't mind having to walk a bit further for her 'creature comforts'.

Dad scoffed at Irene and Donald's modern caravan, but I liked it because there were lots of comfy seats with big cushions. When I sat down I sort of sunk in.

'Did you see my picture in the paper, Auntie Irene?'

'Yes I did, and I saw that your face could have done with a wash!'

'It said I looked authentic! Mum says it means I look as I'm supposed to. What am I supposed to look like?'

'You're supposed to look like you and that's all,' Auntie Irene said.

But later on, when I was playing frisbee behind the beer tent with Teddy he said, 'Authentic means you look like a gypsy, Uncle Donald said. You could be a gypsy, because you've got black curly hair.'

I thought this was great. Carlotta, my favourite Enid Blyton character, was a gypsy and a daring tomboy.

'I am a gypsy,' I said as I turned a cartwheel. 'I might tell fortunes when I'm older, or I could join a circus.'

'I'm going to join the circus and do stunts on a motorbike,' Teddy said.

'Well you can't, because you've got blond hair.'

I read 'The Snow Queen' by torchlight, knowing I shouldn't. Mum would go mad if she found me with a light on. But Mum and Dad had gone to the beer tent. I'd heard them leave.

It was a bit scary in the creaky cupboard bed, even with Teddy next to me. I shone the torch at him, almost wishing he'd wake up, but he had already dreamed himself far away.

I found myself thinking of Teddy when I read about Kay, the boy in the story, but then I cried when the queen kissed him. I even had to lift the bedcovers to check Teddy hadn't turned blue. Maybe I could be Kay instead, and Teddy could be Gerda? Dad would be the wicked magician and Mum the Snow Queen. Or was it the other way around? As I read on, I imagined myself being those characters too.

But after a while I got scared, wondering whether it was possible to imagine things into existence. I was afraid and tired and I tried to stop reading but the words pulled me on.

When I reached the end I was still worrying. In the morning I'd need to find the caravan woman again; I had an important question to ask her. Could a story, or reading a story, make things happen?

Camden, London 1986

While they were in the midst of their play, a large sledge painted white passed by . . . When the sledge had driven twice round the square, Kay bound to it his little sledge, and was carried on with it.

T he Camden Palace nightclub was packed full of posers like me, pounded by the music, cooking in the heat on the dance floor. When it got too hot I walked up the central steps to the Star Bar. The cast iron stairway ran straight upwards from the centre of the room, with a narrow platform at the halfway point. It was the only place to get some air, away from the push and jostle of sweaty bodies, and it was a great place for being seen. I was wearing a black bra, a tiny, black, see-through tutu, French knickers and fishnet tights.

As I reached the halfway platform a man approached me. He was about ten years older than me, tall and thin, with frizzy blonde hair and steel-framed spectacles.

'Hi! My name's Jasper, I'm a photographer. Can I talk to you for a sec?'

'Yeah – sure.'

'You look great,' he said.

'Thank you.'

'Look – I'll come straight –' He was shouting to be heard above the music and people were bumping into us as they tried to get past. He beckoned and I followed him up the next flight of steps.

The Star Bar had sofas, but they were all full. He found a corner and stood in it, facing me.

'I'll get straight to the point. I'm a photographer. I work for several magazines, all men's magazines, and I'd really like to get some shots of you.'

'No, I don't think so – not for men's magazines.'

'Why not? You'd get paid well.'

'How much?

'Two hundred quid a shoot.'

'And what would I have to do for that then?'

He shrugged. 'Just have some photos taken.'

'What would I wear?'

'Just as you are now. What you're wearing now is great.' He grinned, 'I mean – you're not wearing much are you?'

'No, I suppose I'm not.'

There was a pause during which I thought about two hundred quid. Then Jasper said, 'Oh look, leave it. Don't worry about it. It's just a few photos, that's all. And you can earn good money for it. But if you don't want to do it, I'll go and find someone who does.'

I think it was his displeasure that clinched it, following so quickly on the heels of his approval. I didn't like the way he spoke like he'd given up on me, like I was no good after all.

'Hang on. I'm just thinking about it, that's all. So you're saying, just have some photos taken, dressed exactly like this, and then I get two hundred pounds?'

'If you want, yeah.'

'Alright then,' I said.

Jasper produced a notepad and pen, scribbling quickly.

'Okay, that's great. Meet me here, this is my address, tomorrow morning. Is tomorrow okay for you?'

The next day was Saturday and I had nothing to do all day. 'Fine,' I said, trying to sound business-like, decisive.

'Okay, see you at ten o'clock then.' He gave me the piece of paper and left.

The next morning I made my way to Mornington Crescent. At a tall terraced house with lots of doorbells I rang flat number nine.

After a minute Jasper appeared. He was wearing camouflage gear and he looked much scruffier than when we'd met the previous evening. He nodded, said hi and turned, making a follow-me gesture with his head.

He marched off down the narrow hallway and started up the stairs. I hurried after him, taking in the smell of dust and the threadbare carpet.

We went all the way to the top of the house, where he had a room in the attic.

My stomach had been churning on the tube journey, and now his scruffiness and the dingy building unsettled me further. I wondered whether it was sensible to follow this man I didn't know, but I was more worried about what would happen if I backed out now. When we reached an attic room, I was relieved to see a girl sitting in a gloomy corner, sewing.

She stopped when she saw us, and Jasper said, 'This is my girlfriend. She's a make-up artist.'

The girlfriend wore jeans. She had dark hair like mine, but short and straight.

'You can sit here,' she said, positioning an old dining chair under a skylight.

She spent ten minutes doing my make-up, touching up what I already had on rather than reapplying it. Then she put her pencils and brushes back into a blue plastic box and called to Jasper, who was sorting through camera equipment by the bed at the other end of the long room.

'She's ready.'

Jasper picked up a large silver camera case and a tripod. 'Okay, come on,' he said to me, then, '*Ciao, ciao*,' to his girlfriend.

I was surprised when we went back into Camden Palace, which was a short walk from Jasper's house. He let us in through a side door with a small key.

Inside we walked onto the dance-floor and I thought we might be heading for the posers' stairway of the previous evening. But instead we went through a door to one side of the huge empty

27

room, where a red-carpeted corridor lead to the loos. Jasper stopped and unpacked his camera equipment.

'Here?' I asked, surprised.

'Yes,' he said.

I took off the long coat I was wearing. Underneath I had on the same outfit I'd worn the previous night. Jasper glanced once at me, then looked again through the lens of the camera.

'Okay – now lean up against the wall, like you're waiting for someone . . . yeah, that's it.' He snapped away. 'Okay, put your left arm down.' *Snap snap*, went the camera. 'Can you do that with your legs apart?' *Snap snap snap snap.* 'Great, okay, what about turning round – yeah – yeah.' *Snap.* 'And show me your bum?'

I looked round at him.

'Look, just hitch your skirt up a bit there, so I can see the shape of your bum, that's all.' I hitched the tutu up a bit. 'Okay, bit more – bit more.' I hitched it up a lot more. 'Great, that's it. That's great.' *Snap snap.* 'Now just turn slightly, one hand on your hip. That's it. Keep the skirt there, great.' *Snap snap.* 'Come round slowly.' *Snap.* 'And sink down against the wall.' *Snap.* 'Okay, hands on your thighs, elbows out, that's it.' *Snap.* 'Crouching position. Great.' *Snap snap snap.*

And so it went on for forty minutes. There was a kind of rhythm to it, and although I felt very awkward when we started, I began to move more easily after a while.

The movements seemed to flow into each other and Jasper kept saying, 'Great, great,' so it seemed to be going okay. I didn't mind when he asked me to show my breasts. And seeing a bit of my bum wasn't too bad, my outfit had revealed a lot of it. But then, without breaking the rhythm, Jasper said, 'Okay, we'll do some with your knickers off now.'

I stood still and wooden again. 'No, I don't think so!' I tried to laugh it off, but Jasper looked deadly serious.

He said, 'Aw, come *on!*'

'You said I could wear what I wore last night. And I was definitely wearing knickers last night!'

'You know it's for men's magazines. How d'you expect me to sell them if you won't take your knickers off?'

'What do you mean *sell* them? I thought you'd already sold them?'

'Look, come on. This is about us both getting paid.'

'I'm sorry. I can't. You said I didn't need to.'

'Come on! I just need *one* shot, one, that's all, to make sure we get our money. What's the big deal?'

I wanted a cigarette, time to think. It had taken me two hours to get ready, I had paid the tube fare and now wasted most of the day, for what? If I left now I'd have nothing, in fact, even less than I started with, and this bloke would have photos of me for free. I'd felt so happy about my two hundred quid. And I'd already been spending the money in my head, thinking about a holiday, new clothes.

I glanced at my bag, which stood to one side with some of Jasper's camera equipment. I could see the outline of my cigarette packet in the zip pouch at the front. Jasper didn't smoke.

'I don't think it's such a big deal to take your knickers off for one shot,' he said.

It's funny, the first time he told me to take my knickers off I was shocked – not just by the idea of it, but even just by him saying it. Now he had said it so many times I was getting used to it. And in getting used to him saying it I was becoming less shocked by the idea, as if him saying it, and me doing it, were the same thing.

He spoke again. 'I can't believe you would come along here and do all this, and think you wouldn't have to take your knickers off.'

I felt ridiculous now, or that I had been dishonest in some way.

'Look, I can't sell these photographs, any of them, unless I get a shot of you nude,' he said.

I looked at my cigarette packet. I could feel them, taste them.

Jasper tried again. 'Look, we can do it tastefully – it doesn't have to be anything . . . just take your knickers off. You can put your hand over a bit – with those velvet gloves on – it'll look great.'

So I did it. And it was painless. I stood stock still, my hand on my stomach, legs together. *Snap snap snap snap.* 'That's it,' Jasper said.

I had a cigarette while he packed up his gear.

'Okay, *adios!*' he said as we made our way out of the Palace.

My heart was banging away inside my ribcage as I thought about the money. Why hadn't he paid me?

On the pavement he turned to walk away. I swallowed hard.

'Will you pay me by cash or cheque?' I said.

'No, no, no,' he shook his head. 'You'll get the money when I sell the photos. And you get the money from them, not from me.'

Nottinghamshire 1973

'Can the Snow Queen come in here?' asked the little girl.

I was nine when, like all good genies, Thor disappeared in a puff of smoke. Just like that, it seemed the glory days were gone.

Dad decided to become self-employed, and in order to raise some capital he sold the engine. The money provided some savings to lean on while he built up his client base (he would specialise in tax consultancy work for corporate clients). He also purchased a couple of classic motorbikes which he intended to race, and a stair carpet because Mum said we couldn't do without one.

Now, instead of rallies, we went to motorbike races or trials at weekends. For Dad motorbikes were as all-consuming of his time as steam engines had been. If he wasn't at work or at a motor-bike event, he was in his workshop as usual.

But Mum didn't like motorbikes, and I didn't like them much either. No matter how often they were called 'dream machines' they were still just machines. Only Thor had managed to bridge the gap between mechanics and magic.

Mum said motorbikes were too noisy and she took to wearing earplugs. Once we were at the events Dad never took any notice of us anyway. Teddy and I would take the frisbee, we'd run on the grass and loiter around the paddock, while Dad had valves-and-cylinder conversations with fellow fanatics.

Not many wives went along so there wasn't anyone for Mum to talk to, and soon she just stopped going. She accused Dad fairly frequently of not spending any time with her, and they rowed.

'It's true, Duncan. You're always shut up in that workshop – and to hell with the rest of us!'

'I organise entertainment for the weekends. It's you that chooses not to come.'

'You call that entertainment?! Listening to a bunch of motorbikes tearing round a track? It's not entertaining for me, Duncan – or for the children.'

'It's my interest! You're welcome to spend your time as you please.'

'Oh, you think so, do you? And what about the children – who's going to feed them and clothe them and everything else that goes with it?'

'The fact is there are things available to do together. But you don't want to take part.'

'No! And mostly I don't have time to take part I'm so busy acting as your skivvy! I'm not at liberty to lock myself in a room on my own for several days on end, I'll tell you that!'

Their rows always culminated in Mum screaming about housework and Dad walking off. This was followed by weeks during which they spoke to each other only when absolutely necessary, in tones of icy civility.

One weekend at the end of just such a long, icy week my mother left us.

Teddy and I were arguing over the ownership of a yo-yo we had found in a flowerbed when she interrupted. 'Right, I'm off now. Your Dad can look after you two – and see how he likes being driven up the wall!' Then she got into her Mini and drove away.

Dad arrived two minutes later.

'Mum's gone, Dad! Mum's gone!' we screamed.

'What do you mean she's gone? Where's she gone?'

'She's gone. She said you had to look after us.'

In the middle of the night I woke to find Dad sitting on the side of my bed. 'Do you know where your mother is, Arabella?' he asked.

I didn't but I wished I did. He looked less upright than usual and I suddenly felt so sorry for him sitting there in the dark.

'Maybe she's gone to Auntie Irene's?'

'Is that where she said she was going?'

'No. She just went.'

My father sat staring straight ahead. I had never seen him like this and I felt privileged, amazed and sad, all at the same time. He cleared his throat, and spoke again. 'When I was in the army I was engaged to be married. To a girl called Diana. But she was hit by a car. My mother telephoned to tell me about it. Diana was killed straightaway.'

I imagined a long-ago voice on the phone saying it. *She was killed straightaway.* Maybe Dad heard the voice too, because he stopped and sat silently for a moment, just staring into the dark. When I heard him draw breath I realised I'd been holding mine, and released it.

He rubbed his sideburn with his knuckle and continued. 'I was sitting exams in the army at the time and if I didn't do them I wouldn't become an officer along with everybody else. I don't know how I got through but I did. I stayed where I was, and I sat the exams, and then I got compassionate leave to go home.' He pressed his left palm over his left eye and when he spoke again his voice seemed to come down his nose. 'But by the time I got there they'd already had the funeral. It was as if she'd never even existed.'

He moved his hand from his eye and used it to massage his forehead. Then he let it drop to join the other in his lap. He said, 'I do love your mum, you know.'

'Don't worry, Dad. We can look after you. I know how to make toast, and baked potatoes.'

He held on to my shin for a moment through the eiderdown. 'Go to sleep now.'

He got up and walked to the door. It was tight in its frame and made a gentle woofing sound as he pulled it closed behind him.

★

33

Mum came back on Monday while we were at school, and everything seemed okay for a short while.

It wasn't though. Over time the rows became more intense, if less frequent, and the freezing silences hardened and thickened in the spaces in between.

Mum and Dad never really 'chatted' to us. They either reported events, made statements of future plans, or asked questions borne of necessity, which required a correct and prompt response. So when the silences happened, somehow Teddy and I were muddled up in them, and all but the most necessary exchanges stopped. We stuck to routines which kept us busy, adults and children alike, passing each other in the corridors of the house without acknowledgement.

If Dad wasn't at work or in his workshop, he was taking the ash out, laying the fires or stoking the boiler. Mum ran around the kitchen reciting shopping lists or murmuring recipe instructions.

I tried to look purposeful while keeping out of the way, and I suppose Teddy did the same. We didn't speak to each other.

Instead the silence crashed through the house, and it felt fraught with danger. When I did have to speak, even phrases like 'pass the sugar' felt like knife blades in my throat.

Dad started to take Teddy with him when he went into his workshop. He showed him how to take things apart, and how to put them back together. I had to stay and help Mum with the housework, and I learned how to put sheets on beds with hospital-bed folds at the corners; how to peg washing (socks by their toes, shirts by the seams, underpants by the gusset); how to clean a room so that nothing was missed.

Our house was large by most people's standards – Dad was fond of saying, 'You could drive a coach and horses down the hall!' – and my mother had set herself the task of cleaning everything in it once a week. This included brushing the ceilings and dusting all the staves and legs of every chair. Skirting boards, light fittings and door panels were all polished and the insides of windows cleaned.

We did spring-cleans once a year and then the insides of cupboards had to be washed and the contents reorganised. Bedding and table linen not in use were brought down from the loft and laundered, walls were washed, carpets shampooed, chimneys swept and wardrobes moved to clean underneath them.

Mum had come to housekeep for Dad before she married him. According to Dad he bought our house at an auction when he was still a bachelor. It was too big for him to look after on his own so he advertised for a housekeeper. When the housekeeper arrived it was Mum and they fell in love and got married to each other. This story wasn't strictly true, but we children didn't know the rest until much later.

When Mum went away, Dad spoke to me as if she and I were somehow together – a team. But although there was a definite male/female divide in our house, I wasn't in Mum's camp any more than I was able to join the world of Dad and Teddy.

My mother was worn down by illness: a variety of minor, but continual ailments. Whether or not this was the reason for her anger and careless brutality towards me I didn't know. But much that I did was clearly wrong, and nothing I did pleased her.

Not the least of my wrongdoings was bedwetting. At nine years old I was still, frustratingly and inexplicably, unable to stay dry at night. At least once a week I woke up to find myself lying in a sodden puddle. I would get out of bed, take off my wet nightie, put on clean pants and my school blouse, and pull the soiled sheets onto the floor. Mum would appear in the doorway. 'You dirty girl! What's the matter with you?'

I was glad to escape to school while she washed the sheets.

In fact, Mum worked much harder than necessary – she ironed all our pants for example. And she continued to cook, clean, launder and iron, no matter what illness besieged her. Whenever she was ill she tended to wear the same polo neck jersey and I came to dread seeing her in it; it was a glowering red, with lots of little bobbles that stood proud of the material, like tiny warts.

The jersey seemed to pulse with the colour of the aggressive energy in her body as she worked, and it pulled her neck tight, so that she sounded ever more frantic as she marched and span through her daily tasks.

'Arabella, you need to *wipe*. Wipe like this.' Mum was wearing the red jersey and I was cleaning the hearth in the lounge. She showed me the exact motion and gave me back the cloth, continuing to watch me out of the corner of one eye. 'Not like that. It'll take all day at that rate. Give it to me.' Her arm jerked red as she wiped. 'I'll finish it,' she said. 'You go and start cleaning the bathroom.'

I went up to the bathroom, grateful to escape her supervision, and took the cloths and cleaning materials out of the bottom of the airing cupboard.

I cleaned the sink, toilet and bath, polished the mirrors and dusted the top of the cabinet. Then I stood back and looked around the room. I had forgotten the skirting board and door panels so I did those. Only the hoovering left; I ran downstairs to fetch the machine from its cupboard in the hall.

Our Hoover was very old, very heavy, and as big as I was. I had to pull it upstairs step by step. When I was halfway up the stairs, Mum called to me from the bathroom. 'Arabella, what have you used to clean the bath with?' There was an edge to her voice.

'The stuff from the bottom of the airing cupboard – in a plastic bottle,' I shouted, striving to maintain an even, carefree tone. My mother appeared then, in four swift strides – Fee! Fi! Fo! Fum! – like a giant at the top of the stairs. Her face was red with rage and her voice came out strangled by the jumper. 'You stupid girl! You've cleaned the bath with toilet cleaner! Are you trying to kill us all? Are you trying to kill us all, you stupid, spiteful, little girl?'

Soho, London 1987

The person who drove the large sledge turned round and nodded
kindly to Kay, just as if they had been old acquaintances; and every
time Kay was going to loosen his little sledge, turned and nodded
again, as if to signify that he must stay: so Kay sat still, and they
passed through the gates of the town.

After a whole load of phone calls to Jasper, he finally came
up with a name and address. If I wanted the money I needed
to see a man called Wesley Fox at Vince Veroni Magazines. The
address was an office on Wardour Street.

I took care getting ready to make myself as attractive as possible.
In between applying mascara and blusher, getting dressed and
doing my hair, I had to keep rushing to the loo. I was terrified
of going to see Wesley Fox.

I left my hair loose and I wore a black beret to smarten up
my old leather jacket. Then I got the bus to Piccadilly and walked
to Wardour Street. The buildings all looked so official and everyone
on the pavement seemed to know exactly where they were going,
except me. I stood out, as usual, feeling lost as I scanned the gold
plaques on the anthracite marble walls, looking for one that said
'Vince Veroni Magazines'.

By the time I found it I wanted to go to the loo again, and I
wouldn't have gone in, except that a grey-suited man with a
George Best hairstyle came out, and held the door open for me.
I felt obliged to enter.

Inside it was all chrome and dark glass. I walked through another
door, and then up to double doors with an intercom. I pressed a
button and spoke my name. The door buzzed open.

There were calendar-type pictures of semi-naked women on the walls, nothing too obscene. A receptionist with lots of green eye-shadow smiled. 'To see Mr Fox?'

'Yes.'

'What's your name again?'

'Arabella Cordon.'

'First door on the right, he's waiting.'

He had one of those massive dark-wood desks that took up most of the room, and he sat behind it, overweight, tanned and smiling. He spoke with an American accent. 'What can I do for ya?'

'Er . . . my name's Arabella Cordon. Jasper . . . er' – I realised now I didn't even know Jasper's last name – 'sold you some photos of me and he told me to come and see you. About getting paid.'

'Oh yeah! I recognise you now. You look much better in real life. I mean the photos weren't bad – but wow! You look great in the flesh, you know? Can I get you a coffee?'

I had expected hostility, and I was so relieved to find him friendly that I accepted the offer of coffee, and sat down to chat.

Wesley wanted to know all about me and how I met Jasper. After coffee he gave me a cheque for two hundred pounds and I felt drunk with success. Then he showed me round the building.

It all looked very professional. There was a huge white table for viewing slides in one office, and framed men's magazine covers all over the walls. Wesley showed me an empty office, bigger than the rest: Vince Veroni's. Actually it was more like a sitting room. Instead of a desk there were black leather sofas and three black-wood coffee tables, each with a white telephone on top of it. Along the walls were lots of black shelves full of magazines.

On one of the shelves I noticed some children's drawings, which seemed completely out of place. I was going to ask Wesley about them, but he was gesturing to the far wall. 'Veroni's girls,' he said.

There were lots of black-and-white photos, the kind newspapers take of male celebrities. Most of them starred a man in a suit, short with a round face, and receding hair. He was pictured guiding a woman's arm as she played golf; standing at the centre of a group of girls in swimsuits; sitting in a café with a buxom blonde and with his arm around two women on a quayside. There were others in the same vein, and this, I gathered, was Vince Veroni.

Wesley pointed at the right-hand wall where Vince was not in evidence. A colour picture of a red-haired girl in a full-length green sequinned dress stood out. Next to her was a picture of a girl jumping out of a cake, wearing an American-flag bikini.

These pictures were all in colour, and the girls were different to the others. Everything about them was extraordinary and extravagant. Their clothes looked like they cost a bomb and fitted like they were tailor-made. And the girls sparkled. Their clothes, make-up, hair and skin glittered and shone as if reflecting some great bank of lights. They were like film stars, the old, femme-fatale variety. The sort Dad liked.

'Which magazine are they from?' I asked Wesley.

'Oh that's not a magazine. That's the Pageant.' Wesley said. 'Vince Veroni's Pageant of Venus. You musta heard of it?'

I shook my head. I was looking at a photo of three tall, attractive women, all carrying imitation machine-guns and wearing black PVC cat-suits and peaked caps. They looked like Bond girls or Charlie's Angels.

'The Pageant's pretty famous,' Wesley said. 'You'd go real well in it – you're just the sort of girl we look for. Hey, if you're interested, you can audition. Do you take *The Stage?*'

I said I did.

'Well we got an ad out now,' he said. 'And the Pageant's a theatre, so you get your Equity card if you do it for a while.'

When I left Wardour Street I bought myself a pizza and a Coke to celebrate. I had two hundred pounds in my pocket, and a dream to look like the glamorous women I had seen on the wall in Vince Veroni's office.

Nottinghamshire 1974

The snowflake appeared to grow larger and larger, and at last took the form of a lady dressed in the finest white crêpe, that seemed composed of millions of star-like particles. She was exquisitely fair and delicate, but entirely of ice – glittering, dazzling ice; her eyes gleamed like two bright stars, but there was no rest or repose in them.

She nodded at the window, and beckoned with her hand.

The pictures in Dad's newspaper were all of Richard Nixon. I heard the word 'Watergate' over and over, but I didn't understand it, even when Teddy and I were dressed up as Watergate bugs for the village fancy-dress competition. That had been Dad's idea – he thought Americans were a laughable lot, always leaning about and chewing gum. He listened to the radio more than usual around this time and I caught the odd sound-bite here and there. Most of the time the radio talk just washed over me like a foreign language, but I did want to know what Watergate was about.

One day the announcer actually spoke the words 'what it's all about' and I pricked up my ears. 'What it's all about,' he said, 'is this sense that nothing is really the way one thought it was.'

Dad left the *Daily Telegraph* on the breakfast table every day when he set off for work. 'You ought to get into the habit of reading this,' he'd tell me and Teddy.

'Can't you just tell us what it says?'

'Read it.'

It didn't look much fun and I had no desire to read it, until Mum said I was too young to understand it anyway. I decided to prove her wrong and began poring over the words, trying to astound my parents with my comprehensive knowledge of everything that was going on.

Mum and Dad were never astounded. But my teachers were impressed when I regurgitated stuff about all the strikes, the petrol and electricity shortages, the two general elections. I was, however, more interested in a murder suspect called Lord Lucan, and in IRA bombs. I began counting people killed by the IRA. By my reckoning there were more than a hundred that year, including one of their own.

Dad was conserving electricity and hot water. He shouted at Teddy and me when we left lights switched on, and caned us both one Sunday when he discovered the bathroom taps had been left running for several hours. His rows with Mum got worse as he refused to heat the house sufficiently and we kept running out of hot water. Dad stoked the Aga and fiddled with the boiler. He gave the impression of hurrying from one crisis to another, asking the same question of the radio in between times, 'Who's running this country anyway?'

In March of that year the new Labour government stopped the miners' strike by giving them what they wanted, and my father's wrath went on for months. He was only distracted when Mum gave birth to my sister, Lucy.

Lucy was born at home at five o'clock in the morning. Her presence eased the relations between my parents, if only by keeping them apart. My mother was infatuated with her new child, rarely leaving Lucy's room, although she never gave up cleaning. She would emerge during the day whilst my baby sister slept, or at odd hours during the night, to iron, dust and hoover as before. Dad, pleased that mum had found an interest as all-consuming as his own, holed himself up in his workshop with Teddy.

Mum was, in her own words, 'worn to a frazzle'. The birth had not been easy and she had to keep going back to the hospital – I wasn't sure what for. Now with more work and lack of sleep, she developed tinnitus and suffered frequent migraine attacks.

She coped by ignoring those things that were not strictly cleaning, cooking or baby-related, and that included me. So paradoxically, I was no longer required to help in the house, nor was I encouraged to play with or care for my baby sister. Lucy was precious: I could tell from the way Mum and Dad stood close to each other on the rare occasions they were together in Lucy's room. A couple of times I hovered behind them as they looked at her in her cot and they seemed like people standing round a fire, getting warm. I would've known Lucy was precious anyway, just from seeing her tiny hands and feet. If I smiled at her she'd get a certain look in her eyes, like she was smiling back. But Mum said it was too early for her to smile and she shooed me away if she saw me near the pram.

That summer I wandered round the village feeling smaller, as if some imaginary camera trained on me had suddenly zoomed out. The village lanes were curiously empty of people, as if deserted streets were a requirement of the Keep Britain Tidy contest, or as if Woodstowe were a toy town where, behind closed doors, people were positioned and re-positioned according to rules I knew nothing of. Certain objects and places became familiar old friends: the marigolds in a garden on Main Street, the climbing frame at Round Parks where I hung upside down, blood running to my head. There was a black gate beyond which lay mysterious private woodland, a water splash and a giant's head the weather had carved from an old tree stump. On Monk's Lane there was a conker tree, the massive trunk of which divided into two branches only a few feet up. Between the branches was a nestling place, where I could rock forward to embrace the branch in front, or lean back supported by the huge branch behind.

I sat for hours in my tree, and I chanted to myself, 'I believe in fairies, I believe in fairies.' It was because of the bit in *Peter Pan*, where the children have to clap their hands to save Tinker Bell's life. The first time I read that, I swore I'd always believe in fairies, even when I was grown up. Chanting, I could believe there was more to the world than I could see and that the more was good. I felt too that I was helping someone, somehow, the way the children in the story helped Tinker Bell.

Sometimes I watched the donkeys in the adjacent field. I was fascinated by the crosses on their backs. A long time before a teacher told me about the cross being a mark which appeared on all donkeys after Jesus sat on one. I would've liked to ride the donkeys but I was too scared. Peter Pan would ride the donkeys definitely – he wouldn't think twice – then he'd fly off to Neverland. I didn't want to stay a child like Peter; I knew I had to get older before I could fly away.

I daydreamed, and I looked up at the sky. The tree was somewhere to go and it was a refuge from home, where I found myself increasingly in the wrong.

Mealtimes especially were tense when Dad was there. Sometimes Teddy and I would laugh and laugh for no reason, and then we'd be sent to stand in the hall. But usually there was just the clock ticking, the scrape of knives and forks, chewing noises and a paralysing silence zinging underneath.

Dad would bark instructions: 'Elbows off the table. Sit up straight.' Then, 'Keep your mouth closed when you chew, Arabella.' A few more awkward seconds and, 'I've never seen anything like it – you chew like a camel! Look, this is how normal people chew their food,' he would say, pointing at his own mouth and mimicking an almost imperceptible chewing action, 'and this is how you do it,' he slid his bottom jaw from side to side in an exaggerated way, 'like a camel.' The meal would continue in silence and every so often he would rap on the table so close to my plate that I jumped. 'Arabella! Stop shovelling!' We weren't allowed to leave the table until we had eaten everything. Dad never threw food away. 'You can sit there until you eat it,' he'd say and I'd remember the turkey incident the previous Christmas.

A few days before Christmas, Dad had taken Teddy and me to pick up our turkey from Uncle Donald's turkey farm near Lincoln. Uncle Donald usually brought the turkey to us, but he had just bought a steam-powered car he wanted to restore, and Dad was keen to see it.

The car was in a brick outbuilding with no door on it. It was freezing standing about waiting for Dad and Uncle Donald to finish talking and looking at the car. Teddy didn't want to play, choosing instead to join the men peering under the bonnet, and even prolonging the waiting time by asking questions. So when Uncle Donald finally suggested we go and find ourselves a turkey, I was very glad.

He opened the door to a long, low-roofed shed. Hundreds of turkeys called to each other with tremulous voices, like crowds of old people all complaining. It smelled like a hundred wet beds, but at least it was warm.

Uncle Donald approached one of the pens holding the birds and the noise got louder. There was some flapping as he pulled one of the turkeys from the throng of its companions, and placed it on the bench in front of us.

'Do you want to see how we wring their necks?' Cheerfully he placed his hands under the anxious face of the bird, provoking a high-speed version of the wobbly sound it was making. One twist like wringing out a cloth and the neck was slack, the head swinging down like a conker on a string.

The body remained standing up, like a comic-book cartoon, and Dad said, 'Well, he won't be coming out with any more fowl language!'

Uncle Donald grinned. 'It's a good 'un. Lots of good breast meat on that.'

On Christmas Day we took our places in the dining room around the polished mahogany table, and I tried not to look at the glistening centrepiece, our turkey, sitting on a silver platter. Dad poured drinks. We raised our glasses and said, 'Cheers!' before we pulled crackers and read the jokes inside. Dad put on his purple party hat and everyone followed suit. Then he stood up to carve.

'I've carved you some breast, Eileen. Would you like a leg as well? Now, who's going to have the wishbone?' He held it up and I concentrated hard on the fast-rising bubbles in my lemonade, but I still heard the crack and tear as he and Teddy used their little fingers to pull the bone apart.

'Arabella,' Dad said.

I was hugging my lemonade, dipping my tongue into the sweet liquid.

'Move your arms away from your plate,' he continued, and I sat back as he put two slices of turkey in front of me

'You've made a good job of stuffing this, Eileen,' he said.

I couldn't eat it, so I covered it in gravy.

I ate everything else. Then I put my knife and fork together to show I was finished. Everyone pretended not to notice, but there was a sense of impending doom.

Dad said, 'Arabella, aren't you going to eat that lovely piece of turkey?'

'No, Dad, I can't. I don't like it.'

'You haven't even tasted it. It's absolutely wonderful, that is. Your mother's cooked it to a turn.'

'I don't want it, though. I'm full up now.'

'Well, if you're full up you won't be able to eat any Christmas pudding and ice cream.'

'I know. That's okay.'

'Look, Arabella, you need to eat this. Your mother's gone to all the trouble of cooking it for you. What's wrong with you? You ate it last year!'

'I keep thinking of it being strangled.'

Dad hooted, 'It's dead now! You can't hurt it!' He made his own version of the turkey noises, 'Obble bobble obble obble bobble bob!' Then he told a joke. 'Doctor! Doctor! I swallowed a turkey bone! Are you choking? No I'm serious!' He threw his head back and laughed, 'Gobble obble.' He flapped his arms like wings and made the noises some more until Teddy joined in. Dad looked over at him. 'I say, I say, I say! On which side does a turkey have the most feathers? On the outside of course!'

After a while he stopped laughing. 'Come on. Eat it up,' he said.

'*I can't.*' I burst into tears.

'You will sit there until you eat it,' he said, all humour gone from his face.

So I sat looking at my plate, and Christmas continued in a more subdued manner around me.

I sat at the table for two hours. Then, when Mum and Dad went to the door to welcome guests, I filled my mouth with the meat and ran and spat it down the loo.

Dad pretended he thought I'd eaten it, but after all that time I don't think he cared about the food. We were in combat, and what mattered was saving face.

I kept quiet if Dad was there to eat with us. Mealtimes with Mum were usually much more relaxed, but then came an exception.

We were having boiled eggs for tea when I found that mine had a clot of red on the yolk. Mum said something about eggs being fertilised, baby chickens, and things 'going wrong'. I was disgusted at the idea of dead baby chicken and blood in my food. I leapt up in horror and when she tried to insist I eat another egg I ran from the kitchen out to the road, across the fields and down Monk's Lane to my tree.

Sitting in the branches I visualised the egg waiting for me on the table in its white plastic cup. Mum had sliced the top off. Now the yolk would be congealing. If I waited she would probably throw it away, then it would be safe to go back.

I must have fallen asleep in my tree because it was getting dark when I climbed down to walk back through the fields. The air was heavy, and agitated swarms of flies formed nets which fell over my head and face. The trees on my left leered over the barbed wire fence at me, and I started to run.

I lost my footing a couple of times as my feet caught in the long grass and I was sweating when I came in sight of the house.

47

I paused when I saw the darkness at the windows, and Dad's car parked outside.

The door of our house opened silently on well-oiled hinges, and I took off my shoes in the utility room, cold from the tiles seeping through my socks. I opened the kitchen door, hardly breathing, and moved forwards on tiptoe into the humming darkness.

My thighs hit a barrier and I lurched and fell. *Crack!* My head hit the legs of a stool. *Slam!* Pain across the tops of my legs. *Slam!* Across my buttocks. My head was jammed down between the legs of a stool, close to the floor. *Slam!*

It was a belt. My father was belting me.

He had placed a kitchen stool in the doorway, and had sat with his belt in his hand and the lights out, waiting for me to come in. When he was finished he released me, and I ran upstairs in shock.

The next day Mum was sick again, and I met Dad on the landing on my way to the bathroom. 'You're making your mother ill,' he said.

When I was allowed, I escaped to Julie's house.

Dad didn't like my school-friend because she was fat. He made jokes about her spacehopper bursting and called her mum 'The Pink Hippo'. But in his mind Julie was still the best of a bad lot. There were only seven girls close to my age at the tiny village school, and Dad's other prejudices against people living on council estates, and against Smiths, meant most of them were unsuitable friends.

Julie's house was very different to ours. Her mother swore and yelled things at her like 'Julie, have you fed those bloody rabbits yet?' But she didn't seem cross. She gave us Jaffa cakes to eat while we sat in the lounge on a carpet covered in dog hairs, listening to Julie's record player.

We listened to Abba, and it was magic.

Julie put the needle carefully down, and we grinned madly at

48

each other for those first few crackly seconds. When the singing started I sprang up and mimed the words. *My my! At Waterloo, Napoleon did surrender, woah yeah!*

Every time I heard this record the air turned electric, charging me up as I breathed it in. It was like a message from the gods: there was a world out there, which could be mine one day. I only had to be worthy of it – and at such moments I was convinced that I was.

Afterwards I skipped home resolving to be better and brighter.

One Sunday I hung around the door to Dad's workshop whilst he and Teddy were working inside. Here they crouched and peered together at engine parts, or passed wrenches, socket sets and adjustable spanners between them, as they bent over their separate projects. Teddy had the language of machinery now and there was a boast in his voice when he used it: 'Is this where the brake hose attaches, Dad? Do you think that's got enough torque in it?'

Sometimes Radio Four was on, and I heard the rehearsed voice of Dad's new obsession, Margaret Thatcher. But today there was just the rawk-rawk of the vice, the little crick of wire snapped by pliers, the ting of metal on concrete when something was dropped and the occasional clang-crash of a hammer.

I looked at the grey puzzles of metal on the oil-dark wooden shelves, rows of heavy tools on racks, a pile of tyres and a big drum of metal rope. Pieces of machinery queued on Dad's bench, waiting their turn, and a film of sticky black grime covered everything. There was no colour except for the red petrol tank of a Triumph Tiger Cub, and the calendar in the doorway.

The calendar drew my eye, though I didn't want it to. I didn't want Dad and Teddy to see me looking at it. It was embarrassing. On every page there was a picture of a woman with her breasts showing.

The August woman had red trousers and no top. She was sitting on a motorbike holding a blowtorch and smiling. There didn't seem to be any reason for the blowtorch and I thought I must have missed something about the picture, but I could never really study it with Dad and Teddy there. My eyes darted to it, and away again. Dad just acted like it wasn't there, but Teddy had a special laugh he kept for when he looked at it.

I skulked uncomfortably under the calendar. I was waiting for them to finish, as I knew they must, because it was time to eat. Dad said, 'Arabella, shouldn't you be helping your mother lay the table or something?'

'No, she doesn't want me to,' I said. 'I've been practising diving.' I thought this would please Dad, who always admired physical prowess and feats of daring.

Teddy said, 'How can you practise diving without a swimming pool?'

'Miss Linley said you can practise it anywhere. It's important to get the start position right.' We were walking up to the house now, around the edge of a huge boggy dip Dad said had once been a lake. Teddy looked at the dip and said, 'If we had a bull-dozer we could dig this out and go for a swim.'

Dad nodded. 'We could do that. It would soon fill up – there's a well up there.' He pointed beyond the apple orchard. 'You know, when I was a lad we used to swim in the river at the back of my Grandma's house. We dived off the trees on the riverbank.'

Teddy jumped alongside him. 'Didn't they have strong currents?'

'Nobody ever thought about it. We didn't have the nanny state we've got now, you know. People just got on and did things.'

'What else did you do?' I asked him. Conversations like this were rare and I wanted it to continue.

'Well, I was from the town really. There wasn't the freedom you have to run about the fields and climb trees. At home we used to test our nerve by jumping off buildings –'

Mum came out to the doorstep. 'Duncan! I've been waiting for you to come in. Your food's been on the table for ten minutes! You all think this is a hotel, I'm sure!' She marched back into the kitchen and we hurried to wipe our feet on the mat before going inside.

But what Dad had said about jumping off buildings stuck in my mind, and it grew. I practised in my mind's eye jumping from the church tower, the roof of our house, the top of the school, the village hall. In my imagination the jumping took on an air of drama and heroism. I dreamed of an admiring crowd who ooh-ed and aah-ed and applauded. Finally I convinced myself that if I leapt off the roof of a building and Dad saw me do it, I would be showered in glory and assured of his rapt attention forever and ever.

Spurred on by the bravery of kamikaze pilots on TV, I made my plans. The village hall was the best place to jump from because it wasn't too high, about twenty feet, but still impressive, and it had a flat roof I could climb onto easily via drainpipes. Best of all, Dad would be sure to see if I timed it right, because the village hall was on his way home from work.

I decided to do it on Tuesday evening, the only week-night Dad came home early enough. He would pass by the village hall at about half past six, so I would have to leave our house as soon as I could after tea.

When I got home from school on Tuesday, I crept into Mum's workroom and found an old white T-shirt in the ragbag. In my own room I cut a strip off it, stuck a circle of red paper to it with some glue and tied it around my head. It looked good, and I put it in my pocket for later.

Tea was fish fingers, which were difficult to swallow in my nervous state. I contemplated making an announcement to Mum and Teddy about my forthcoming leap. It seemed a shame they'd miss it. But I knew that if I did I wouldn't be allowed out, so I kept quiet.

I ran all the way to the village hall after tea: six o'clock – I was early. I climbed onto the roof to wait, and lay flat on my stomach behind a ledge that ran all the way around the perimeter. I could feel the fish fingers halfway between my stomach and my throat. I remembered my kamikaze scarf and got it out of my pocket, then turned on my back, and half-sat up to tie it. The red paper was a bit crumpled.

Back on my stomach I peered over the ledge. What cars there were appeared from over the brow of the hill, and then headed straight for me, slowing down for the sharp right turn in front of the village-hall car park.

If I put my head further over and looked straight down, I could see the small area of grass I was hoping to land on. I could feel my heart thumping but I took a deep breath, thinking, *to die will be an awfully big adventure.* That was from *Peter Pan.*

Six twenty-five. My eyes were fixed to the brow of the hill. Suddenly Dad's red Jaguar was there, and advancing all too quickly.

I stood up, waved and jumped.

Soho, London 1987

The snow fell and the sledge flew . . .

'Have we really got to take all our clothes off?' I asked a girl next to me with a blonde bob, who turned out to be Saf. We were backstage for the first time, auditioning for the Pageant of Venus.

'Yeah,' said Saf who was huddled in a white fur coat and sitting on a shiny purple poodle, apparently one of the props. 'Didn't you know?'

'Yes, I saw the advert. I just thought, maybe not at first . . .'

In fact, despite the words in the ad, 'artistes will be required to appear nude', I had been out and bought some spectacular new underwear for this occasion, clinging to the hope that perhaps not everyone would need to be completely undressed.

A tall, top-heavy woman in jeans and a baggy T-shirt appeared from the other side of a curtain separating us from the stage.

'Come on out as soon as you're ready,' she said, and disappeared again.

'That's Tracey Veroni,' Saf told me as she shrugged off her coat, and headed, starkers, for the stage.

About twelve naked women followed her and I scrambled to take off my frilly cerise high-legs and catch up with them.

I cast around for a moment for a suitable place to put my knickers, then tucked them under my coat, and followed the others.

'Facing front, legs apart, hands on hips. *So,*' said Tracey Veroni. She was fully clothed in jeans, and what I saw now was a Motorhead

T-shirt. She did a few simple moves, all dutifully copied by the line of naked women in high heels.

Through the glare of the lights we could make out the heads of the watching men: Wesley Fox and three others, one of whom I recognised from the photos in his office as Vince Veroni.

Gradually the group dwindled as girls were asked to leave. Tracey slid into the gloom at the edge of the stage to speak with the men. Each time she came back after less than a minute.

'Thank you, you can go now,' she said to the girls they didn't want, and I watched, amazed, as women I thought utterly lovely were turned away.

Saf must've seen my face, because she started giving whispered explanations. 'Tattoo' she said of more than one girl, and 'inverted nipples' of another. When a girl with peroxide hair on her head and dark pubic hair was sent off, Saf said, 'Someone should have told her she needs matching collar and cuffs.'

A girl with bright red hair stood at the front now, and Tracey stayed off stage for longer than usual. We could hear the low tone of the men's voices conferring. Then Tracey was back with, 'Thank you. You can go now.'

As the redhead turned to leave I saw that her pubic area had been shaved. 'Ah, bald eagle,' murmured Saf wisely. 'They've already got one.'

In the end, to my amazement, it was just me and Saf they took on, and Saf had worked at the Pageant before. We went to a tiny Soho café together after the audition, where a tall, good-looking man behind the counter held his arms out and spoke to Saf in an Italian accent. 'Sapphire! You should always be in dresses! These trousers, they are not good for your legs!'

'How's it going?' Saf said to the man.

'That's Delilah,' she said to me as we took our seats in the window. 'Delilah's a transvestite. When you see him in the evening you won't recognise him. Will she, darling?'

'The evenings! In the evenings I am truly amazing! *Magnifico!*' Delilah said, winking at me. I grinned at him, and he grinned back. He looked pretty magnificent already, I thought. He turned back to the coffee machine and Saf and I sat sipping celebratory cappuccinos. I looked at all the black-and-white posters framed on the walls: Marlene Dietrich, Judy Garland, Brigitte Bardot, Marilyn Monroe.

'Sapphire's not my real name,' Saf said. 'It's Saffron, but I'm usually Saf. My parents were hippy chicks. My Mum . . .' She stopped, her gaze caught by a couple walking on the pavement opposite. She nodded towards them. 'There's Vince and Tracey Veroni.'

We watched them pass. Tracey looked very thin next to the barrel-like body of her father. She was taller than him but when she stumbled on the kerb, he put a protective arm around her.

'They're like that,' Saf said, twisting two fingers together.

'Of course! He pay her rent!' said Delilah from behind us.

The next two weeks were spent rehearsing. I had to learn the bits with all the girls together first: the parade, a kind of pornographic barn dance which started the show, and the finale, for which we were dressed in fantastic headgear resembling Quality Street chocolates. The finale involved girls appearing from a larger-than-life chocolate box, wearing only fake jewellery and fake grins.

The night I made my debut, I stood in formation with thirteen other girls ready for the parade. We all wore the same high gold T-bar sandals, and gold ra-ra skirts made from layers of lurex and stiff gold net. Round our necks were ruffled collars made of the same material attached to a loop which you had to shrug on like a jacket, except it didn't cover our breasts. During the course of the act we would take these two items off, ending the performance wearing just our gold harnesses, and our earrings.

There were a few bars of music at high volume, and then a male voice came on over the PA system.

'Ladies and gentleman, Vince Veroni presents his Pageant of Venus!' It sounded like something from *Sale of the Century*.

As soon as the announcer finished speaking, 'Material Girl' started up, the music whirling out as the festoon curtain rose slowly to the sides and in front of us. The curtain rose completely during the musical intro, and I stood motionless waiting for Madonna's voice, my cue to move.

The auditorium looked full and, disconcertingly, I could see some of the men in the front row clearly. They stared up at me, their faces lit in garish colours, a reflection of the lights we ourselves were bathed in. Looking down, I met the eyes of a man examining me curiously, like I was a cake on a plate. I lifted my head, fixing my gaze towards the back of the auditorium, where there were just shapes in the dark.

On the first words of the song I moved forwards. I had been told to keep my hands on my hips whilst moving my shoulders back and forth, and now I was trying to remember this as well as where to move my feet next. I was too busy to notice the audience anymore, or even think about them.

There was an intricate crossing and interweaving with the others, pairing up, and moving on. I was terrified I might suddenly find myself facing in the wrong direction as I once had in rehearsal, when I had crashed into Liz coming the other way, banging our heads together so hard it was a wonder we weren't concussed.

We ended up in one long line and this was the cue to rip off my skirt and sling it to the back of the stage. All the girls did this move at the same time, revealing ourselves in our naked splendour. I felt a flash of power as we did it. We were beautiful and shocking. It felt like we were in charge.

Centre-stage was a wooden chair, a little too wobbly for my liking, but nevertheless once our skirts were off we took turns to do high kicks whilst sitting on it, the choreography changing slightly for each performer. I had to turn and slide on the chair, one hand on the floor and one leg in the air; I kicked one leg over the chair back and sat for a moment, my back to the audience, looking over my shoulder. Then I kicked my leg back over the chair, placing myself sideways on for a few more kicks. After that I was off parading around again, and the next girl began.

Of course every part of my anatomy was on display throughout this acrobatic performance, but I never gave it a thought. It was fast, and I had to concentrate, not only to remember what I was supposed to do and when, but so I didn't knock the chair over.

At the end of the song the dry-ice machine puffed out cold, white cotton-balls as we left the stage one by one. The ice added a sense of mystery, Tracey informed us.

Nottinghamshire 1975

Kay exclaimed, 'Oh, dear! What was that shooting pain in my heart?'

I was in a wheelchair for six weeks as a result of my kamikaze jump. I broke my right ankle and my left heel bone. Dad said he'd nearly crashed the car and why didn't I think? Didn't I know I could have ended up brain-damaged? Mum said it would have served me right if I'd ended up paralysed instead of just in plaster.

I felt like a hero sometimes though, with all the signatures on my plaster casts. And I loved it when Dad told other people the story, making it sound funny, and describing me as 'a complete lunatic'.

Towards the end of the summer holidays I was in the library with Mum when she ran into Mrs Post, head of the local WI.

I'd just had my plaster casts removed, and Mum told Mrs Post it was lucky, because I was starting at Tiley Green Comprehensive the following week. Mrs Post took hold of my hand and led me outside to where her daughter Jo was sitting on a wall waiting.

'Jo's at Tiley Green already,' she said, and left us there. The girl on the wall looked at me and her lip curled. 'What's your name?' she asked me.

'Arabella.'

But this was wrong. I could see her face re-arranging, as if she would say something not very nice. I remembered a girl at the village school saying I was stuck-up because of my long name. 'You can call me Bell if you like,' I offered. Jo grinned, but she still didn't look friendly.

Mum came out of the library.

'Well, see you at school then,' I said to Jo.

'Yeah, see you,' she said.

On the first day of school I walked to the top of our road to get the school bus. On the bus I walked along the aisle looking for somewhere to sit.

'Bell! Ding-dong Bell!' It was Jo. She and her cronies were on the back seat.

'Ding-dong! Avon calling!' someone else shouted, and they all burst out laughing. They kept going most of the way to school,

'Bell! Bicycle bell!' Then they sang all of 'My Ding-a-Ling'.

Jo and her crowd were third-years. They wore tight skirts from Chelsea Girl, and their hair was short, grown-up. They shimmied off the bus when we got to school, chewing gum and exaggerating their gestures to show off painted nails.

Little had I known how the rules of 'big school' would differ: that the crimplene skirt, royal blue V-neck and big plastic brown satchel from Bestman's Schoolwear, all holding the promise of 'big girl, big school', would be articles correct enough to shame me.

Tiley Green was a world away from the tiny village school I'd attended before. There were a thousand pupils, and lots of long corridors and stairs. There were science labs and language labs, even classrooms with kitchens in them.

At break-time, boys chased each other around a playground at the back of the school. Girls strolled to the patio at the front and sat on benches talking. The patio was bordered on three sides by the school building, and on the fourth by a row of three-foot-high cylindrical posts, beyond which was a car park.

At lunch break I sat on the posts with another new girl called Victoria. There was a man in a yellow van in the car park smiling and winking at us, 'Come on over here,' he kept saying. We smiled back but we wouldn't go.

The day was mostly taken up with form-filling and being shown around the school. In the afternoon teachers gave speeches and I had my first French lesson.

I got the bus home with some trepidation, but Jo and her
friends had forgotten me. They shared a cigarette, and flirted with
the bus driver until he turned the radio up. Then they sang along
to a song by The Sweet called 'Block Buster': *You better beware!
You better take care!* I relaxed a little and looked at all the forms
I'd been given. I had been allotted a sitting for dinner, a form
tutor, a year tutor, a house and a head of house. There was a
dinner ticket, timetable, lists of PE kit and books, information
about swimming classes and parents' evenings, homework from
my first French lesson. And a request for my birth certificate.

That evening after *Blue Peter*, Mum walked into the lounge with
milk and rich tea biscuits. Something was up.

She switched the television off and moved to the window. 'I've
got something to tell you, something that concerns both of you.
I'm going to tell you this now, because it's better you hear it from
me than from somebody else.' She had a good look outside,
pressing her face close to the glass to peer into the twilight, then
shut the curtains carefully, furtively, as if she suspected someon
of spying on us.

She came back towards us, smoothed her skirt, and sat in
armchair. 'This is important and I want you to listen caref
she said. Teddy and I waited on the sofa, hands under our k
heads forward.

'Sometimes grown-ups do things by accident. And the
have to make the best they can of the situation.' She sm
her skirt again. 'When your dad and I met, I already had
then, like the baby I've got now. The baby I had then w
girl too. She was a very sweet little baby with jet-black (
she was called Arabella.'

At this point, even though she had said my na
convinced she was talking about someone else.

'Yes, you, Arabella,' she said. 'So I brought you wi
I married your dad. Then your dad thought so mu
decided to adopt you!'

Mum had been looking down at her hands. Now she looked up into our blank faces. 'I'm telling you this because you need your birth certificate, Arabella. And I haven't got your birth certificate, but I've got your adoption certificate, to take with you into school tomorrow.'

'What about me, Mum?' said Teddy.

'Well, Ted, you came along a bit later. After your dad and I were married we thought we would really like to have a little boy as well as a little girl, and so we had you.'

'I'm not adopted then?'

'No, Teddy, you're not adopted. Your daddy adopted Arabella to make us all a family.'

'So who's my real dad?' I asked.

'Well, Dad is your real father really, because he's always been your dad, from the day you were born, almost.'

'Who was my dad before I was born then?'

'He was someone I used to know but don't know anymore. He left when I was pregnant with you, Arabella. Dad is your dad, and he's always been a good dad to you. Being adopted doesn't make any difference really. It's just a piece of paper.'

'Is Teddy my stepbrother then? And Lucy's my stepsister?'

'Oh, Arabella, now you're being silly. Teddy's your brother, and I'm your mum. And your dad's your dad, and Lucy's your sister. Everything else happened a long time ago, and it's not worth worrying about.'

Most of the questions came to me a long time after the subject was closed. At first there were just the words Mum had said and it seemed a huge effort to think about them, so I didn't. Instead I followed my usual bedtime routine, getting into bed, asking God to prevent me from wetting it, hollowing out a space in the pillow to put my head in. I lay on my back, pulling the covers up to my neck.

The Sweet song was still running through my head from the ss journey, and I sang it quietly to myself:

You better watch out if you've got long black hair!
He'll come from behind, you go out of your mind,
You'd better not go, you'd never know what you'll find.

Soho, London 1987

'I will put on my red shoes . . . and then I will go down to the river and ask after him.'

M y second week at the Pageant I learned the double act I would be doing with Saf. We were given a pink tandem which we had to cycle onto the stage, dressed in pink tennis outfits. I was very disappointed to have missed out on a sequinned dress.

The rest of the act involved playing tennis whilst gradually shedding clothes, and hanging from the branches of a plastic tree in the nude, apparently trying to rescue a ball. To Saf and me it was hilarious, and the biggest problem was trying not to laugh.

Tracey Veroni watched us carefully with dark haunted eyes. She wasn't keen on us laughing while she tried to teach us our moves, and since she was the one who had the ideas for the routines, it must have seemed like an insult. The first time we collapsed laughing she didn't say anything and just waited for us to stop. But the second time she said, 'If you want to work, work. If you don't, I can arrange unemployment.'

Unemployment was such a terrible, serious word; it stopped us laughing straightaway.

At breaks and lunchtimes we bought bacon baps or cheese toasties, cappuccinos and hot chocolate at Delilah's café. I had introduced myself to Saf and Delilah as 'Harri', a name I'd picked up in London. But, after the first time, Delilah insisted on calling me Arabella. At first it struck me as strangely old-fashioned, maybe because Delilah was forty-something, but then I realised he just liked to make everyone sound glamorous. His Italian accent was strong, despite having worked in London more than twenty years. I think he kept it that way to seem more exotic.

After rehearsals and before work, Saf went home for her dinner, but I got into the habit of staying at Delilah's. Sometimes on quiet days I'd sit at the table nearest the bar, and Delilah would drink an espresso and tell me a story while I ate my meal.

He told me about beautiful Tuscany, where he grew up hunting wild boar, and the Isle of Elba where rich people threw fabulous parties for artists. Delilah's father was a sculptor, and his mother came from Elba. They were invited to lots of parties, and Delilah (who was Franco then) would go with his parents. According to Delilah they never had much money, so on party nights they skipped dinner and ate lots of canapés instead.

Delilah told me the dramatic story – in fact all Delilah's stories were dramatic – of the masked ball he attended on Elba, how he was stuffing himself with canapés when he saw his mother walk into the garden with a man whose mask was a big yellow sun covering his whole face.

'I follow them, my mother and this sun-man. I saw them with their arm around each other. And then, my father – running across the grass. He ripped the mask off the man. And he was not a man. He was a boy, just a boy, about nineteen.'

Delilah slapped the bar top he was leaning against, 'My father became anti-sun! Yes! He shut himself in the house. He close the shutters. And he paint the moon. More and more. Just the moon.'

In the end, the boy with the sun mask turned out to be Delilah's half-brother, Antonio. The paintings of the moon were snapped up by galleries and art collectors. The money cheered up Delilah's dad, and paid for Delilah to go to drama school.

Delilah was very fond of his half-brother. Every now and then he declared to anyone listening that upon his death he wished to be buried on the Isle of Elba, next to Antonio.

From the way Delilah spoke, I thought maybe Antonio was dead, but Saf said he was alive and kicking and came to visit Delilah for three weeks every year.

66

I wondered why Delilah had chosen me particularly to be his confidante. He'd known Saf for longer, but it was me he told his stories to. I came to the conclusion he'd built one of his stories around me. He'd taken the little I'd told him of my past and injected his own brand of romance to create an Arabella–Cinderella story. For him I was a kind of princess who'd become displaced.

Sometimes he called me 'Little Flower' and I could picture the rose-petal border of the frame in which he placed me. I liked it, except I could never really confide in him, because I didn't want to say anything that might cause the petals to disappear.

Nottinghamshire 1977

'. . . and now again, something has certainly got into my eye!'

N *ow Gods, stand up for bastards!*
I am a bastard. This startling piece of information came to me in the middle of Mrs Carter's English class, where we were studying *King Lear*. It was the first time I had heard the word 'bastard' used in its proper context, and I wasn't quite sure how I felt about being one.

Bastard was a word used freely in the playground, a tough-nut word used mostly by boys, to apply to the perpetrator of some practical joke or worse. Older girls spoke of men who were bastards and apparently more desirable than those who weren't. The maths teacher, who liked whacking hands with a ruler, was a 'real bastard', and then there was the 'bit of a bastard', which was what I supposed my real father to have been. But although he left my mother when she was pregnant with me, I forgave him because he was young and wild – I had simply assumed he was of a similar age to my mother.

In my imagination my real father was Robin Hood and Casey Jones, he was Starsky, James Bond, or Rocky. He grinned and winked before racing full-throttle into a sunset on his motorbike, he stood in the centre of the room at expensive parties drinking champagne and raising one eyebrow, or he strolled down alleyways with his coat collar up, looking mysterious and drawing on a cigarette.

I had also taken it into my head that he was Italian, which made him more exciting in my eyes, and I was curious to know whether or not I was right.

I decided to approach my mother for more information. It was difficult to catch her standing still. She ate tea with Teddy, Lucy and me, but I didn't want to talk in front of Teddy. I felt very distant from him now. I knew that he was studying *King Lear* too, prior to a show which the whole school was to see, and I wondered what he thought about bastards. Did he see me as a pretender to his father? Did he resent me for all the time he thought he'd had to share Dad with me, compete with me for him, when all along he didn't really need to?

In the end I caught Mum while she was bathing Lucy. I sidled up feeling apprehensive, not too close. 'Mum?'

She didn't say anything, just continued rinsing the soap from Lucy's arms.

'You know about my real dad?'

I watched as she lifted Lucy out of the bath and wrapped a towel round her, but she still didn't reply. I ploughed on. 'Well, I was thinking about him, and I thought he might be Italian . . .' Mum glanced round at me, then reached up to get the shower hose as I continued, 'because some people think I'm Italian, don't they?'

Now she sloshed the sides of the bath, rubbing with a cloth at the same time.

I waited.

She rubbed harder in one spot. Then, 'Your Dad was a liar and a thief!' She shot the words out so suddenly and forcefully, I flinched. 'And he was certainly not Italian – his name was John Dodd, and he came from Sheffield. There!'

She wrang out the cloth, hung the shower hose back on the wall, and ushered Lucy out of the room.

'Come on, you'll get cold,' she said to her.

I never asked about my real father again, and she never spoke of him.

I lived more and more inside my head. In my fantasies I ran away to the circus, and became a star of the flying trapeze, or I moved to Italy to become a nun. I held pictures in my mind like movie stills, so I could press 'play' anytime. In one of my fantasies I died in what I thought was a glorious and spectacular manner, driving over the edge of the white cliffs of Dover in a gleaming white Daimler. In another, I became the beautiful girl on a motor scooter I had seen in an army promotional video, riding to work in a hot country alongside a vivid blue sea.

My real father starred in my imaginings: he was cheering in the circus audience, solving murder mysteries with the nun, or delivering a heartfelt eulogy about an heroic young girl who had given her life for her country.

Sometimes he stood in a village square on a foreign island, surrounded by girls in grass skirts, and he laughed as he threw stolen banknotes into the air.

I was thirteen and innocent as only a village girl can be. My idea of sexy was Abba, and a boyfriend was so far unknown. But my body was revving up for change. I had a constant, undefined urge to take some sort of action, and stuff that looked like snot in my pants.

School was really only about best friends and boys, no matter how much we were tutored and tested. My new best friend Linda and I read and re-read our copies of *Jackie* magazine, where articles like 'How to be a Glamour Girl', or '20 Ways to Get Your Man' had us completely hooked. In Linda's mum's *Cosmopolitan* there were tons of women with flawless skin and perfect breasts, but no explanation for the snotty stuff, no remedies for legs that went all pink and mottled with cold, or breasts that refused to grow.

Linda and I spent our pocket money on blue eye-shadow, and wore it to the school disco. My father said, 'You look like a clown,' but he didn't make me wash it off.

From *Cosmopolitan* we learned that real women shaved their legs, and I noted the tiny black hairs, like a film of dirt on my own skin. Linda and I both decided to shave, even though she was blonde and hers didn't really show.

71

That evening while Mum was busy putting Lucy to bed, I locked myself in the bathroom and got Dad's electric shaver out of the bathroom cabinet. I took off the transparent plastic cap and switched it on, but the noise was so loud it made me jump. I switched it straight off again. Flushing the toilet to mask the sound, I tried again. This time I moved the silver foil against my skin. It worked, and once the cistern had refilled I flushed the toilet again, and continued. Five flushes later I was finished. My legs felt smooth, bare and cold, even when I put my jeans back on.

I replaced the cap on the shaver and put it back in the cabinet, positioning it exactly where it had been before.

The next morning Teddy and I were sitting at the kitchen table eating cereal, when Dad appeared in the doorway holding his shaver. I wanted to hide under the table.

'Who's been using my shaver?' he said, but he looked at me. I decided to go for casual.

'Oh, I borrowed it last night Dad.' (I was going to add, 'I hope that was alright?' but I dried up after the first bit.)

'What on earth did you use it for?' he said.

I felt my face turn red. 'To shave my legs.' I squirmed and sweated to say it in front of Dad and Teddy.

Dad came and put his face too close to my face. He held the shaver between us, right in front of my nose, and spoke through gritted teeth. 'This is my property, d'you hear? And you never ever use my property without my permission, d'you hear?'

'Yes, Dad.'

He turned to go. 'You dirty little girl,' he said as he went out into the hallway.

If Dad had thought I was beautiful it would have been different. But he didn't. In *King Lear* Edmund talked about bastards being 'base', a word which I interpreted as describing the way I felt over the shaver incident, or the time I watched *The Onedin Line* with no slippers on and Dad went on about my huge smelly feet. Linda's family was different. When Linda's sister Sonia had her sixteenth birthday, her Dad woke her up by playing a cassette in her room. The song went, '*You're sixteen, you're beautiful, and you're mine.*' I wondered whether my real dad would have played me a song like that. I tried to picture it and couldn't.

Sonia was very beautiful anyway. She looked like a film star, and she had big breasts which were all that seemed to matter to the boys at school.

''Ere Linda – why d'you hang around with Cord the Board?' Kevin Daley, a boy from our class was asking the question. 'I mean,' he sniggered into his blazer, 'it's not like you need to make your tits look bigger or anything.'

Kevin's mate joined in. 'Yeah. You're a legend in your own lunchtime, Linda.'

'Oh, get lost, Daley.' Linda and I pushed past the two boys in the school corridor.

'You're just a board, Cord,' said Kevin, repeating the insult as I went past him. It meant that I was flat-chested, like an ironing board. It was my regular nickname with the boys at school, ever since Kevin had come up with it six months before. Linda was accorded an odd kind of respect because she'd already sprouted above average-sized boobs for her age. Hanging out together didn't help Linda or me, because it made the difference in our chest sizes more apparent and this resulted in the additional taunt of 'Little 'n' Large'.

At break-time I had to walk to the gym which was on another campus. The walk took about fifteen minutes, round the side of the school playing fields, across the park, then down an alley which led around the back of the high-street shops.

As I walked I thought about my nickname. There, *my* nickname! How could it belong to me? I hadn't invented it and I didn't want it. But there didn't seem to be anything I could do about it. I couldn't change anything – not the things people said about me, not my body, not my family. I was powerless.

73

I compared myself to other girls in my year: Karen, a coy brunette, who had normal-sized breasts and wore fashionable skirts and jerseys in not quite the school colours. She got away with those clothes because, although the teachers didn't like it, her mother didn't think it was important. I couldn't imagine a parent like that but it sounded fantastic. And boys adored Karen.

Then there was Jane who was very tall and looked about twenty. She hung around with Jenny who was of a similar height. Those two were at least a foot taller than the tallest boy, and perfectly capable of pulverising any lad who insulted them. Result: they were left in peace to do their thing, which was dating much older guys.

Deborah, Amanda and Katie: average-looking, well-behaved girls with normal-sized breasts. There was very little comment from the boys about them. Perhaps being ordinary was the key. But then I didn't really want to be ordinary.

Another girl in my class, Juliet, got called Specsy Four Eyes, but she was in a little group of odd-ones-out that included Denise who was in remedial class for every subject and covered in spots, and Louise who smelt funny and lived in a house with windows permanently covered in newspaper. These three probably got picked on about as much as I did, although it didn't make me feel any happier to realise I was somehow aligned with them.

Next to the sports fields I passed Juliet, going in the other direction. Her rucksack was so large she always looked as if she was going hiking. She was pigeon-toed, and she stared at her feet as we walked past each other like she always did. I would've said hello if she did, but she didn't, and the next thing I knew I was holding my breath. I didn't want to breathe in Juliet. I was afraid she would contaminate me, and I didn't want to get worse; I needed to get better. I waited until she was at a safe distance before breathing normally again.

Netball practice that day was with Miss Beasley, who had a habit of scratching her armpits and was about the most unfashionable teacher going. I certainly didn't want to breathe *her* in.

But she was around me a lot and I was huffing and puffing, trying to keep holding my breath whilst running around and throwing the ball and everything. Miss Beasley was giving me funny looks, and seemed just about to say something about my breathing, or my lack of breathing.

Then suddenly I found it wasn't a problem anymore.

My hand went to my left temple where I'd always had a large mole. Now my fingers found, instead of the mole, a switch, like a light switch but smaller and more protruding.

I used the switch on the side of my head to *switch off,* quickly finding myself back to normal, with no worries about breathing Miss Beasley in.

By the end of the day, I found I could switch off instead of holding my breath when I didn't want to breathe someone in, and even better, if I passed someone I *liked* the look of, I could switch on, take a deep breath and breathe a little of them into me.

Next time I saw Sonia coming towards me I flipped the switch on and breathed in as deeply as I could. She said 'Hi,' as she passed by, but I couldn't speak for inhaling.

I wasn't sure what I was doing; I sort of knew I was fantasising, but I kept on. But then the switch went wrong. It kept getting stuck in the 'on' position, which was when I found that there were far more people I didn't want to inhale than people I did. Holding my breath all the time was a big problem.

I told myself I believed in magic, that everything would turn out alright in the end. *I believe in fairies, I believe in fairies,* I repeated to myself like a mantra, practising holding my breath at night under the bedcovers.

The switch was with me through a time of change. It disappeared one day, in the matter-of-fact way it had arrived, when a boy I fancied taunted me for being asthmatic (all that desperate deep breathing). But most of the way down the road from crimplene to condoms, it was there.

Slowly I stopped listening to Abba, in public at least, and learned to like other music. First Sweet and T. Rex, then The Clash, X-Ray Spex and the Sex Pistols. I went to the youth club instead of school discos. There was a small dance floor there where I liked to pogo with the lads. Afterwards I hung about outside on the steps, trying to catch the eye of blokes from Nottingham cruising by in their dads' cars.

At home the house was still freezing over on a regular basis, but the focus of Mum and Dad's unhappiness was no longer each other, it was me. Mum was staying in bed more often, and every time Dad found a way to make me the reason for it. *You're making your mother ill . . . You're making your mother ill*, went the refrain, and I felt guilty when I saw her washed-out face, the way she dragged herself around the house most days.

Dad never talked about his work, but he was in a bad mood all the time, and I knew business wasn't good. In the evenings he listened to the radio. The news was all of riots, bombs and strikes. Dad always turned the radio up for Margaret Thatcher's speeches. She was calling on Jim Callaghan to resign, but he stayed and Thatcher got into trouble for her immigration speech.

Dad liked her speech of course. She had said that people feared being swamped by those of a different culture and I think it was what he felt too. He took the speech as the opportunity to tell Teddy and me, 'Black people have very small brains.' We were in the car at the time and I remember looking carefully at him for a trace of a smile; I was sure he knew he was talking nonsense. I knew what he had said was rubbish. But if he was joking he didn't let it show, and I found myself staring at his short forehead as he drove, feeling glad I hadn't inherited *his* brain.

The newspapers called that winter, the one after I turned sixteen, 'The Winter of Discontent'. The miners were on strike, as were the railwaymen, British Leyland, lorry drivers, teachers, hospital workers and bin men. In the paper there were pictures of rubbish piled up on Clapham Common, which was being used as an

76

emergency rubbish dump. In some places cemetery workers were refusing to dig graves. I was still following the progress of the IRA, and now too there was the Yorkshire Ripper.

Dad became more and more energetic in a desperate kind of way. He never seemed to stop for a rest, and the word he used most was 'chaos'. He got transcripts of Margaret Thatcher's speeches from somewhere and taped them to the walls in his workshop. The bits he liked best he highlighted.

I got myself a Saturday job at Georgie's, a fashion shop in Nottingham city centre. The bus took an hour to get there, but it was worth it for some money of my own. With my first pay packet I bought a small radio. On the long bus journey home I held it close to my ear, tuned to Radio One. Blondie was playing and I mouthed the words as Debbie Harry sang: '*Once I had a love and it was a gas / Soon turned out, had a heart of glass / Seemed like the real thing, only to find / Mucho mistrust, love's gone behind.*'

I was studying hard: where to buy clothes and which ones to buy, how to wear make-up, what to say to boys and how to get out of the house unseen, with the maximum amount of make-up, and the minimum amount of skirt. I read all of Mum's Harold Robbins novels and I practised facial expressions to combat my father's critical remarks, always trying to look as if what he had said was irrelevant and boring. ('You've got to look like you're smelling shit', was the latest advice from school.)

On balance I'd come out in favour of bastards. In fact, I was aiming for bastard bad, and it felt exciting.

Soho, London 1987

'In the kingdom in which we are now sitting there dwells a princess – a very clever princess . . . It is not long since she ascended the throne – which I have heard is not quite so agreeable a situation as one would fancy.'

A t least fifty per cent of the time Saf talked about her dad. She had a badge of a silver spider, which used to belong to him. She wore it all the time pinned to her bomber jacket, and she touched it when she talked.

'Dad disappeared when I was eight, and Mum never seemed that hassled about it. She reported him missing, but the old bill came up with diddley-squat. He's got a sister, Lorraine, who's pretty cool and she put posters up all over central London. Then she saw him, Lorraine did, right? A year ago, near Westminster Bridge. She swears it was him. She says she wasn't even thinking about him at the time, he just materialised – walking on the pavement by one of those Souvenirs of London shops, you know? He looked kind of down-and-out, she says. Lorraine was in traffic, she couldn't stop. It blew her away. She had to go all the way over the other side of the bridge to turn round. Of course the traffic was a pisser – that roundabout next to St Thomas's, you know it right?' I nodded; it was on my bus route home.

'Jeez – by the time she got a parking slot and walked back, he'd de-materialised. She beats herself up over it now – like she should have bloody stopped dead in traffic or something. I was going travelling then, I'd just done a stint at the Pageant. I would've stayed, but I'd already handed over the cash for a lot of my tickets

79

and stuff. I started looking for him as soon as I got back, all the Sally army spots and cardboard cities.'

'What's a cardboard city?'

Saf looked at me sideways. 'I can tell you're a northerner,' she said. 'Homeless people sleep in cardboard boxes. Get enough of them together and it's a cardboard city, yeah?'

'Right. Did your mum love him?'

'I dunno. She never wants to talk about him.'

'Do you think she knows why he went away?'

Saf shook her head.

'That's why I need to find him. I mean, if he just didn't dig where he was at – family life and all that, they could have got a divorce or something, right? If he doesn't want to be found, I'm cool with that. But I'm dead sure no one really wants to live on the streets – you should see them! In any case, I'm supposed to find him. It's my destiny, man.'

Saf was a great believer in destiny and the stars, or more particularly the moon. She had a chart taped up on our dressing-room door that told her when the moon was full, or waning, or waxing. She'd try to make sure important events coincided with a full moon. She had a bag of rune stones too – for daily decision making.

'Everyone believes in something,' Saf said. 'What do you believe in?'

'I believe in fairies,' I told her, the words out before I realised I was going to say them. I'd answered immediately, with no hesitation, and Saf looked surprised.

She narrowed her eyes. 'Okay, okay,' she said.

In fact I hadn't thought about it until then. *I believe in fairies, I believe in fairies*; I'd been telling myself this since I was a child.

'What does that mean exactly?' Saf said.

So I explained about Peter Pan. But then I realised there was more to it than that. For me, *I believe in fairies* had somehow translated into trusting the world.

'It's a belief that the majority of people are good and kind,' I found myself telling Saf. I was thinking that I'd pretty much relied on that since leaving home, and overall I didn't consider I'd been wrong. The world was kinder than my childhood experiences had led me to believe. Or perhaps the way I thought transformed my experiences, making them appear more positive. Either way it seemed important, a deliberate decision. I wanted to carry on clapping.

Saf didn't agree with me, she thought it was about half and half: half the world good, half the world bad. Most of the time she just had *feelings* about things, she said. Most people ignore most of their feelings, especially if they're as outrageous as some of Saf's were, but in her case she felt compelled to act on them. She was a bit odd, but I liked her very much. In any case we had a great deal in common, not least that we both fantasised about our fathers. Despite my suspicion that my real father was probably by now a family man, with two-point-four kids and a semi in Preston, I continued to nurture the fantasies I had had as an eleven-year-old, when he was a hero and the amalgamation of every film star I ever admired.

In the Athena shop near Leicester Square I would stand for thirty minutes at a time, gazing at posters of James Dean whose air of mystery and bad-boy glamour captured what I thought of as 'the essence' of my real dad.

If I'd been Saf I probably would have been hunting down celebrities, convinced one of them had fathered me. As it was, I didn't even buy a small picture of Tony Curtis. Maybe because I preferred magic to reality. And the hero of my imagination could never reject me.

'Once upon a time there was a king who had three daughters. The eldest was called Big Boobs, the middle one went by the name of Big Bum and the youngest was Burning Bush.'

Saf and I sat in a tiny theatre just off Covent Garden, watching an 'adult' puppet show, written and directed by Tracey Veroni. All Veroni's girls had been invited by Tracey, and about half had turned

81

up. The rest of the audience were, I suspected, mostly people involved in the production in some way or their friends; it had that kind of atmosphere.

Big Boobs, Big Bum and Burning Bush appeared on stage now, with the relevant features all hugely exaggerated. Big Boobs' out of proportion body parts cast an enormous shadow, only eclipsed by the shadow cast when her sister Big Bum came on stage. The puppets and the audience were gradually enveloped by the shadows of Big Boobs' boobs and Big Bum's bum, until there was complete black-out. When the light returned, emanating this time from Burning Bush's wealth of pubic hair, most of the audience roared with laughter.

Burning Bush's light continued to be the one we saw by, cleverly illuminating the other characters and everything that happened on stage. The narrator continued. 'The three princesses loved their father very much, and he loved them back. He had himself given them their names, names to highlight what he felt were their best and most remarkable qualities.

'Big Boobs, the eldest daughter, sat around eating chocolate most of the time and tended to be rather complacent about her name.'

'It's not an insult to be credited with mammaries which are a tad larger than the norm,' Big Boobs told Burning Bush.

'Big Bum was quite happy to spend all day watching television. Like her older sister she saw her large arse as an asset and didn't mind her name. But Burning Bush, the youngest of the three, a restless creature who went running every morning and spent most of her time consorting with ordinary folk, hated her name. She hated too that part of her which her father most adored. But since the king had ordained that all women, including princesses, were to walk around naked, Burning Bush could not hide her light under a bushel as it were – indeed her light was the bushel. She tried dying it different colours in order to camouflage it . . .' – the lights changed from yellowy white to blue then green then red and back again – 'but this only seemed to draw more attention to her. Finally she decided to wear knickers, men's knickers since these were the only kind available.'

'You can't wear those!'

Now Big Boobs pushed Burning Bush who landed on the sofa next to Big Bum who shrieked and stood up. Burning Bush stood up again too and it became evident that she'd sat in her elder sister's chocolate. The king was alerted and his reaction was to banish Burning Bush from his kingdom. She walked slowly and sorrowfully offstage accompanied by sad violin music, the baggy bum of her white Y-fronts very much in evidence and all stained with chocolate.

Now the king insisted he couldn't see without the light of Burning Bush – although the audience still could because the stage lights had come on to replace hers. His kingdom fell into ruin and the other sisters were deprived of their chocolate and television. It became more and more ridiculous, but the audience were laughing and seemed to be enjoying it.

The king held an audition to see which of his subjects might provide 'new light' in the palace, and we saw a woman who 'smoked after intercourse' but couldn't produce fire. Another woman who answered yes to the question 'Does it burn when you pee?' was able to produce small fires and the king hired her to light up his bedchamber.

In the end, Burning Bush came back to be reunited with her father who was on his deathbed. But when the new light in the king's life missed the chamber-pot, everybody died in the ensuing fire.

'Man, that was weird!' Saf said as we walked out.

'What d'you think it says about Tracey?'

'She's disturbed, with a capital D. The woman's raving. Some bits of it were clever though. Jeez – she stunned me with the humour! I've never seen her even smile, let alone crack jokes, you know? I wonder if she really wrote all of it? Could be someone else did the jokes . . .'

I didn't think we were the ones to judge who was disturbed and who wasn't. Maybe everyone in this whole world was a bit ding-dong. That didn't bother me. The humour had surprised me too, but what had really shocked me was how this play of Tracey's was so obviously about her and Vince; her struggle to survive in a world he'd created.

We were walking up through Leicester Square. 'Did you see Vince there?' I asked Saf.

'Nah, but it'd be a bit strange if he'd turned up. He's a millionaire, he's not going to hang out with a load of hobos and artists, you know?'

'No, maybe, but it was his daughter's play.'

'D'you reckon she'd have wanted him to see it?'

'Maybe not.'

'Well, there's two good reasons why he wasn't there then.'

'But don't you find it strange that she'd do this – it's like, I don't know – exposing herself. And she's not like that – I mean, she doesn't expose herself.'

'You don't mean taking her clothes off right?'

Sometimes Saf could be so dumb. 'No! I mean she doesn't let anyone know where she's at.'

'What, and you think you know now?' Saf laughed.

Nottinghamshire 1979

But the higher they flew the more wrinkled did the mirror become;
they could scarcely hold it together. They flew on and on, higher
and higher, till at last the mirror trembled so fearfully that it escaped
from their hands, and fell to earth, breaking into millions, billions
and trillions of pieces.

Clint was from Nottingham, so he didn't know about me
being 'Cord the Board'. He wore a black cap-sleeved T-shirt.
His mother, he explained, had called him after Clint Eastwood.

'My Mum would like you,' he said.

I'd only just met Clint when he invited me to baby-sit with
him at his auntie's house. When he asked me to have sex with
him I refused. 'I'm a virgin.'

'Oh, don't worry about that. I've been with quite a few virgins.'

We were kissing, I was melting. He had his hand in my pants
and I wanted it there. He said, 'Let's just lie down next to each
other with no clothes on.' This made me feel safe, because I didn't
know yet there was a stage when I wouldn't be able to stop. He
tugged at my jeans. I had to help him take them off because they
were so tight. My body felt hot – no mottled skin. There was no
shame, I felt almost beautiful. I felt *wanted*.

He lay next to me while he took his own clothes off, kissing me,
never losing contact with my skin. When I saw his body, I felt blood
rush to my face, not with embarrassment but with excitement.

I didn't know enough to expect pain, and in any case there
wasn't any. I thrust my pelvis against him wanting him closer,
closer, pleasure building all the time until I was frantic with it. I
was on the brink of something.

But then Clint stopped. I felt him thicken and release. He lay on top of me gasping.

I was disappointed it hadn't lasted longer. But I liked his weight on me, the feel of his naked body against me. He stopped gasping and rolled over and off me. He withdrew, looking carefully between my legs at the same time. His gaze wasn't sexual, it was inspectorial. I wanted to cover myself but I lay still.

'There isn't much blood,' he said.

I sat up alarmed at the thought of any blood at all. Clint looked at my face and I felt immediately conscious of how sweaty and dishevelled, how not-pretty I must look to him now. 'Is there usually much more blood then?' I asked him.

'Yeah, I've slept with loads of virgins and there's normally much more than this. One girl I went with at a party bled buckets – she wouldn't stop. In the end someone went to get her Mum. I had to clear out pretty quick.'

I hated this discussion; it was so unromantic as well as threatening and insulting in ways I couldn't define. 'So, you've had lots of girlfriends?' I tried to sound flirtatious, but it came out sad.

Clint looked into my eyes. 'I have a girlfriend. She's called Brenda. I'm going to have to go back to her after tonight. I shouldn't really be doing this.' He stroked my upper arm.

I started to cry. 'I don't understand why? Why did you do it if you knew you already had a girlfriend?' I didn't mean that, I meant, *you can't be very happy with your girlfriend or you wouldn't be doing this with me, so why don't you stay with me and finish with her instead?* I didn't have the guts to say it.

'I'm sorry,' he said and put his arms round me which felt lovely and made me cry more. 'I'm sorry,' he said again, with a catch in his voice. I looked up from where my head was rested on his shoulder to see that he was crying too. 'I'm really sorry,' he repeated, tears trickling down his face.

I was stunned by his tears. It was all much more complicated than I'd thought. I stopped crying and told him it was alright. He perked up fairly quickly.

'What's Brenda like?' I asked.

'Oh, she's quite different from you. She's got size 38D tits.'

There were lots of things he could have said and I think I would've found a reply to most of them, but even though I was still determined to impress him, I couldn't think of anything to say to this. Maybe my mouth fell open.

'D'you want a cup of tea?' he got up, pulling his jeans on.

As he made the tea he told me about his new motorbike. Here was a subject on which I might make some headway, I thought. I was bound to know more about motorbikes than Brenda did. I showed interest and asked as many knowledgeable questions as I could think of. He was talking more easily now and I started to think he might actually like me. We talked motorbikes right up until his aunt and uncle arrived back. We said goodnight to them and walked out together, but came quickly to the road where he'd parked his bike. He showed it off to me proudly, then put his arms round me and kissed me. 'Goodbye,' he said, mounting his bike. Then, 'I'll give you a tip for next time: always move with the man, never against him.' He kick-started the engine and roared away.

In the space of a few hours I had been reduced from a hopeful, innocent virgin, to a boyfriendless, over-enthusiastic tart.

When I told Linda I'd lost my virginity, she told Sonia. Then Sonia got a friend of hers to take me to the family-planning clinic. My parents didn't know I was no longer a virgin, until I told my mother I was on the pill.

It was one of those days, like most days, when she came downstairs late, looking unwell. She'd been up early with Lucy then gone back to bed.

I felt the full force of my guilt when I saw her. *You're making your mother ill.* I didn't need my father there to say it anymore; it was always there, reverberating through my head.

I think I had some idea of bonding with her, of making up to her by sharing my secret. Maybe this idea even included being women together; we could sit around and paint our nails, have 'girly' chats. Perhaps I hoped for some advice too.

'Mum, if something really important happened to me, something really personal, then you'd want to know about it, wouldn't you?'

'Well, yes, I suppose so, Arabella.'

It wasn't a very promising start, but I was relying on the special nature of my confidence to thaw the ice.

'Do you want me to tell you what's been happening to me then?'

'If you want to tell me.'

'I'm on the pill.'

'Oh.' There was a pause. 'Well, I hope you know what you're doing.'

She turned and opened a cupboard.

It felt just like when I told her I had my first period, less than a year before. I'd wanted some sort of recognition of my passage into womanhood, some form of initiation, however small. But she'd told me where she kept some sanitary towels and that was it.

My mother's back was toward me as she stacked plates inside the open cupboard and I felt awkward. I didn't know what else to say.

She didn't ask me anything so I said, 'I thought you'd like to know anyway.' I finished drying the dishes and walked out.

The following Friday night I came in late from the youth club, where I'd had sex with a boy called Dave, in the dark behind a bush in the garden.

Dad was waiting. 'Where the hell do you think you've been?'

'To the youth club.'

'You've seen the time. The youth club shut hours ago. What have you been doing since then?'

'Just standing outside talking to people.'

Mum came through from the sitting room in time to hear my reply.

'I don't think so,' she said. 'I think you're out there sleeping with every Tom, Dick and Harry!'

Dad's face looked thunderous 'You get upstairs to bed NOW!'

I ran, and he called after me up the stairs, 'And you're not going out at night at all for a week.'

On Saturday I went into Nottingham to work at Georgie's. On Sunday I spent the day reading and sleeping, holed up in my room except for eating, which was a necessary evil, each meal a silent, too-large slice of the day. Mum and Dad made some self-conscious effort at conversation during meals, as if to prove to themselves and us that everything was normal. But Teddy and I never spoke nowadays. We had learned to keep quiet and 'get on'.

My father sat at the head of the table, and now and then when I felt his gaze sweep over me, I could feel the rage that he only just kept in check. I kept my head down.

On Sunday night we watched *The Onedin Line*. Dad loved the energetic and entrepreneurial James Onedin and it was a long-standing ritual, the only time we all sat down and relaxed together. I liked it because it felt like we were a real family then. Mum would bring in a tray of chocolate biscuits and cups of tea, and, as long as we didn't speak to each other, the fantasy could be kept up.

But following the sex row, I found myself standing in the hallway on Sunday evening. I could feel my parents' hostility through the closed door to the sitting room where *The Onedin Line* was starting. I turned and walked back upstairs, the house dead quiet apart from the sound of the television, which faded out as I retreated.

As I passed Mum and Dad's bedroom, Teddy's and Lucy's rooms, I thought for the first time about the way the bedrooms were arranged, Teddy and Lucy either side of Mum and Dad, and my room right at the far end of the house.

★

89

On Wednesday evening I got ready to go out. But Dad stopped me on my way through the kitchen.

'Where do you think you're going?'

'To the youth club.'

'I told you, you're not going anywhere for a week.'

'It's only the youth club, Dad. I haven't been anywhere for nearly a week.'

'I said a week. You're not going anywhere for a week.'

I went into the porch and put my shoes on. Dad followed. When I reached for the door handle he was there before me, his hand huge on the knob. 'You're not going out, I say!'

Anger rose up in me as I contemplated being shut in the house even longer. 'You can't stop me!'

I ran to the other end of the house, to the back door. Dad ran after me. The back door was never used, and there were huge bolts that were stiff. He came up behind me, pulling my hands away as I started to pull at the bolts. Crying, I fought to get free of him, but he had hold of me by the wrists.

'What are you trying to do?' he shouted.

'I want to go out!' I screamed, struggling to free myself. But I was held fast. I looked in my father's eyes and thought I saw that he was enjoying it, the total control.

I put all my strength into wrenching my arms free, and when I couldn't move them even an inch, I thought I would go mad.

I screamed again. My father held on. I was powerless, helpless, nothing.

The fight went out of me then, and he let me go.

Mum and Dad just stopped speaking to me after that.

I think they told Teddy not to speak to me either and Lucy had always been kept so far away from me that I hardly noticed her presence at all.

Mum stopped preparing meals for me. She'd call 'Dinner!' and I'd forget, arriving in the kitchen to find my place wasn't set. I'd casually walk through as if it didn't matter. Or head straight back the way I'd come.

All that week, after my fight with Dad, I stole food from the pantry when there was no one around. I carried it to my bedroom, stuffing bread and biscuits into my mouth with my body on fight-or-flight alert, partly because of the way Dad could creep up and surprise me, and partly because of my guilty conscience.

At the end of the week Dad caught hold of me as we were walking past each other in the hallway. 'You're making your mother ill,' he said, 'and I want you out of this house by tomorrow night.'

He looked at me for a few moments with cold eyes. I could see myself reflected in them, a small blot like a flaw on the iris. 'As far as I'm concerned, I don't have a daughter anymore. And I don't want to see you when I get home tomorrow evening, d'you hear?'

Triumph folded across his face for an instant. Then he pulled his cheeks taut again and strode purposefully away. He didn't look back at me and the door into the kitchen click-clacked closed behind him.

Inside my head something tilted dangerously. I stood still because there was nothing to pull me in any particular direction. I had nowhere to go, neither immediately, nor in order to meet this ultimatum.

The hallway was silent, the curtains still drawn. Dad usually opened them on his way downstairs, with one smart synchronised sweep of his arms. I used to imagine he learned how to do it that way as an officer in the army, alongside the polishing of his leather carpet slippers and the careful origami he practised on enormous white handkerchiefs.

A slice of light slid through a gap in the saggy velvet curtains. It lit the vivid blue of my mother's polling-day dress, which hung, in dry-cleaners' polythene, from one of the giant wooden coat-hooks on the wall. Last weekend Dad had polished the big blue Bentley he kept for special occasions, and this lunchtime he would wear his royal-blue tie to drive it to the polling station.

There, for the first time, my parents, along with the majority of the country, would vote for a woman: Margaret Thatcher.

It wasn't just my world that was about to change.

I must have stood still a long time. Then I heard Dad striding about in the kitchen. The sound of his footsteps made me anxious and I headed quickly for the stairs.

In my room I sat on the edge of the bed. Overcome with tiredness, I just wanted to crawl under the covers and sleep. But I felt too vulnerable.

I sat on the bed and thought. Dad's words were a brick wall.

I fetched the largest suitcase I could find from the loft. It was an ancient beige thing, which might only have been beige because all the colour had rubbed off it – it was difficult to tell. It smelled of the loft. I packed my clothes into it, and a few photographs: Teddy with a pudding-basin haircut, sitting on a tiny sledge, and some old school photos in which Teddy was blond and neat and radiant, whilst my wild black hair looked as though it had never been brushed.

I packed everything I owned, pausing when I came upon a copy of my adoption certificate. 'CERTIFIED COPY OF AN ENTRY IN THE RECORDS OF THE GENERAL REGISTER OFFICE,' I read. My name was given as 'Arabella Cordon' and under 'NAME AND SURNAME, ADDRESS AND OCCUPATION OF ADOPTER OR ADOPTERS' was written 'Duncan Charles Cordon, Lake House, Cherry Tree Lane, Woodstowe, Nottinghamshire. Chartered Accountant, and Eileen Cordon, Housewife.'

Mum had explained on the morning she gave it to me that the law required her name to appear alongside Dad's, even though she was my real mother. It was because they had married before Dad officially adopted me. A ridiculous system, Mum had said, and the law had since been changed. Still, it was odd.

I had to sit on the suitcase to close it. It fastened okay, but I could only just lift it. When I finally got up there were wings beating in my chest. I heaved the suitcase downstairs as noisily as possible, my skin alive at the same time to the faintest squeak not of my own making.

I wanted someone to stop me.

Dad had gone to work, but Mum stood at the kitchen sink, looking out of the window. I dragged the suitcase past her.

I chose a spot opposite the kitchen window to pump up my bike tyres and strap the heavy case onto the bicycle carrier; but she didn't call to me, or even appear to see me.

As I made my way clumsily down the path, and through the garden gate, I strained to hear the voice which would call me back. It would inevitably come, because leaving was an idea, something that was said, but surely, surely, never meant.

It didn't feel real, until I started to walk away down the lane. Then I saw drops of rain on the stone wall bordering our garden, and I felt a chill wind in the nape of my neck. I slipped on the wet tarmac of the road, and the physical world came up too fast to meet me.

I got up and continued along with bloody palms and knee, the confirmation that this was really happening.

Soho, London 1987

Little Gerda began to repeat 'Our Father'.

'Get out! Get out! Get out!' The door to dressing room two, which the priest had opened only slightly, closed again rapidly. 'Fuck! Fuck! Fuck! Fuck!' Grace, who'd been doing all the shouting held her head in her hands.

We had been warned about the priest – it was on the bottom of the running order: *the Revd James Whittaker will be visiting this evening. 8–10 p.m.* I wondered if he'd been warned about Grace.

'It's a tradition,' Saf had told me. 'Because this is officially a West End theatre and West End theatres have priests. It's from the time when people thought actresses were all on the game, you know? Save our souls and stuff.'

'Really? Have you met the priest then?'

'I met the old one. He was bloody awful. This guy's not been here before.'

'And they actually come here – backstage – in the dressing rooms?'

'You don't have to let him in the dressing room if you don't want to. The old one used to just creep around in the corridor for a bit.'

'But what's the point?'

'I dunno. Try to speak to us, you know? Grace always goes mad, because her dad's a priest and she hates them.'

When she wasn't working, Grace always looked like a cross between a punk and a hiker. She was learning how to juggle and ride a unicycle on a circus-skills course and this interested me, but we never really seemed to hit it off, so I didn't find out any more about it. She had a theory that all women who worked as strippers had been sexually abused as children, which I took to mean that she had. Another girl, Elaine, had talked about a friend of her father who used to baby-sit for her and her sisters and did stuff like that. Elaine didn't mind talking about it at all. I asked her once what her father's friend did to her and she said he used to get his cock out; she called it a cock. He'd ask her to play with it, touch her in inappropriate places. Elaine told all this in an amused tone of voice and that was the only thing I felt I couldn't ask her, why she sounded amused when she told us about it.

But Grace didn't talk about stuff. She was a bit different: she didn't buy clothes all the time like the rest of us and she didn't go to beauty salons either. I never saw her in anything other than dirty-looking pairs of jeans, which she wore with plain black T-shirts in summer. In winter she added muddy-coloured woollen jumpers and a tea-cosy hat. She looked more like a young lad than a girl and I wondered sometimes what the punters would think if they could see her like that. If you saw her on the street you'd never imagine her body being so perfect, or that twice nightly she performed an act called 'Lady Jane' in, and out of, a gold, sequinned dress and diamante earrings. She ripped off the huge clip-on earrings and chucked them at the formica make-up bench.

'Pervert!' The priest wasn't there anymore so this was thrown out to the room in general.

'I feel sorry for him,' I said. 'You haven't even let him in the room, so how do you know he's a pervert?'

'Because they're all perverts and weirdos – I should know, my dad's a priest.'

'But this guy's only doing his job. He can't help it if we're all half-naked when he comes in here.' In fact, most of the girls were wearing costume or had towels or dressing gowns wrapped round them, in honour of the priest's visit.

Grace gave me a pitying look. 'So why does he come to see the show?'

'Does he?'

'Yes, they always come to see the show first. He'd just been out there watching you strut your stuff before he came in here to talk to us.'

I considered this. 'Well, maybe they don't want to seem disapproving. And he can't very well talk to us about what we do if he hasn't seen it.'

Grace picked some glitter out of the corner of her eye with a cotton bud. 'That's crap.'

The other girls were quiet, but I could feel that sympathies generally lay with Grace – it was why no one else was speaking. It wasn't my own dressing room; I'd only gone in there for a change of air. But the air suddenly felt a bit hostile.

'Maybe,' I said. 'Anyway, I'm on in a minute.' I crept out.

It was odd how the two dressing rooms had a completely different feel, one from the other. Dressing room two was always a bit darker and quieter. It had an edge about it, or at least for me it did. Dressing room one, on the other hand, my dressing room, was the talkative one. A few months back we'd had a journalist in, and even though Vince Veroni got us all together beforehand and told us to 'be nice', the girls in dressing room two had virtually refused to speak. It must have been a relief for the journalist to come into our dressing room because we all had a bit of a natter. We'd enjoyed answering his questions, collaborating with him in making our job sound like 'the way the daring, naughty girls have fun in London'.

When the article was published in one of the Sunday papers, girls from our dressing room were described as 'beautiful' and 'articulate' whilst a couple of girls in dressing room two, referred to by their real names, were 'miserable'.

Still, I was surprised, when I walked back into my dressing room after my stage act, to see the priest rising slowly from my chair.

'I'm sorry, is this your chair?' He was very well-spoken, but not uptight, and he looked like a priest: grey at the temples, dog collar, fatherly.

'Oh, yes, but it's fine. I'm going out in a minute.' As I spoke I remembered what Grace had told me. 'Did you see the show already?' I asked him.

Seeming almost, if not completely, at ease surrounded by semi-naked women, he just said, 'Yes,' then looked to me for further guidance.

'Oh, er, did you like it?' I couldn't think why on earth I was asking the question.

'It looks very professional,' he said, sounding very professional. 'What do *you* think of it?' He looked at me straight: curious, rather than censorious.

'Oh, I think it's great!' I said and dropped to my knees at his feet to retrieve my street shoes. He didn't respond for a few moments and I found myself feeling uncomfortably false, in a way I hadn't with the reporter.

'I really think I should give you your chair back,' was all he said finally. He got up and stood with his back to the door. 'Well, I've enjoyed talking to you all. Thanks for talking to me. I'll be back in at some point so I hope some of you will still be here on my return.' I felt strangely disappointed and found myself resisting a surprising urge to prevent him leaving, but there was a general chorus of 'Bye . . . yeah, bye,' and he went quietly out of the door.

'What was he talking to you about?' I asked the others when I judged he was out of earshot.

'Oh, just where we live, how we get to work, where we come from originally, stuff like that.'

I struggled with the zip on my jeans – I was getting dressed to go out and fetch coffee. 'He didn't talk about God then?'

'No.'

'Does anyone here believe in God?' I asked, suddenly fascinated. The others stared at me. There was a general shaking of heads and murmuring. But I didn't think it meant no one believed, it meant it was boring, or too deep and meaningful for a dressing-room conversation. Funny how we could be closeted together stark naked night after night, yet never really get to know one another well.

I left the dressing room and headed off. At the top of the stairs to the stage door, Bill, our doorman, a retired seaman who looked just like a retired seaman, halted me with a look and a finger to his lips. I looked at him questioningly and he made the gesture again, then pointed down the stairs to indicate there was some-body there. I stood next to him and waited. 'What?' I whispered, smiling at his unusual request and his serious face, but he just gestured again, *stay here*. Then Elaine came up the stairs looking glowing and relaxed, like she'd just had a full body massage and a milk bath. At the same time, I heard the stage door to the street bang closed below.

Elaine's face took on a closed look when she saw me and she passed through the door to the dressing rooms without speaking.

'What was that all about?' I asked Bill.

He shrugged. 'She asked the priest to bless her,' he said, 'but you didn't hear it from me.'

'To bless her?' *Elaine! Of all people.*

He shrugged. 'Each to their own.'

I didn't think about God again until the night the window blew in. There was noise in my dream; a game on a screen in black-and-white; dark shapes moving too fast around the edges of sleep; a crash, glass all over the yellow-and-white striped duvet. The glass felt sharp, real. Cold night air rushed into the room. This wasn't a dream.

I sat up and moved the duvet to one side. It was covered in pieces of glass which crashed and tinkled together as I moved the covers over. There was a hole where the window had been; wind and cold night air invaded the room. Now I became aware of the noise. Planes? Explosions? I had the impression the building was moving.

I didn't think about the danger of treading on glass. My bedroom no longer felt safe and I raced into the sitting room to look out of the window there.

The sitting-room window boomed as the wind hit it repeatedly like an invisible fist. I stood back in case it blew in.

I caught sight of something flying across the road below. It looked like a motorbike. I checked my watch, as if knowing the time would bring back a sense of normality. *The end of the world? Always happens at this time in the morning.*

The end of the world. Was that what this was?

I turned on the TV – only fuzzy black-and-white lines. I changed channels but it was the same. The building seemed to be rocking. There was banging above me, as though the whole structure was preparing to take off. The window boomed again. I knelt down on the floor leaning my hands and head on the sofa. 'Our Father who art in heaven, hallowed be thy name. Thy kingdom come, thy will be done, on earth as it is in heaven. Give us this day our daily bread and forgive us our trespasses, as we forgive those who trespass against us. Lead us not into temptation, but deliver us from evil . . .'

Deliver us from evil.

'For thine is the kingdom, the power and the glory, forever and ever. Amen.'

Had I got it right? I wasn't sure. I tried to remember more prayers and realised I didn't know any. The Bible? *If thine eye offend thee, cut it out,* was all I could come up with. Not particularly comforting. It made me think of Dad. *As far as I'm concerned I don't have a daughter anymore.* He was a man of the times. IRA bombs. The Falklands War. *If thine eye offend thee, cut it out.* The gunman at Hungerford who walked into a school and killed fourteen people. If thine eye offend thee, blow it up, pretend it doesn't exist.

But this kind of thinking wasn't going to do me any good. I

tried the Lord's Prayer again: 'Our Father, who art in heaven, thy kingdom come . . .'

There was an almighty tearing and crashing of metal. I raced back to the window to see the roof of the bus shelter across the road fly off, like a kite ascending. It went up, up, about twenty feet, then sped across the road in a downward trajectory, smashing into the side of a parked car. Windows broken and roof dented, the car turned over on its side as if in surrender.

Now there was a loud bang like a bomb going off. I couldn't see anything but it sounded like more windows being blown in above me.

War? Wouldn't I know if war had been declared?

But I knew it wasn't really war, it was *it*, the end of the world. I knelt again, racking my brains for the words that would save me. The Bible, the Bible; why couldn't I remember what I'd been taught?

At school, when I asked my RE teacher why he taught RE, he'd told us a story: 'I was in the desert, serving in the military. I caught some kind of disease out there and I was taken to an army hospital. Some very basic place, a camp, in the middle of nowhere. The illness I had made me unable to sweat. I was burning up and I couldn't sweat. They put me in a bed in a ward, not that I was aware of it – I was too far gone. That night, the first night, was the decider for me. If I managed to sweat I'd live, if not, I'd be dead by morning.

'During that night I became aware of my soul leaving my body. I looked down on myself in the bed. I could see my body. I was somewhere in the air above the bed. Then there was someone else there with me. It was the bloke from the bed opposite mine. He had burns, very severe burns all over his body; I don't know how I knew that. But he was like me, he wasn't in his body now, he was floating above it. We were both just our souls, hanging in the air between the beds. But this other chap started to fight me and I knew what he wanted. He wanted to get inside my body, to escape his own and take mine instead. We fought – our souls fought – this fight, up in the air in the middle of the ward, between our two beds, and I knew that if I lost I would be dead, and he would be in my body.

'I was struggling, losing. He was going to win. I was afraid, but I didn't have any strength left to fight. So I cried out, "Jesus, help me!" Not in the manner you usually would. I meant it, I really meant it. And the minute, the *second*, I used Jesus's name the other chap vanished and I was back in my body, in my own bed.

'In the morning my sheets were wet through. I had sweated all the heat out and I was on my way to recovery. The chap in the other bed, who did turn out to have severe burns, was dead.'

It was quite a story; it was why I was praying.

I tried to imagine being outside my body; seeing myself as others saw me. But my body just seemed to take on more prominence than it had when I was inside it.

And what was God to me? I'd never believed in anything, except fairy stories – and John Dodd maybe, who was a kind of fairy story as well. I thought of Elaine, being blessed on the stairs at work, and the peaceful expression on her face afterwards, before she saw me. Faith: the faith of Elaine, the faith of my old RE teacher, where did it come from? Saf had asked me what I believed in and I'd said Peter Pan. I found comfort, not just in the story, but in the sight and feel of the book I'd had as a child, the fantastic blue or sepia drawings of Peter, wearing pixie boots and a little skullcap with a pointy bit on the crown.

A great crashing came then from the roof; it seemed as though a giant stood there, pounding his feet amidst the cracking and splintering noises. I had no way of knowing that what I was experiencing was a hurricane, the worst storm in England since 1703. 'Our Father . . .' I began again.

I continued to say the Lord's Prayer into the early hours, as the unseen force outside ripped and slashed. But in my head there were only those beautiful pictures of Peter Pan showing Wendy how to fly.

Nottinghamshire 1979

He felt the pain no longer, but the splinter was there.

Some people sense that you have no protectors, no fall-back, no way out. Like Sharon's teacher did.

Sharon was a girl I knew from Georgie's, and I lived with her and her family for about three months, in a council house in Beeston. I went to Linda's first but her mum took one look at me and my suitcase, folded her arms and said, 'We're having nothing to do with this.'

'One night only!' she allowed in the end, after much pleading on my behalf from Linda. So I stayed there the first night, a Friday, and went to work with my story on the Saturday morning.

Sharon was seventeen, and she had worked at Georgie's full-time for nearly a year before I started there. She liked showing me what to do, tidying the rails, replenishing stock, unpacking new stuff as it came in, and putting security tags on all the clothes.

I liked Sharon because she liked me. A lot of the girls had snubbed me because of my 'posh' name and accent. For Sharon, these attributes of mine were attractions. She called me 'Bella' for greater intimacy (soon the other girls followed suit) and she treated me like a rich relation fallen on hard times.

When I told Sharon I'd been thrown out of home, she was excited. She phoned her mum straightaway, then offered me a bed at her house.

Sharon had a tiny pink room with tiny pink bunk beds, and she let me choose bottom or top. I chose top, thinking it would be less claustrophobic, but once in bed the ceiling was too close.

Sharon talked until midnight and I talked back to be polite.

She had plans for me: she would introduce me to all her friends; I could be the sister she'd never had; we could go clubbing together every Saturday; we would have double dates; maybe even a double wedding.

I lay in the tiny bed listening. I felt like a Sindy doll in a mousetrap, and even when I closed my eyes I could feel the pink ceiling pressing in on my head.

Part of Sharon's plan for me was that I should go full-time at Georgie's. I thought this was a good idea. There was no question of continuing at school without the means to pay for anything, and the manager at Georgie's was happy for me to go full-time from the following week. There was so little work around I counted myself lucky to have a job.

Georgie's was deep inside an indoor shopping centre. The lights were dim, and cover versions of pop songs played loudly all day. The clothes squatted heavily together in a dozen huge carousels on the shop floor.

There were no real windows, only a display window and the yawning rectangle which allowed the shoppers in, and through which it was possible to pass at lunchtime onto the main drag of the indoor shopping centre.

We stood for hour after hour in that dimly lit room with very little to do, listening to the interminable tapes until we knew every word of every song off by heart. After one week as a full-timer I felt as though I'd been there a year.

One afternoon Sharon and I were trying to work close enough together to chat, singing along to the piped pop tunes in spite of ourselves, when she waved at a man who'd paused in the shop doorway.

The man waved back and came towards us, winding his way around the circular stands full of pleated skirts and jerseys with glitter on them. Sharon said, 'That's my teacher! He's a teacher at my old school!'

I watched them talking. I couldn't hear what they were saying, because they were on the other side of a carousel, and the music was too loud. He wore a fairly smart green shirt with a really battered denim jacket, and he was handsome in a smooth, grown-up kind of way.

I couldn't imagine myself chatting to any of my ex-school-teachers as casually as Sharon seemed to do, and I wondered what she found to talk to him about.

After a few minutes they turned to me and Sharon introduced him by his first name. I had been expecting her to call him 'Sir' but his name was Steve and he said, 'Hi! So you're Sharon's new mate! Are you working here full-time?'

'Yes.'

'What's it like?'

'Okay.'

'Yeah?'

'Yeah.' I felt I wanted to explain that this wasn't all I was capable of, so I said, 'I was going to go into the sixth form at school, but I've left because Mum and Dad threw me out. So I had to get a job. I'd like to be an actress really.'

'Yeah?' He sounded impressed with me. 'Well, I teach Drama and English, Sharon's probably told you. I might be able to give you a few pointers. Introduce you to a few people.'

He didn't talk like a teacher. But he was a grown-up, and I knew I wasn't. There was a line between him and me. Then he said, 'Would you like to come out with me tonight?' And the line disappeared.

He said he was going to see some friends for dinner. 'We can have a chat. Someone might know something, take you in the right direction. And we'll have a good meal.'

I was flattered, and in need of a good meal.

I met him at his place, a small flat in Nottingham city centre. It was quite difficult to find – I hardly knew the city at all. Steve – I still felt as if I should be calling him 'Sir', or at least 'Mr' – let me into a tiny dark hallway. Then he stood arranging his hair, looking into a cabinet mirror on the wall in a bathroom, just to the right of where I came in.

I waited, awkwardly casual in the doorway.

To stand at such close quarters, forced to watch him perform such a personal task, repelled me. I found myself holding my breath and I was relieved when we left.

Steve's friends, a couple who were also teachers, were about the same age as him and lived in a flat a lot like his. They seemed slightly amused all the time we were there. The woman, whose name I didn't catch, had long hair and didn't say much. But I didn't feel unwelcome.

Apart from being nervous because they were all older than I was, I felt okay, until the meal arrived. I was horrified when I saw it was spaghetti bolognese. I pictured what might be my slurping attempts to eat it – tomato sauce on my chin and clothes. It was scarily unattractive and I was in a sweat just thinking about it.

I glanced at the long-haired woman. She had put candles on the table. Her face glowed and her blonde hair shone in the light. She held her hair back over her shoulders in a graceful pose, somehow managing to pop in a neat mouthful of spaghetti and still look amused.

I got a bit of sauce on my fork and sucked it in what I hoped was a foxy way. Then I feigned an all-consuming interest in the conversation the others were having, although I'd missed the start of it because of my panic. Now I didn't have a clue what they were on about.

After a few minutes during which I watched the others eating and talking, Steve turned to me.

'Look, here, like this,' he said, digging into my plateful with his fork.

I thought I would die of embarrassment, but Steve's friends took no notice at all, just continued to talk with each other.

Steve used a spoon to support the fork, which he twisted round with spaghetti. For an awful moment I thought he would feed me, but instead he ate the mouthful on his fork, gesturing at the same time towards my own cutlery. I found it easy enough to copy him. I was very hungry and I ate all the spaghetti and every-thing that was put in front of me after that.

Everyone drank lots of wine. They talked about teaching, and about Margaret Thatcher. Apparently her father had once been mayor of Grantham, although before that he was a grocer. They said she'd been encouraged by her father, inspired by him.

I thought of Dad wanting me to run faster, dive more perfectly, or hold my breath longer than other kids. But maybe Margaret Thatcher had another type of dad, gentle, sympathetic, sharing: the stuff of my dreams.

Thatcher had won the election on the day I left home. I'd seen TV clips of her, waving as she entered Number Ten, moving into the most prestigious home in the country just as I was being turfed out of mine.

'She might change things for women,' Steve said.

But his friend replied, 'Nah, don't be silly. She's a man with a handbag.'

I didn't contribute anything to the conversation, but Steve squeezed my hand every now and then, and kept topping up my wine glass, so I could tell he wanted me there.

When it was time to go everyone kissed each other. Steve put his arm round me as we walked off down the road. He did it easily and naturally, like he'd been doing it all his life. It didn't feel natural to me, but I let him lead me through the dark streets and the little alleys that linked them together, until we were almost back at his flat. When I recognised his road I stopped and said, 'I'd better be getting back.'

In fact I wasn't at all sure of the way back to the bus station or if the buses were still running, but I thought Steve would help me get back to Sharon's somehow.

I had moved away from under his arm, and now looking up at him I was surprised to see him looking puzzled and irritated.

But he spoke gently enough. 'The buses will have stopped running by now. Why don't you sleep at my place? I can walk you to the bus station in the morning.' He smiled.

I wanted to be wanted and I was an easy lay. It would have been difficult to go off on my own, to try and find a way back to Sharon's place in the middle of the night. And I was worried too about getting in once I got there – I had no key and they might be all locked up for the night. I didn't want Sharon's teacher. I wasn't even sure I liked him, but I wanted to keep his approval, and he had saved me from the spaghetti.

Afterwards it was comforting too, to be held in his arms in his warm, cosy flat.

In the morning he made tea, which we drank as we dressed. It was Saturday, but he said he had an appointment. He would walk me to the bus station first. It was obvious to me that I would never see him again, that his business with me was finished.

The bus to Beeston was already waiting at the station, and as I sat down next to a window, the driver revved the engine. Steve stood on the platform and waved. Just before the bus set off he came close to the window.

'I love you,' he mouthed, as the bus roared away. I couldn't understand why he did it. He must have thought I was stupid.

Soho, London 1987

'I always sleep with my dagger by my side,' replied the little robber-maiden. 'One never knows what may happen.'

The Pageant's thirtieth anniversary party was planned for the third week of my employment there. It was a double celebration because it was Tracey's thirtieth birthday too. Vince had commissioned life-sized cardboard figures of all of the Pageant girls in costume. A room at head office was completely redecorated in red and all the cardboard women were displayed there.

Four real girls from the Pageant, including me, were asked to go along to serve champagne. We didn't have to do it, but we would be well-paid for it, and it was just a couple of hours on Friday lunchtime.

On the day, there weren't very many people there, although the room looked pretty full because of all the cardboard cut-outs. We four girls had been told by Vince to avoid talking to people. 'You're here to look beautiful, not to make conversation,' he had said.

Everyone soon had their drinks, so it was incredibly boring.

I went to the toilet after an hour, just for something to do, and while I was in there, I heard someone come into the next cubicle and do some really obvious sniffing. When I came out, Tracey Veroni was standing at the mirror, dabbing at her nose with her fingers.

'Hi,' I said, but she didn't speak. It was as though she didn't see me at all. She just flicked her hair back and left.

After that I played 'spot the people coked up to the eyeballs' to pass the time a bit. But I came to the conclusion that unless they were playing with their nose, you just couldn't tell.

Vince Veroni and his girlfriend, Trudy, stood in a corner of the room, with a load of guys who I supposed were business associates, all quite close together. The media people stood a little bit apart, in ones, twos and threes, with bigger gaps between them. Tracey sat on one of several big red couches along the wall at the back with one of the men I saw at the audition.

A man came over and introduced himself to me, even though I was holding my tray like a barrier. 'Hi, my name's Rob,' he said, holding his hand out and waiting. I felt forced to put the tray down on the bar and shake it.

'Fruity Tootie, I presume?' He must have read it on my cardboard cut-out, which, like Saf's, was emblazoned with the name of the act we performed together.

'Yes,' I said, trying not to grit my teeth.

'I have to admit I've never seen the show, is it good?'

'It's difficult to tell when you're in it,' I told him, 'and I haven't been in it very long.'

'What makes you want to be in it? Is it something you always wanted to do? Or er . . . ?'

I looked at him to see if he was taking the piss. But he seemed genuine, so I held back from saying sarcastically that it had been my lifelong ambition to be a stripper.

'It's a way to get an Equity card,' I said – saying I was doing it for the money in any other job might have been okay, but in this one, it made me sound like I was for sale.

'Oh, the stage is definitely your thing then?'

'Yes,' I said. Over his shoulder I could see Vince Veroni beckoning to me from the other side of the room. 'Excuse me.' I picked up my tray and went over.

'Just see if anyone wants more champagne, will you?' Mr Veroni's voice was muted, a kind of mutter in which the words were nevertheless distinct. On that occasion I thought it was his 'discreet' voice, but actually, I realised later, he spoke like that all the time.

I thought he must have cultivated it, in the same way Maggie Thatcher had hers.

I did another tour of the party. Tracey had moved to the centre of the room and was talking to some guy I hadn't seen before.

'If I stripped off, would you give me an audition?' the guy said to her. 'We could star together, or branch out into movies. What do you think?'

'I think I've heard that line before,' Tracey said. 'But it is more original than asking if my father knows what I do for a living.'

I turned away to serve a drink, then got back within earshot to hear the bloke say, 'I never thought I'd be here, mingling with the clitterati!' He laughed. 'Perhaps you can school me, I'm only an amateur. The difference between vulvas, for example, what does one need to look out for?'

'Oh, they're all very different,' Tracey said. 'Actually, in my line of work it's arseholes you've got to look out for, and I can spot one a mile off. Excuse me.' She turned and put her glass down very carefully on my tray, then made her way around the other guests, to go and stand by her father.

The arsehole put his drink down too. He went to speak to some other guy, and they left.

I stayed in town after the party and ate dinner at Delilah's before going on to the Pageant. After work I got the night bus back to my Deptford bedsit, arriving about half past one – my usual time when I didn't go clubbing.

I made tea before bed and I was really pleased to see, next to the kettle, a new mini-cooker, which had been delivered while I was out. The maintenance man had left it as a gift when he'd learned mine had packed up.

'Don't worry love, I've got one of them Baby Bellings you can have for free,' he'd said, introducing himself as Roger. 'Bung me your spare key, and I'll leave it for you – I can chuck the key back through the letterbox after.'

He'd been as good as his word, and it looked nice and clean too.

I took my tea, lit a cigarette, and went to sit on the bed. On the sheet covering the mattress was a bit of paper.

I didn't remember leaving it there.

I put my cigarette in the ashtray, and leaned over to pick the paper up. It was a tiny picture, torn from a magazine. A headshot of a girl, taken at an angle. She had her mouth open very wide. Almost touching her lips was a large, erect penis.

I froze, like an animal locked under the gaze of its predator. My ears buzzed and my heart started banging hard and fast.

The familiar traffic noise outside the window faded, and I had a mental image of my room spinning away with me in it, away from cosy Earth into cold, dark space.

The picture revolted me and I put it down quickly as if holding on to it could stain my hand. Obviously it was Roger, the maintenance man who'd left it; no one else had a key.

I had been stupid. To give my key away like that! I'd given it to someone who wasn't normal. Someone who might be very dangerous. I'd put myself at risk.

The key! I stood up too fast. Darkness closed in round my head. I stood still. Swayed. Fought it. I didn't pass out, but the effort of not doing so made me sweat.

I needed to see if he had posted the key back through the door. I looked down at the floor. But I couldn't see because my eyes were full of water.

Tears always accompanied fear for me. It wasn't crying, it was something involuntary, like sneezing. Now water was running from my eyes like from a tap, brimming and falling on the carpet, where I searched in vain for the key.

Instead of concentrating on the key, I was imagining Roger. Not the Roger I'd met, but a monstrous version. He would be on his way up the stairs, with my key.

'Where's the key? Where's the key?' I murmured out loud, trying to drag my mind back to serve me.

There was a clunking noise from next door, and my spine went rigid.

At the same instant, I saw the key.

I bent to get it, and I held it. Hard. Metal. It helped. I checked the door was locked.

But turning to face the room again, I had an awful creeping feeling, as if things in the room were really alive, just posing as inanimate objects in order to watch me.

I caught a glimpse of a movement in the wardrobe mirror, and I jumped.

But it was just me, wild-eyed. My eyes stayed on the wardrobe door though, travelling down to the lock. And then I knew.

He was in the wardrobe.

I looked at the chipped, gold-coloured knob, and underneath, the small lock without a key. I felt him watching me through the keyhole. That's what it was about for him. He wanted to see my reaction to the picture.

My eyes fixed on the black hole of the lock. I put the key down on the breakfast bar. I unhooked a saucepan from the rack on my right and held it up, ready to strike. Keeping my eyes on the lock, I moved to the wardrobe.

I took a breath and put my hand on the knob. The door opened on a quarter turn, and I flung it back.

There was no one there.

I stuck my free hand inside and batted about among the clothes. Nothing. I turned and scanned the room with frantic eyes – wall to wall, around the perimeter, up to the ceiling – looking for the places someone might hide.

My room was so small there wasn't really anywhere else. But I opened all the cupboards, just in case, and I checked the door was locked again.

I threw the picture in the bin, and washed my hands.

My bed looked the same as when I'd left it. The pillow a little depressed where my head had been, the bottom sheet creased and the duvet halfway down. I yanked the duvet off completely, in case something was hidden underneath it. There was nothing, but my mind was busy. Had he sat on my bed? How long was he in my room? Did he just bring that picture, or the whole magazine it had come from? Did he lie down on my bed? Did he have a wank?

I looked at the sheet again. I couldn't see any stains. I didn't want it near me though. I took off the sheet, pillowcase and duvet cover. I bundled them up and threw them in a corner. Then I washed my hands again.

I put a clean pillowcase on the pillow, and laid a bath towel across the mattress, because the spare sheet was in the wash. Then I put a clean cover on the duvet. I'd been holding myself so tense, my limbs ached now as if I'd been lifting weights.

Sitting down on the bed I lit another cigarette.

What if Roger had had another key cut? Was he planning to come back? What did he want? What was in his mind when he left the picture? Did he think I'd like it? Could I go to the police? What if they didn't believe me?

They'd want to know where I worked, and then they'd think I'd done something to encourage him. Had I given the wrong impression to Roger somehow?

I went over the day I met him in my mind, what I had said; the clothes I was wearing. I had been wearing my old black dungarees. My hair had been a mess, but I was wearing make-up, just eye make-up, no lipstick.

I imagined saying it in front of a judge and jury.

They would wonder why I was so het up of course, someone with a job like mine. But at work the men were away in a pit at my feet, and I was secure in the knowledge they could never come close. Now – this obscene message – it was like a hand in the dark reaching out to poke me, the ugly thoughts of men that I held at a distance rearing out of a nightmare to invade my real life, my personal space.

What if Roger knew where I worked and that had given him ideas? But how could he? There was nothing in my room to tell

114

him. Even my wage slips only said 'V City' on them – some tax dodge company set up by Vince Veroni, no doubt. It wouldn't have meant anything to Roger though, surely?

Nottinghamshire 1979

Every snowflake seemed much larger, and resembled a splendid flower, or a star with ten points; they were quite beautiful. 'See how curious!' said Kay. 'These are far more interesting than real flowers – there is not a single blemish in them. They would be quite perfect if only they did not melt.'

Sharon was waiting when I got back to her house, eager to hear all the details of the big date. I didn't know what to tell her. I had the same feeling I had when I once lost my purse, kind of sick in my stomach. So I kept it short.

'We went to his friends' for a meal, and then I slept with him. It wasn't very good.'

I watched myself go down in Sharon's estimation, and I wished I'd made an effort to make it more entertaining. Perhaps she would have forgiven me then, for being a slag.

Sharon was more streetwise than I was – at school she'd been offered five different kinds of drug, and said no to them all. But she had a close family, and family values. And she was still a virgin.

I already knew I didn't fit in at her house, and now she knew it too. But she would feel bad if she asked me to go – I'd only been there just over a week, and she'd been so enthusiastic about having me there in the first place. So we continued on together for a while.

Sharon had a brother, Warren, who was nineteen. Sometimes, when Sharon's mum was on an evening cleaning shift, Sharon and I would hang out with him and his friends in the cramped kitchen at her house. We got chips from a chippy round the corner, and ate them either sitting in one of three chairs round the small kitchen table, or leaning against the wall. The others shared cigarettes and we passed round cans of lager.

One night in the kitchen, everyone was giving each other shoulder massages. Sharon was playing her mum's Tom Jones LP on the stereo for a laugh. Warren's friend Martin wrapped a tea towel round his head, for some unexplained reason, and massaged me. At the same time he pretended to be Tom Jones, with me a fan in ecstasy. Everyone was laughing.

At the end of the evening Martin led me out onto the doorstep with him and we had a snog. He asked me to go to the Cave with him the following Saturday night.

I was hugging myself with glee because I really liked him, and Sharon was excited for me, even though things had been a bit cool between us. She helped me plan what I would wear: a leopard-print dress I already owned, fishnet tights I could buy, but I didn't have any shoes. I remembered Linda had some shoes that were black with a leopard-skin pattern on the heels, so I phoned and asked to borrow them. Linda said she'd drop them off at work for me on Saturday when she was in town shopping. So I was all set.

Except that by a quarter to six on Saturday Linda still hadn't come in with the shoes, and the shop was due to close at six. Sharon's shoes were too small for me and no one else seemed to have shoes to lend. I was going mad because I'd have to wear my cloddy old school 'pork-pie' shoes with the leopard-print dress.

When the shop closed I went to the toilets to change, as I was meeting Martin straight from work. Sharon and most of the other girls left while I was still fighting with the fishnets. I bundled up the clothes I'd taken off to shove into a locker.

There was a whole wall of lockers, none of which locked. It was just a place to stow our stuff. A couple of people had claimed particular lockers as their own, by putting stickers and postcards on them, but most of us just used any that were free. So I opened a locker at random, and to my surprise and relief, Linda's shoes were sitting neatly inside. Linda must have called in while I was on lunch and left the shoes with someone.

I put them on, emptied my bag for the obligatory security check at the door, packed it again, and ran off to meet Martin.

The Victoria Centre clock was chiming six when I got there. Martin was leaning on the first-floor railing looking down on it. We watched the clock perform its hourly dance, the golden petals opening to reveal metallic creatures dancing and playing musical instruments. The fountain splashed gold and blue reflections and we listened to the tinkling music.

Then the petals closed and there was only the sound of the water.

'I love this clock,' Martin said. 'I remember when it was put in. My auntie brought me to see it. That flower made of metal, all the gold and colours, like. It was the most beautiful thing I'd ever seen then. I'd never seen metal look like that before. I mean, it's just there to do a job usually.'

'But someone made something beautiful out of it.'

'There's something a bit magic isn't there? Rods and cogs and things. Like you could make a car for Noddy out of those bits.'

'Yeah, I can see that!' I was amazed. Men didn't, in my experience, talk about things being magical or beautiful, (not voluntarily anyway). I'd love for him to talk about me like that, I thought, eyeing the curious structure in front of us, wondering about its appeal, and looking for any clock-like qualities I might be able to assimilate.

Martin was still gazing at the water. 'It'd look good if there was steam coming from the pool at the bottom. Or ice,' he said. 'D'you know what the triple point of water is?'

I shook my head.

'It's when you get ice, water and steam all at the same time.'

'I don't see how that could happen.'

'You have to have a particular temperature, and pressure, that's the triple point. If you do it as an experiment in a lab then you start with water and water vapour, then change the temperature slightly to add ice. I reckon I could use that to make a really wild kind of fountain.'

We leant over the rail and looked at the clock together in a companionable silence. For some reason, the triple point made me think of 'the Father, the Son and the Holy Ghost', but Martin's little science lesson also reminded me of Dad and how he used to go on about engines. In a funny kind of way I suppose Martin talking like that made me feel at home. I found myself telling him about Thor and steam-engine rallies as we left the shopping centre.

At the Cave there was live music, and we danced and snogged a lot. Around midnight we went and stood in the car park to cool down and smoke. Martin said he'd left home because his parents were boring. He was signing on, but he worked now and then as a DJ, with a friend who owned decks. He went on about musical taste for a while, and a lot of bands I'd never heard of. He said Abba were awful and that John Peel was the best DJ. I didn't want to admit to liking Abba, and I'd barely heard of John Peel, so I just listened to his enthusiasm.

We stayed at the club until it shut, and then we stood in the car park again. I told Martin the circumstances of my leaving home. '*I wonder . . .*' he sang to me, '. . . *why she ran away, and I wonder where she will stay . . .*' When he hit the high notes for all the 'why's in the song it made us grin, but his voice stayed strong, '. . . *my little runaway.*' The last three words he sang quiet and so close I felt his breath on my face. Then he kissed me tenderly and I surprised myself with the forcefulness with which I kissed him back; it was because he'd sung 'my' as if I really had somewhere to belong.

About three in the morning, we went back to Martin's squat, which he shared with two other guys.

'We can just sleep together. We don't have to do anything,' he said, as we tumbled onto his single bed, unable to keep our hands off each other. 'Easy! Easy!' he said as the bed rocked and he pointed underneath. There were bricks piled up at each corner to support the frame.

Once he was inside me he slid back and forth, rather than pounding up and down like the other men I'd slept with. It made a difference. I came noisily, and for the first time, bar masturbating. At the same time the bed toppled over onto the floor and Martin slipped out as we fell, his semen escaping in little spurts all over my belly. I laughed until I fell asleep, and I slept deeply for the first time since leaving home.

When we woke up the following afternoon, Martin asked me to go out with him again on Tuesday, and I skipped back to Sharon's to tell her my news, leaving out the sex part this time.

On Monday I left Linda's shoes at Sharon's, because I wouldn't be able to get them back to her for a week. I went to work in my 'pork-pies' as usual. I arrived a bit late, and ran straight downstairs to put my coat and bag in a locker. Then I went back up to the shop floor. The shop was still closed and our manager Lyndsey was standing by the counter with one of the other workers, Alison, and Alison's friend, Little Min. I smiled, but they didn't smile back. 'Why did you steal Alison's shoes?' Lyndsey said.

I looked behind me to see if she could be speaking to someone else. She continued, 'You were seen on Saturday night at the Cave, Bella.'

I couldn't think what to say first. There was a logical sequence of events I needed to explain, but this accusation was already so off the mark it confused me.

'I – who? The shoes I wore were Linda's shoes!' Their faces took on a disgusted look. I carried on, 'Linda is my friend, you don't know her, but they were her shoes. I asked her to bring them, and then I thought she must have brought them and given them to somebody, who must have put them in a locker, and not told me.'

It sounded weak, even to me. And at the same time I was remembering how tight the shoes were, even though Linda was exactly the same size as me. The three of them just stared.

'I didn't realise! I wondered why they were so tight!' I said.

Lyndsey said, 'Where are Alison's shoes now?'

'At Sharon's house. That's where I'm staying.'

Lyndsey folded her arms. 'We don't like thieves here, Bella. Go and get your things. You can ask Sharon to bring Alison's shoes when she comes in tomorrow, and if we don't see them, it'll be a matter for the police to sort out.'

'But don't you believe —'

'Go and get your things. I don't want you working here.'

A few minutes later I was sitting in a coffee shop, wondering where to get another job, and how to survive until then. I sunk my head down over my coffee to feel the heat on my face, and thought about my real father. A liar and a thief, Mum had said. Was he also accused of something he didn't do? Or was I on a slippery slope, made slippery by bad blood, leading God knows where?

Sharon tried hard to be on my side. I think she believed me, but I knew the other girls at Georgie's would rip me apart as soon as I'd gone, and Sharon had to work with them every day. In addition, I'd been paying Sharon's mum rent, and now I didn't have any money. I had to ask her to wait until I got another job.

But unemployment was nearing the two million mark, and young people were among the worst hit, especially those without qualifications. Martin and I searched the local and evening newspapers every day for jobs but it didn't make it any easier to stay with Sharon, or face her mum who was feeding me.

One night, a week or so after I got the sack, Sharon and I were lying in our bunk beds. She said, 'You don't want to live here anymore, do you?'

It was difficult to reply because it was true; I didn't want to live there. I'd never wanted to live there really. But where would I go?

Sharon had already worked it out. 'You can live with Martin.

You two are going steady now, and I'll be glad to get my room back. It's a bit small for two, isn't it?'

So I lived at Martin's, and signed on the dole. The bed on bricks continued to collapse regularly, and the filthy flat was made filthier still by the addition of a kitten, which shat under the sofa and rooted through the bin when there was no cat food. The kitchen was too dirty to cook in so we lived on chips and bread, and large mugs of sweet tea. On the day we cashed our dole cheques we'd celebrate with a Chinese takeaway. We didn't budget at all, and often ran out of money completely. Then we would visit Martin's elderly auntie who gave us tea and fruitcake, and I would beg milk and bread on credit from the corner shop.

Geographically speaking, I was much closer to Mum and Dad now than I had been at Sharon's, but like Kay, the boy in 'The Snow Queen', I was all ice and I never thought about them now.

In 1980, unemployment topped two million. One of the guys we lived with left and went to live in a squat in London. He sent us a postcard of Trafalgar Square. He'd got a job as a courier – there were loads of jobs in London, he wrote.

I'd never been to London, but the idea of it contained a variety of colourful images, which, for me, combined to create a kind of English Disneyland full of characters from Oliver Twist, palaces, red soldiers with black fur hats, talking cats, Big Ben, the BBC and streets paved with gold. And so Martin and I left Tiley Green for a space on the living-room floor of a Peckham squat.

Soho, London 1987

Then spoke the wood-pigeons, 'Coo, coo, coo! We have seen little Kay. A white fowl carried his sledge; he himself was in the Snow Queen's chariot, which passed through the wood while we sat in our nest. She breathed upon us young ones as she passed, and all died of her breath excepting us two.'

D elilah came to my rescue.
The night after I found the picture in my bedsit, I went with Saf to Auntie's, where Delilah sang most evenings.

Auntie's was short for The Man from Auntie's. It was a gay nightclub in Soho, popular with Pageant girls, due to its proximity to work. There were no lager louts, and I guess we felt relaxed. But also I loved the intimate decadence of the place, the gold panelling, crystal chandeliers and the waiting staff, made up entirely of beautiful young women, who were really beautiful young men.

There were a dozen small round tables, each with its own light glowing, a heart-shaped dance floor and a tiny stage. From midnight to two, five nights a week, there was a show starring several larger-than-life transvestites.

Rose in June, the MC, whom everyone called 'Rosie', was huge and round, like Humpty Dumpty. He wore an electric-blue dress to match his electric-blue eyes, and a blue Ascot-style hat, with pink roses round the brim. Rosie told jokes and introduced the singers, who were all rather more sophisticated and apparently feminine than he was.

Delilah appeared in high heels beneath a long gold lurex dress with glittering sleeves. His turban-style hat was also gold lurex, and he sparkled with diamante.

He sang jazz, standing centre-stage, crooning into the mike. A handsome young man in a tux accompanied him on piano.

When the show finished, Delilah went around the room chatting to people. He smoked a dark brown cigarette in a long cigarette holder, and his face was beautifully made up in pink, blue and gold.

Eventually he came to Saf and me.

'Darlings, my feet are killing me! The heel broke off my usuals, and I have to wear these things instead.' He pulled gently at the material of his dress, ruching it up to expose large stockinged feet, clad in silver sandals. 'Well, it should be okay – these are my size. But they belong to Rosie and they're all out of shape, because she's got bunions.'

We all contemplated the sandals while Delilah talked, twisting his feet this way and that. I'd never seen such massive feet in such dainty shoes.

Delilah gossiped a bit about the people in the club and then Saf told him about the caretaker at my bedsit, and what had happened to me the night before. I was scared to go home and Saf had offered to put me up for the night. It wasn't a long-term solution.

'Where does this jerk-off live?' Delilah asked.

'In a flat, on Blackheath,' I said. Roger had told me where he lived; that he'd got a flat to himself as part-payment for his job.

'Darling, Blackheath is too huge!' Delilah said.

I thought back to what Roger had actually said: 'I used to live in a council place, but this place I've got now is much nicer. Much more yuppie type of thing, you know? It's right overlooking the heath, and it's even got a pub next door – load of tossers trying to be Elvis on Saturday nights – now that's a laugh, that is.'

I related this little speech to Delilah who said, 'If we can find his flat, I will go and see him and make him a scare.'

I had visions of Delilah, decked out in gold lurex, turning up at the door of Roger's flat, and I wasn't sure about what effect it might have.

'Yeah? Thanks,' I said. 'Er . . . how do you mean?'

'I will be pretending to be your dad,' said Delilah, and I stared. It was the last thing I would've thought of.

'I can be the big man if you want,' he said, tossing his head a bit.

Next morning at ten, I left Saf and her boyfriend Simon asleep and crept out to where Delilah was waiting in a purple MG Midget.

The fantastic make-up of the previous evening was gone, and he looked all male in a black jersey and black jeans. There was a shadow of stubble on his beautiful face. I thought how kind he was to help me. Looking at him, I realised he was attractive to me in this mode, and I wondered about his sexuality. Saf said he wasn't necessarily gay – she'd never seen him with anybody. But I only considered his possible straightness for a moment, before I realised that I preferred to believe he was gay. It made me feel safe.

Delilah was playing a Billie Holiday tape. She had style, he said. During the journey he talked about other famous women he admired: Ella Fitzgerald, Jackie Onassis, Francesca Annis and Princess Diana. He said stylishness was often the result of people being brave enough to be themselves. I wasn't sure I agreed, especially as I found myself fighting an urge to sit up straighter in my seat with my toes pointed.

We passed the Elvis pub as we came onto Blackheath. It had banners up above the windows which read 'ELVIS HERE EVERY SATURDAY!' and 'BE ELVIS FOR A NIGHT!' Next door was a tall, thin building painted beige – an old place, converted into flats. Delilah parked up a little way on, and we climbed out of the MG.

There was a lot of wind, and the clouds were moving fast over a June sun too feeble to heat the shady side of the road. The streets were quite empty and eerie without the constant drone of traffic. Was it because it was Sunday? Or being so far out of town? It made everything feel a bit unreal. Some children shouted on the heath, running after a kite with a long pink tail, while their dog kept its distance, barking. Delilah put on a pair of mirrored Ray-Bans and said, 'Call me Dad.'

We set off down the street, and I noted how Delilah changed his walk to a swagger to match his new persona. He was big, and he looked authoritative and fit. Trotting along at his side, I felt a swell of pride in my chest. It was a glimpse into another world, where dads called their daughters 'Princess' and jumped immediately to protect them, like handsome Alsatian dogs.

The door to the flats was ajar. It was battered-looking, with opaque glass panels set into the upper half. Inside was a narrow windowless hallway. A flight of stairs with a grey banister climbed the wall to the right. The hallway continued on the left, a grey door at the end.

Delilah marched straight to the grey door and knocked. The wood was so thin it sounded as though he was trying to break the door down.

I grimaced, whispering fiercely, 'We don't even know if it's his flat!'

Delilah looked perfectly relaxed. 'We try all of them,' he said calmly.

He was about to knock again, when a woman came to the door. She was wearing a mauve tracksuit and lots of gold necklaces.

'Hello. Does the caretaker live here?' Delilah said.

'Yeah, he's not in,' the woman replied. She sounded northern.

'I have a message for him,' Delilah said. 'Will you mind if we come in?' I stood open-mouthed at his daring.

'Yeah, alright,' the woman stood to one side to let us in.

Delilah went through first, filling the doorway in front of me for a second. I followed in his wake and the woman led us to a grey-carpeted sitting room with two large grey sofas in it.

She reached down and picked up a new pack of Embassy Red from a low glass coffee table. She took the cellophane off, gesturing at the same time to the grey sofas. 'Take a seat if you want,' she said. She lit the cigarette with a gold lighter produced from her trouser pocket.

Delilah remained standing, so I did too. The woman took a long toke on the cigarette and blew it out again.

'Roger's gone to see his mam in Bromley. He doesn't work Sundays,' she said. From another room, there was the sound of a child screaming, 'I can't get it off! I can't get it off!' followed by a long, drawn-out wail.

'Wait a sec,' the woman said, disappearing through one of the grey-painted doors that led off the sitting room.

'He said he lived on his own,' I whispered to Delilah.

The noise from the other room stopped and the woman came back.

'Which flats are you from?' she said.

'My daughter has a bedsit in Deptford,' Delilah said.

'Well, he only goes out there on Fridays. I don't think you'll get him there sooner because . . .'

'Roger has been leaving obscene pictures in my daughter's bedsit.'

The woman's eyes widened. She brought down the hand holding the cigarette and spoke quickly, her voice suddenly shrill with anxiety.

'Not Roger! He wouldn't do that. He'd never do such a thing. It must've been somebody else.' She looked at me then, and spoke slowly, as if to a simpleton. 'It must've been somebody else, love. It wasn't him.' She sounded phoney.

Delilah stood still in the centre of the room. He spoke calmly and evenly. 'Unfortunately we know it was him. So, will you please tell to him to leave my daughter alone? I don't want him to come closer than twenty miles. I don't want that she will ever have to see him again. Tell him that if he comes to her again, if she sees him again, I will find him. And I will deal with him myself.'

'I'll tell him, I'll tell him – but it wasn't him. It wasn't him. He won't know what you're talking about . . .' The woman continued her nervous denials on Roger's behalf as we walked slowly out.

On the way to my place, Delilah said he was sure Roger wouldn't bother me again. He said he knew that type of guy, and he'd be prepared to bet on it.

We talked about Saf and Simon. Delilah liked Simon, but he thought he should be more concerned about Saf wandering round London at night, searching for her dad.

'I don't think there's much Simon can do to stop her,' I said.

'He can go with her.'

'Yeah, I suppose so, I hadn't thought about it. I wonder why he doesn't?'

But Saf was so sure of herself, so organised about her search, so seemingly unafraid. It had never occurred to me to go with her either. Now I felt as though it should have.

Delilah asked me about my parents. It was a long time since anyone had, and I was embarrassed to find I choked up as soon as I began to speak about them. He waved his hand in the air. 'Another time.' Then he pulled a small pink box of tissues out of the glove box and handed it to me. 'You want to come with me, and I make you beautiful brunch?'

'Yes. Yes, thank you.' I realised as I responded that I was dreading going back to my bedsit where there was no food because I hadn't got around to buying any, and only the day stretching ahead, endless and empty.

Delilah's flat was in a small private block in Islington. The five-storey building was red brick with lots of shiny black railings and his place was on the fifth floor.

As soon as we were inside Delilah said he needed to change, and he left me to take a look around. Each room was painted an intense colour, brilliant orange in the hallway, Caribbean blue in the kitchen, forest green in the sitting room.

But more surprising than the colours were the sculptures. All over the walls in the hallway and sitting room were sculptures of different shapes and sizes. There was a bull made out of metal and a thing that looked like a robot with a feather duster. There were heads in metal and stone and a strange smooth shape that reminded me of the way I felt when I was dancing. There were lots of animals too: tigers and storks, frogs and dogs. Their shapes spoke so well of their characters they made me laugh.

'My father,' said Delilah, reappearing in a long light blue kaftan, 'gives me one sculpture every year, on my birthday. So there are forty sculptures now. The animals came when I was a child.'

'They're lovely,' I said. 'Can I touch them?'

'Of course.'

I picked up a marble woman. She was hugging her knees.

'She is beautiful,' Delilah said. He turned to go into the kitchen, and I followed him.

'The beautiful ones are picked up more times from the shelf. They will wear out before,' he said.

He put a white apron over the kaftan, and started to cook bacon and scrambled eggs. Then he made fresh orange juice and toast, which I carried to the table.

For years I had eaten breakfast on my lap or in greasy spoons. More recently my habit was to skip breakfast altogether. But Delilah and I ate at a table with a tablecloth and thick cotton napkins. There was even a toast rack.

Afterwards I washed up while Delilah made us mugs of hot chocolate. Then we sat in the green sitting room in huge terracotta-coloured armchairs, and he showed me a photo of his mother. She showed her love for him through food, he said. He had been a fat child and it wasn't until he came to England that he lost weight. He told me she still talked mostly about food on the phone; it was her way of communicating her affection.

'And when you see your mother and father?' he asked me.

'I haven't seen them for nearly eight years.'

'What happened?'

I told him about the day I left, my father's ultimatum.

'Why was your father so angry with you?'

I shrugged, 'I lost my virginity. That's what sparked it off, in the end.'

'Yes. Is difficult for fathers.'

'It's difficult for daughters.'

'But now you have a life of your own.'

'Yes,' I said. But it felt like a little, falling word.

'When I was a small boy,' Delilah said, 'I used to watch my mother getting ready to go out. Or just in the mornings, putting the pins in her hair. She had ribbons and little brooches. I liked to put those things in my hair, and she would help me. And I wore her jewellery. Sometimes she let me put on make-up. Then there was a day I not allowed to do this. I had to wait for stage school to do it again. But I wasn't really free until I came to England. Now I live the truth, and I am glad to be myself. And you, you do not have to be what the others say you are. You can be yourself.'

'I'm not sure I know who myself is,' I told him.

There was the sound of a key in the lock and feet being wiped on the mat. Then the door opened, and a young guy in a white shirt and a black blazer stepped into the room.

'Oh hi,' he said when he saw me.

'Hi.' I recognised him as the piano man from Auntie's.

He walked over to the TV.

'There's a programme, *All the Violins*,' he said to Delilah. 'Three of the best composers and that conductor you like.' He flicked on the TV, but it was Margaret Thatcher's face that appeared on the screen.

Elected for the third time, she smiled and waved three fingers in the air. The number-one song 'Nothing's Gonna Stop Us Now' was being played over a collage of triumphant Maggie scenes.

I squirmed.

The images piled up, Maggie's face always a reminder of Dad's.

She had unhesitatingly sunk the *Belgrano* and completely crushed the miners. She had remained inflexible as ten hunger strikers died. People said she was more like a man than a man.

I thought she was being her idea of what a man was.

Thatcher's dad, I knew now, had been harsh, strict and unbending; not unlike my own. So maybe she was just trying to be like him, the way she saw him, anyway. But she loved her father, by all accounts, and he loved her. Was that the difference between a prime minister and a stripper? And would my real father have inspired me to achieve more, or less?

Delilah picked up our empty mugs to take to the kitchen, and I left to go back to Deptford.

When I arrived at work the following evening, there was a brown paper parcel on my dressing-room chair. Inside was a men's magazine, *Razzamatazz*, and a note from Wesley Fox: *You're in this issue.* I had opened the parcel in front of everyone as I didn't know what was in it. Now the other girls crowded round, as I leafed through the pages to find the pictures of me.

They were near the end and had been presented as six individually framed snapshots, a style that suited their amateur appearance.

I looked awkwardly posed, like a doll bent into position.

In the last shot, the only fully nude one, my hand crept across my stomach ready to hide my exposed pubic area.

The other girls murmured politely.

'Your hair's grown since then.'

'You look a bit serious, Harri.'

'Yeah, couldn't he have told you a few jokes or something?'

They were curious too.

'When did you do these?'

'Have you done any more?'

The photos wouldn't have been so bad, but someone had written a story to go with them. It was called 'A Sucking Good Night Out', and the narrator, purporting to be me, was an obsessive

133

cocksucker who went to a nightclub and gave blowjobs to a dozen men in one evening.

I turned back to the front page to see the date of publication. Last Thursday.

It wasn't hard to see where Roger had got his inspiration.

Peckham, London 1982

'Why do you cry?' asked he. 'You look so ugly when you cry!
There is nothing the matter with me. Fie!' exclaimed he again.
'This rose has an insect in it, and just look at this! After all, they
are ugly roses, and it is an ugly box they grow in!' Then he kicked
the box, and tore off the roses.

In London you could spend years doing nothing you'd ever
wanted to do.

Martin got a job as a courier and I worked as a dental nurse
for a humourless man called Sadin.

If a patient didn't turn up Mr Sadin would ask me if I wanted
my teeth done. He gave me eight huge silver fillings, two of which
were on the outside of my molars, so they showed up when I
smiled. My teeth had been pain-free and snow-white prior to this
treatment, and I started to suspect that the work, still in progress,
wasn't really necessary. So I told Mr Sadin I had to stop having
my teeth fixed at work. I was worried I'd be pressured to finish
the treatment already started, so I said that Martin had objected.
In reality Martin had only just enough energy to listen to my
worries before falling asleep, as black as any Midlands coal miner,
coated with London grime from a day on the motorbike. In fact,
he got so tired and filthy each day that he'd given up showering.
It wasn't worth it until the weekend, he said.

Eventually we saved enough money for Martin to buy decks
and he started to work as a DJ in the evenings and at weekends.
After a while he gave up his job. We didn't see much of each
other because of the hours he kept.

I was unhappy at work. Mr Sadin was an unpredictable person.

135

Perfectly affable most of the time, he would suddenly throw a probe or a drill-bit across the room in a fit of temper. It was my job to pick things up and sterilise them.

After two years in London, I was desperate to leave the place, but unemployment was higher than ever. There were riots everywhere and the government tried to say they were started by the black communities, but it was really young people and the jobless.

Martin, who liked to think he was into anarchy, said the government was at war with youth. He even had a little speech he'd put together for the beginning of his set at the wilder gigs. 'Youth is another problem for this country,' he declared, holding forth into the mike in an imitation of Thatcher's voice. 'Like broken families, blacks and beggars. These people are responsible for holding Britain back! They are preventing the others from being great again.' Then he played a clip of the Daleks from *Doctor Who*: 'Exterminate! Exterminate! Exterminate!'

But Martin and I weren't strictly part of 'the Youth' anymore. We were another category, called 'Lucky to Have a Job'. We could be somewhere worse, and we knew it.

I went along to a lot of Martin's DJ evenings in the beginning, hoping we'd get chance to talk. But he was caught up in what he was doing, and there wasn't time to spend together. We saw each other less and less, and we rowed a lot. Most of our fights were about money: our wages were low and we lived on baked potatoes and baked beans, moving from one shabby rented room to another, dreaming of the foreign holiday that we never saved enough money to go on.

In 1982, Irene Cara's hit 'Fame' reminded me I wanted to be an actress, and around the same time I was handed a leaflet on the street for an amateur drama group called Zen. They were looking for new members, so one Friday night when Martin was working, I decided to go along.

The drama group met in a church hall in Greenwich. There were about twelve people in the room when I arrived. Most of them were sitting at one end, watching a tall guy on a stage at the other end cracking jokes. A pretty, overweight girl in one of those huge shapeless Indian dresses got up when she saw me and introduced herself as Jackie. She directed me to sit down with the others. The tall guy was just finishing and everyone else started to applaud, so I joined in.

Jackie introduced me to the group as one of two new members. The other was a mentally handicapped forty-year-old in a suit.

'We're asking everyone to get up on stage tonight and do something funny,' Jackie said. 'It doesn't have to be jokes, it can be anything you like. Something funny that happened to you or that you know about. Just improvise. But if you can't think of anything except a joke then you can stand up and tell that. Everyone knows at least one joke, don't they?' she said. She thanked the tall guy, Jimmy, for his contribution, and she nodded at the new guy in the suit. 'You now then, Fred.'

She stepped towards Fred, who immediately stepped backwards shaking his head, 'Oh no, I can't . . . not . . . I don't . . .'

'Don't worry, don't worry,' Jackie said straightaway. 'It's supposed to be enjoyable. You don't have to do it if you don't want to. You can do yours another time.' She looked at a lad with blond hair tied back in a ponytail. 'Peter, you do something!'

The lad stood up revealing blue trousers tucked into stripy socks. He grinned, 'Oh alright then,' and headed for the platform.

'Quiet, please!' Jackie held up a hand to the rest of us, and Peter began.

'Well, I thought I'd tell you about when I was with my mum one time in France. My auntie used to live there, and we went to see her . . .'

What the hell was I going to do, I wondered, trying to listen at the same time to Peter. I hadn't expected to be asked to actually perform, not on the first night. It might have been alright if it didn't have to be funny. I didn't think funny was my forte.

Peter talked on, 'So then she took us to this lotto thing, bingo to you heathens . . .' The story was about how Peter and his mum had inadvertently, and very publicly, eaten hard, shrivelled-up corn, provided for the purpose of covering up bingo numbers. It wasn't particularly funny, but it was interesting and Peter told it with a great deal of charm.

Next up was a girl called Sue who recited a Pam Ayres poem, and then a bloke who told jokes about lending money to his friend. 'And when I finally plucked up courage to ask him for it back, I said "Have you forgotten that you owe me ten pounds?" And he said, "No, but give me time and I will."'

After each one we all applauded. Then it was my turn.

By this time I had decided on a few things. Number One: all the acts were pretty bad, so one more catastrophe wouldn't really make any difference. Number Two: I liked the people here (especially Peter who lit the room up when he smiled), they were all happy to have a go and they didn't seem to worry about making fools of themselves. Number Three: they had treated Fred normally and kindly. Number Four: I was enjoying myself and I had nothing to lose.

'Arabella?' Jackie smiled, holding her hands out at waist height, palms up, and sweeping them in the direction of the stage.

'*Ging gang gooley gooley gooley gooley watchit! Ging gang goo, Ging gang goo!*' I sang when I got up on the stage. I didn't know where it came from. I made silly gestures to go with it, and then told a bad joke – it was the only one I could remember: 'Humpty Dumpty sat on a wall, Humpty Dumpty had a great fall. All the king's horses and all the king's men trod on him.'

After that I told them that I half remembered a joke about tap-dancing and falling in the sink, and I kind of tap-danced my way off the stage. Everyone applauded as they had for the other acts, and Jimmy stood up and said, 'Ladies and gentlemen, our last performer was told by doctors that she'd never dance properly again – and she hasn't.'

Jackie instigated a discussion then about the acts we'd seen, different types of comedy, comic timing and so on. Then we did directed improvisations. She gave us different scenarios to act out and I was paired with Peter. Jackie told him he was returning to his wife after ten years away fighting a war. I was the wife and when Peter arrived I flung my arms around him straightaway.

Jackie stopped us. 'No, no, it wouldn't be like that,' she said. 'There would be a lot of distance. He's been gone ten years, and they may have loved each other wildly when they got married, but that's a long time ago now.' She turned to me. 'You've moved on, you've got a new life now. You might even have a new lover.' Our audience murmured their approval, but I disagreed.

'No,' I said. 'I loved him enough to wait for him and I've spent ten years waiting for him, thinking of him every day and dreaming of him coming home to me.'

'Okay,' said Jackie, and I understood why she commanded the respect of the others, 'Peter, you're the one with another life. Whilst you were away you met someone else, and you have a child by her.'

So we played out the scene, and at the end of it I persuaded my 'husband' into my bed. 'One last time,' I said gently, realising suddenly how quietly attentive our audience had become. Then we wrapped ourselves around each other and that was the end.

We all went to the pub afterwards and it was lovely. It made me realise what a lonely existence I'd been leading, staying in every night and waiting for Martin, or trailing after him to his gigs where I just hung about, always on the edge of someone else's party.

I went to drama group every Friday after that. I told them all about Martin, but after a few weeks I found myself more and more with Peter. Peter played the part of my boyfriend in a full-length improvisation we were eventually planning to stage.

Peter and I talked a lot about our acting in the pub afterwards. He wanted to go to stage school, he'd already applied to some, and he kept asking my advice about the monologues he was practising for his auditions.

One night he asked me to go back to his flat with him, to

help him rehearse, and I went, knowing it was going to be more than that.

Shortly afterwards, things came to a head between Martin and me.

We were living in two rooms above a Chinese restaurant, sharing the kitchen and bathroom with another couple who lived on the floor above. The smell of food cooking in the restaurant below was strong and constant; it put me off eating a lot of the time and made it difficult to sleep somehow too. Martin and I ate lots of toast – in fact toast-making became an art.

'Butter it! Butter it now while it's hot!' Martin yelled as I got the toast out from under the grill.

'I'm going to butter it, give me a chance!' I said. I scooped up huge slices of butter and pushed them over the bread with a knife. Martin stuck another knife into the bread to make holes for more butter to soak into, then we took our plates into the sitting room and sat down to eat.

'The cash–point machine swallowed my card today,' I said, 'when I went to get some lunch money. I can't understand it! I know you paid the rent on Saturday, but we definitely had a bit extra in there. Is your card working?'

'My card is working, yeah,' Martin said. 'Maybe we've got less than you thought.'

'Less maybe, but not nothing! It would only swallow my card if we were overdrawn, surely?'

'I dunno. Maybe it's a mistake.'

'It must be a mistake.' I picked at the crumbs on my plate. 'I know for a fact there was at least another twenty quid in there, on top of the rent. You haven't bought anything have you?'

'Nah, it must be something wrong with the machine. Here, I took some out when I paid the rent on Saturday.' He handed me a fiver. 'Use that.'

But three days later our Chinese landlord arrived on the doorstep, and he wanted the rent.

'Martin's paid the rent,' I said. 'He paid it on Saturday.'

Mr Chan shook his head. 'No, he didn't. It's two hundred pounds and you need to pay it now.'

I'd just come in from work, and I was tired and fed up. 'Look,' I said, 'Martin's not in at the moment, but he told me he paid it. Maybe he saw your wife?'

'No,' said Mr Chan. 'You need to speak to him. I'll come back on Monday.'

I had an ache in my lower back after talking to Mr Chan, but I was asleep by the time Martin arrived home from a gig in the early hours of the morning.

The next day was Saturday and I had to work a half day. I left early, while Martin was still asleep. I could have woken him, but I didn't want to face a money conversation at that time in the morning.

At lunchtime I went to the bank to ask about my cash card. But I didn't get it back, because our account was overdrawn.

The pain in my lower back was worse, and I found it difficult to stand for as long as I had to that afternoon.

As soon as I got home I confronted Martin.

'Martin, Mr Chan came round yesterday. He said we haven't paid our rent, but we have, haven't we? I don't understand why he'd think that we haven't! We always pay it on time.'

Martin was fiddling with some wires attached to his music equipment, but now he turned to look at me and I continued. 'Also, I went to the bank today about my card, and they say we're a hundred and fifty pounds overdrawn.'

I wanted Martin to say everything was okay, Mr Chan was mistaken, the bank was mistaken. But instead he said, 'I didn't pay the rent. I bought some new speakers. These things.' He tapped the black box next to him.

'You bought them with the rent money?' I was incredulous. I trusted Martin absolutely. He would never do such a thing.

'And a little bit more – yeah.'

'How much more?'

'A hundred and seventy quid.'

'You're joking!'

'No.'

'But how are we going to pay it back? And how will we pay Mr Chan? And what about being able to live for the rest of the month? I would have done the food shopping today – what're we going to eat?'

'I don't know. But we can make it up, darling, we'll sort it out. Mr Chan can wait, he's not going to chuck us out just for this; we've never done it before. And the bank'll wait too.'

'Wait for what? What're we going to live on? What am I working for? You know I go to work every day, and I fucking hate it, and now I can't even afford to buy myself a bloody sandwich at lunchtime! I can't believe you did this.'

'I'm sorry. I'm really sorry. I just saw the speakers in the window, like, and . . .'

'It's not just spending the money, it's the lies you told me! You said you'd paid the rent! I told Mr Chan you'd paid him. I feel a right idiot now! Why did you lie to me? You could have just told me what you'd done! Why didn't you tell me when I was on about my cash card?'

'I was worried what you'd say, I suppose, and I didn't feel that good about it.'

'So you just told me a load of lies? And I believed you.'

'Look, I just told you why. I didn't feel up to telling you at the time.'

'So telling the truth or not depends what mood you're in now? Martin, I just can't believe you'd deceive me like this –'

That's when it hit me about who was deceiving whom. I sat down heavily, and put my head in my hands.

Martin was already sitting on the sofa and he leaned towards me, reaching a hand out to touch me gingerly on the shoulder. He could see the anger had left me. He must've wondered why.

'You know, we will manage,' he said.

142

I replied from behind my hands, 'No, it's not that. It's just . . . it's me who's been deceiving you.'

'How do you mean?'

'I slept with someone else.'

Dead silence. Neither of us moved. I continued. 'It was only once. I won't be doing it again.'

In fact I had regretted sleeping with Peter as soon as I'd done it. He wasn't a generous lover – more wham-bam-thank-you-ma'am. And now we didn't even talk much.

I didn't dare look at Martin. I hoped he would say something, or put his hand back on me.

But there was only stillness and silence.

Behind my hands I had my eyes closed. I was alone in the hot dark there. *Please say something, please speak*, I begged him from an empty, numb area inside my stomach. I felt a tearing in my chest, my eyes and my jaw ached, my whole body sinking and dying into this realisation – that what I had done would end us.

Then he moved. The small sound of his trouser legs brushing against one another gave me hope for an instant, because surely there was a chance he'd move towards me.

But he went quickly out of the room. And when he came back into it the next day, it was only to say that he should be the one to stay put, and I needed to find somewhere else to live.

Thatcher won another general election then and UB40 sang 'Red Red Wine' as if drink were the only solace left.

I didn't feel anything about splitting up with Martin. Or rather I did, but I shut it off. I put my feelings concerning him in the same icy place I kept those concerning my parents. Martin didn't love me anymore and that was that. It never occurred to me that he'd just been terribly hurt. The solution as I saw it was to pack up and move on.

Old Kent Road, London 1984

'Are you still cold?' asked she; and then she kissed his brow. Oh! Her kiss was colder than ice. It went to his heart, although that was half frozen already; he thought he should die. It was, however, only for a moment; directly afterwards he was quite well, and no longer felt the intense cold around.

S inging telegram or 'kiss-a-gram' companies were all over the place, so there were plenty to choose from. I'd been looking at the ads in the *Standard* for ages, trying to pluck up the courage to respond. In the end I chose a company called Wow-a-gram on the Old Kent Road.

I called and spoke to a girl called Sophia, who asked me to come to an interview.

Wow-a-gram was a short bus ride away from my bedsit in Deptford, but I got off at the wrong stop. Sophia had said the office was above a dry-cleaner's, and I thought I could visualise where it was, but I got the wrong dry-cleaner's.

I ended up walking for ages, and before I was even in sight of the Wow-a-gram office the left heel of one of my stiletto boots snapped off. I tucked it in my pocket, but this meant I had to tip-toe with my left foot to get it to match the height of my right. I felt ridiculous doing this, trying not to limp in my eye-catchingly short mini-skirt. I must have looked pretty stupid to anyone who noticed that my left heel was actually missing, to say nothing of the difficulty of performing this balancing act.

Finally I found the Wow-a-gram office at the top of a three-storey building which also housed the dry-cleaner's and a courier office. A girl of my own age, with bright red hair and a nose stud, welcomed me at the top of the stairs.

'Hi, you must be Arabella, and I'm Sophia,' she said. 'Did you get lost?' She guided me into a tiny office and offered me a cup of coffee. She chattered on about the office location – good because it was so close to central London, bad because it was a skanky area. I asked about 'skanky' because it was a word I hadn't come across, and she said maybe it came from the south coast where she was from.

She asked me about myself, and I told her I'd just moved into a bedsit down the road. I told her I'd been doing dental nursing. Then I found myself telling her about the broken heel on my boots, and I demonstrated my new walk, which made her laugh.

Sophia told me about the different types of telegrams: singing telegrams, kiss-a-grams (same as a singing telegram but with a kiss on the cheek at the end), Jane-a-grams (opposite to Tarzan-a-grams), traffic wardens, sexy waitresses, custard-pie-a-grams, and others which might involve posing as a secretary or a sales rep. I would have to provide my own costume for the singing telegrams, kiss-a-grams and custard-pie-a-grams, to consist of a black basque, black knickers, stockings and suspenders. Likewise for the Jane-a-gram – Sophia suggested strategically placed leopard-print scarves. Secretaries and sales reps would also come out of my own wardrobe, but sexy waitress and traffic warden costumes were hired by Wow-a-gram, who charged the client.

If I was in costume, then I would be expected to strip down to the black basque and French knickers when it was time for all to be revealed.

'What makes you think you can perform singing telegrams?' Sophia asked me then.

'Well, I belong to an amateur drama group, and I like people. I'm good with people,' I told her.

'Take me through what you would do if I sent you somewhere to deliver a kiss-a-gram,' she said.

I'd been thinking about this and I knew my singing voice was terrible, but I had chosen a couple of songs I thought I could get by with.

'I think it's important to make an entrance,' I said. 'I was thinking about how to do that on the way here, and I thought I could start with that song, you know, "Big Spender"?'

'Yeah, that sounds good. Can you sing?'

'No, but I think it's more about how you present it. I don't think Mick Jagger can sing, but he's great, isn't he? It's the way he is, all that strutting about. I can strut!' I said, and I laughed, partly from relief because it seemed to be going well, and partly at my own audacity.

'Okay,' said Sophia, 'What I want you to do . . .' She described the layout of the courier office on the floor below us. In it she told me I would find two guys sitting at their desks. I was to deliver a kiss-a-gram to the one on my right, and he would be expecting me.

So I made my way downstairs. And with Sophia hot on my tails, I wobbled into the small entranceway outside the courier office door.

Sophia counted to three, and I flung the door open, and marched into the room.

Walking carefully on my imaginary left heel, and pointing at the same time at the guy on my right, I launched myself towards him singing. The guy was tall, young and good-looking. He smiled when he saw me.

I shook off my leather jacket and lay across the guy's desk for the last line of my song, finishing on '*Spend a little time with me*', delivered in what I hoped was Monroe style. Then I stood up and pecked him on the cheek.

'That was great!' chorused the two guys, as Sophia applauded me from the doorway.

'Yes, fantastic! Nice one! You're hired!' said the guy I had kissed, who turned out to be called Dave, and was in fact the overall boss, owning both the courier company and the kiss-a-gram company.

'This is Terry,' he said introducing the other guy, and Terry and I shook hands.

The three were all good friends and Sophia seemed chuffed to be introducing me to the two guys. She kept leaping in to answer Dave's questions about where I came from and what I was doing in London.

I stayed another twenty minutes then limped off home feeling, ironically, like a success.

Five o'clock in the morning at Victoria coach station and I was freezing to death. The sexy waitress outfit I was wearing was so thin you could almost see through it. I buttoned my coat right up to the neck, but it wasn't much warmer.

For this, my first *real* telegram, I was posing as a hostess accompanying a team of international rugby players on a coach journey to Heathrow airport. But neither coach nor rugby players had turned up yet.

When I finally heard the welcoming drone of the coach, the rugby players also arrived all at once, as if by some secret signal. I struggled to find an appropriate facial expression and greeting for them as they filed passed me up the steps and onto the coach.

'Good morning!' I tried to smile at them, but like after anaesthetic at the dentist's, my mouth was numb with cold and I wasn't really sure what my expression was. The guys smiled back and said good morning. They didn't look cold, so I guessed they'd all been in a waiting room somewhere.

Once the journey was underway I took orders for tea and coffee, then disappeared into a curtained-off bit at the back of the coach.

When 'Uptown Girl' came on the stereo, it was my cue to reappear and stroll down the centre aisle, dancing and taking my clothes off until I was down to my underwear.

I thought the guys would be cross because it was so early in the morning, and most of them looked in need of the strong cup of coffee they'd been promised. But instead they laughed and talked with me until we got to Heathrow. Then they hoisted me up onto their shoulders and carried me through the terminal.

They set me down at the gate to the departure lounge and as each guy filed past me towards passport control, they left a ten- or twenty-pound tip. It was a good deal more lucrative than dental nursing.

The rugby team was a bit of a one-off: the telegram jobs were mostly for the city: EC1, EC2, EC3 and EC4 over and over, until I knew my way around really well. The male recipients were those the papers had branded 'yuppies': Young, Upwardly mobile, Professional Persons. Sophia received some good reports about me from happy customers, and she kept me busy. She also gave me anything that promised to be a bit special.

Of course I couldn't sing, which was a bit of a drawback, but I could act – people always looked amazed when the 'traffic warden' took her uniform off.

I was proud of my lyrics too.

Most people wanted their song personalised, so Sophia would get some information about the man the telegram was for: 'He's going bald. Likes working out in the gym. Never washes his car,' that sort of thing. And I'd make up songs to the tune of Alvin Stardust's 'Coo Ca Choo':

> *Brian Smith, you are such a dish,*
> *You know you don't have to fish.*
> *Clean your car and I'll give you a kiss,*
> *Oh Brian be my coo ca choo.*

> *I love-a you, I love-a you, I really do aah.*
> *I want-a you, I want-a you, I really do aah.*

> *Ooh ooh, you were in the gym,*
> *Lots of sweat on your head and your chin,*

> *One look and you'd reeled me in,*
> *Oh Brian be my coo ca choo.*

My dad would have thrown a fit, if he could have seen me in my underwear, serenading Smiths for a living.

Deptford, London 1985

. . . she flew with him high up into the black cloud while the
storm was raging.

'*H*elter skelter *na la la la la la la . . .*' Siouxsie and the Banshees
belted out from the bedsit above mine as I applied make-
up, put on my 'Jane' outfit, and packed a black backless dress for
later.

I had a telegram to do in the city at nine, then I would meet
up with Sophia's crowd in Covent Garden to go clubbing. Not
having anyone else at home I had taken on more and more
telegram work and I was doing a lot of clubbing – at least three
times a week – with Sophia and her friends. They were all
wannabe singers, actors, musicians and designers, currently doing
nothing of the sort. Sophia was the only one with a nine-to-
five job. She wanted to be a costume designer really though.
And she did at least sell the extravagant hats she made, at
Greenwich market on Sundays. The others did telegrams like
me, or were unemployed.

The girls all did topless telegrams now. They had become Wow-
a-gram's biggest sellers, and I was already so blasé about wandering
around London in my underwear, I just went with the flow. I
might have felt differently if I'd had big breasts, but an A-cup
didn't seem worth making a fuss about. Standing half-naked in
front of most of the population of the City of London, I got used
to shocking people and even quite enjoyed it. As time went by,
I wore fewer and flimsier clothes to go clubbing in; after all I was
used to wandering round in nothing more than a pair of pants.

I was, however, constantly anxious about my appearance, upon which everything seemed to depend, and I went to great lengths to make sure I looked right.

I worried about my uneven skin tone, and it was therefore essential for me to cover my skin completely in make-up called stocking cream, which I bought from Boots. It had to be mixed with water and I smeared it on before a telegram or a night out.

Occasionally I had panic attacks – I would be on my way somewhere when I started feeling anxious, sweating and trembling. When this happened I took deep breaths, and tried to distract myself by noticing my surroundings.

Dancing in the clubs was a great release. Dancing I felt alight and alive. I lost myself in the music, feeling it go through me, letting it dictate my movements for me.

Often a small crowd gathered to watch me and I loved it. I played up to it, spending all my money each week on increasingly outrageous outfits. I had a mini-dress made of black lace cobwebs with spiders stitched over the nipples, a top-hat with long green feathers – one of Sophia's creations – and my black, leather, thigh-high boots. Then I bought tiny white shorts with a white bikini top, so I'd stand out from the goths. I stuck white stars on my skin and bathed in strobe lighting.

I was something of a regular feature at the smaller clubs and I enjoyed the sense of belonging, living for this small power I owned, to hold the floor and be considered outrageous, even by my contemporaries.

My friends snorted speed to keep them going into the small hours but I never did – I was frightened of drugs. I think I had some dim awareness of the emotions I was clamping down on: rage, grief, the fear that love, wherever I found it, could be switched off as suddenly and completely as a tap.

From the outside I must have appeared free and easy, high even. My friends laughed when the guys trying to score approached me, always me, the least likely person to know where to get hold of anything. I never even touched dope after the first time. I was unwilling to let go of my control and travel to some place I might not like or be able to return from. Besides, my high came from the music and the attention.

Towards the end of the evening I usually found a man to take me home, or I'd go back to his place. Without Martin I'd become extremely promiscuous, grabbing any available male who came my way. Once, this even included a surprised and delighted middle-aged bus conductor from my regular route into town. I wanted a connection desperately, but I could never find anything to say to the strangers in my bed the next morning.

I lived life at one remove from myself. Sex made me feel better and helped me avoid thinking. I didn't want to think. But sometimes pictures came into my mind involuntarily, my thoughts in metaphor. The image I saw most often was of a boat torn away from its moorings. The boat had lost its anchor, and I knew the anchor was Martin.

I no longer saw anyone from Zen. They all had nine-to-five jobs, and when they were free I was working. Once I went to the Midlands to look up Linda. (I had long since lost touch with Sharon.) She was married to an electrician. They were doing up a house in a village just outside Derby. Her conversation was all loft conversions and where to source old radiators, and we struggled to find common ground.

Back in London the telegrams and clubbing filled my time. I never talked about Martin or my family with anyone, but sometimes, returning to my bedsit like a spent firework in the early hours of the morning, I cut my arms before I went to sleep. Then I had to improvise with long gloves, or bracelets, so I could still do the telegrams, and, later, to pose for the photos Jasper took at Camden Palace. The day I auditioned for the Pageant I was lucky the cuts weren't too fresh. I smeared stocking cream over them and nobody saw.

Soho, London 1988

Gerda then remembered how large and curious the snowflakes had appeared to her when one day she had looked at them through a burning-glass. These, however, were very much larger; they were living forms; they were, in fact, the Snow Queen's guards. Their shapes were the strangest that could be imagined; some looked like great ugly porcupines, others like snakes rolled into knots, with their heads peering forth, and others like fat little bears with bristling hair.

One of Thatcher's favourite words was 'entrepreneur' and everybody I saw was trying to be one, including most of the girls at work.

Being an entrepreneur meant looking for ways to use things to make money. And you had to have a Filofax. Excepting Saf, everyone in my dressing room had a Filofax. We were supposed to fill them with important appointments, but mine was pretty empty.

Elaine was the biggest convert to entrepreneurship. She used magazine-words in all her conversations, always talking about being more *creative*, which meant thinking harder about ways of making money. We had plenty of *money-making options,* she said, and time during the day to make the most of them. More money would give us more options. But before that we should work on *image.*

'Look at Thatcher,' said Elaine. 'Attention to appearance: that's one of the reasons she is where she is. She looks like she looks on purpose . . .' Saf threw her arms in the air and laughed like a child at a clown. Elaine persevered, '. . . because that's right for the job. Think Queen Elizabeth. *Power-dressing*. Get the clothes right and you're halfway there.'

Saf didn't like Elaine. She said she had a yuppie's soul. She called me naïve and she read out an article from the paper:

YUPPIES PUT CASH BEFORE COMPASSION

Compassion is out, conspicuous consumption in, and the Puritan work ethic is back at the helm as far as Britain's under-25s are concerned, according to a new survey, published by the advertising agency McCann Erickson.

Money, above all, is what 'Yuppies' – Young Upwardly Mobile Persons – want, to the dismay of critics who condemn those they call 'Thatcher's Children' for selfishness.

'Is that us as well then? *Thatcher's children?*' Elaine, who was actually quite pleased with Saf's 'yuppie soul' theory, was exploring other labels.

'No!' Saf said scornfully. 'They're saying *yuppies* are Thatcher's children. We're not yuppies. We don't earn enough and our jobs don't go anywhere. Jeez – this is hardly a career, is it?'

'So whose children are we?' I knew she'd have an answer.

'We're nobody's. We slipped through a hole in the net. There are lots of people like us, and that's whose side we should be on right? Not trying to be yuppies for God's sake.'

Nonetheless, perhaps because I craved respectability – although that's not what Saf would have called it – I was influenced enough to go to what Elaine called a 'business meeting'. Some of the other girls came with us, to a function room in a hotel in the West End.

There was a bar area outside the main room, where a woman in a red suit came up to greet us. She shook our hands firmly one by one, making good eye contact each time. 'Would you like a glass of bucks fizz?' We hesitated – we'd come to hear what she had to say, not to spend money. 'I'll just go and fetch you all one. Complimentary of course.' She walked off, and was soon back to hand the glasses round. 'You all look fabulous!' she said. 'I bet you work in fashion or something like that. Am I right?'

I was feeling uneasy; I wasn't used to being in hotels. The hushed carpets and champagne, the polished doors and churchy atmosphere were all disconcerting.

'Bits and bobs,' Elaine said, in reply to the question. The woman nodded as if that explained everything, then went off to greet some new arrivals.

After about five minutes, during which we murmured together in imitation of the other little groups standing about nearby, we were ushered into the large function room, where a white pull-down screen had been set up.

We were shown a video, which mostly consisted of people sitting drinking champagne next to swimming pools in luxurious settings, saying how lucky they were and how easy it had been to make their millions. Between each scene a logo appeared in a shower of stars: 'Loving It'.

When the video ended we were instructed to shake hands with our neighbours and share our thoughts. Elaine was on my left. 'What is "Loving It"?' I asked her.

'I dunno, but it's easy to sell,' she said. 'The sea looked so blue,' she added with a nod at the video screen.

My right-hand neighbour leaned towards us and stretched out a hand. A middle-aged guy, in a suit which had seen better days, he had some facial eczema and wispy hair. He smiled. 'What did you think? Good, wasn't it?'

'Yes,' I told him. The video had made me feel good, and it had obviously done the same for others; everyone looked happier and more relaxed. I shook the guy's hand. A frizzy-haired blonde woman in the seat in front of me said, 'Florida, here we come!' Then Red Suit appeared to address her audience.

Ten minutes later Elaine paid Red Suit fifteen quid for a box full of cheap perfumes, made and packaged in imitation of much more expensive ones. About three-quarters of the people in the room did the same. The idea was that they would sell the perfume to friends and family, eventually also recruiting others interested in selling it.

I saw the man who had shaken my hand walk up to buy his share and I felt sorry for him, without really knowing why. Maybe just that he looked old and dull next to Red Suit, his movements slow and visibly full of effort, whilst she was quick, sharp, spick-and-span.

I didn't buy the perfume. The video had been a real feel-good success – it made me feel high. So much so, that when Red Suit appeared afterwards talking about selling fake perfume – it just seemed ridiculous. I couldn't marry the two things together.

It was my first brush with pyramid sales. A month later, I would attend another meeting that was every bit what I imagined a gospel church service to be, including lots of cries of 'Alleluia!' People came out of that one armed with toilet cleaner.

If it wasn't fake perfume or Betterway cleaning products, it was slimming aids, Tupperware, sexy underwear parties – people trying to claw their way up, or just pretending they were already there. Elaine was a prime example with her deep tan, her flat in Docklands, and the Porsche key fob she carried around just for show. (She didn't own a car and her boyfriend drove a clapped-out Mini.) Elaine had a dozen suits with huge shoulder pads. I had a couple of jackets with those big shoulders too, starch-stiff. They were essential at the time. I looked in the mirror and wondered if the point was to make oneself feel fortified, or to discourage others from crying.

It struck me that the Pageant was a world of its own. Whatever we were, we were old enough to know we were Lucky to Have a Job but still young enough to be infected by a fame and fortune fantasy. A lot of the time we were aspiring actresses, dancers, singers and models. We were comfortable in a material sense, but also uncomfortable because none of us actually wanted to be there. We were chickens in a battery farm, where each chicken sat planning her own individual escape. We knew our looks had value and tried to use them to make money for ourselves, but we always ended up as products in someone else's factory, or fantasy: the easy meat of Thatcher's world, waiting to be spotted and whisked away by some man on the make.

I wasn't the only girl from the Pageant who'd appeared in a men's mag. Elaine and her friend Lynne did regular glamour modelling to supplement their income. They had glossy portfolios, full of professional-looking nude shots they had paid to have done. Lynne, like Elaine, spent more time than the rest of us taking care of her hair and paying for sunbeds. When they weren't working for men's mags, the two girls did the rounds of the camera clubs.

After I'd been at the Pageant about a year, Elaine asked me to go to a camera club with her. 'They need nude models. It's like for painters, but with photographers instead.'

I said I wouldn't do nude. Nude for a photographer would be different from nude in a theatre. I remembered that from last time.

But I said I'd do topless, and Elaine said that would be okay.

The photographer was a small, polite man in his late forties. He selected outfits and accessories from the bag of things I'd brought with me, and I changed in a small dressing room off to one side of the studio.

There was a break during which we chatted in a fairly formal way. He did the topless shots all at once near the end. The session was for an hour and I got paid twenty pounds, cash-in-hand, which was good money I thought, especially as it was on top of my usual wage.

The second time I worked at the camera club, a different photographer brought a suitcase full of clothes with him. He asked me to put on a pair of shorts with a bikini top and scarf, which I did, but the clothes smelled terrible, like they'd been stored somewhere damp. This man was about fifty, with a wavering voice, like someone much older, and he seemed distracted, his attention darting everywhere, like he was really stressed out.

Although he never made eye contact with me, the room felt strangely intimate with only him and me in it, in a way it hadn't the last time. He didn't chat, just told me what he wanted me to wear.

I posed in the horrible-smelling shorts and bikini top and consoled myself with the thought of a shower when I got home.

Several times he came towards me, breathing heavily, to adjust the scarf.

He asked me to wear a swimsuit next, but when I came to put it on I saw the crotch was white with the discharge of the last woman who'd worn it. I refused to wear it, and the session continued awkwardly with me in my own clothes. He seemed to lose interest after that, and we finished early. I didn't go back.

A year or so later Elaine told me that she paid for her posh flat by sleeping with the landlord. It made me wonder what else she did at camera clubs, and what might have been expected.

All of the girls at the Pageant wanted to get out of the sex industry. We were convinced that if only we could earn enough money and find the discipline to save it we would eventually feel secure enough to make the break.

Of course we never saved any money. We used it instead to buoy ourselves up with new clothes, to make our bodies perfect, to pay the living expenses of the lost boys we went out with, and to stem the tide of bad feelings we had about ourselves.

Most of the Pageant girls bought *The Stage* every week and scoured the ads for auditions that might provide the magic leap to wealth and fame.

Armed with my new Equity card, I went with Saf or one of the other girls to auditions for dancers and 'models who move well', for bit parts in music videos and on TV. I went to a big open audition for game-show presenters and another for a children's storyteller. But it didn't take many auditions for us to realise we weren't professionals. We could never learn the dance pieces fast enough, and I felt somehow unworthy too because of what I did for a living, not quite as pristine as those smart pony-tailed girls slick-stepping in unison, whilst Saf and I lumbered around at the back.

It made me wonder why Tracey Veroni, who was a proper choreographer, would slum it with us. It must have been frustrating for her when it took us days, rather than hours, to learn our routines. But then maybe she felt unworthy too.

At auditions I felt as though my crimes – being a stripper, going topless in the city of London, posing for a men's magazine, sleeping around, and something else I couldn't quite identify, something horrible but almost intrinsic to myself – were listed on my forehead. Unsurprisingly, given my feelings of inferiority, I was consistently turned down.

Saf and I sat in a café we hadn't been in before. We'd been to an audition, and had a couple of hours to kill before work. It was a tiny place and we perched on high stools next to a couple of guys in suits.

The café was between the Wardour Street junctions with Old Crompton Street and Oxford Street. The businesses there were mostly to do with film and the rag trade. A lot of the business people wore jeans, although there were still a few suits here and there, like the ones sitting next to us. The suits tended to be sales people, but I didn't know that.

Of course the other business of the area was sex. A few yards up the road there was a phone booth stuffed with cards advertising escorts, private massage and dominatrices. But the prostitutes themselves were invisible.

On TV, prostitutes always wore tight, shiny, brightly coloured clothes; very short skirts with lots of brassy jewellery. But the reality was that, in this area of town, they were indistinguishable from businesswomen and secretaries. So it was an environment in which every woman was suspect.

'Do you work around here?' said one of the suits next to us.

'Yes,' said Saf. 'Why? Do you work around here?'

The two suits were in their forties, their bodies and faces bloated with the effects of too much food and booze. The one who had spoken looked like Terry Wogan; the other had reddish hair and a nose to match. They sat with their feet on the stainless steel bars of the stools and slurped their coffee,

'We work over the road there,' said Terry Wogan, nodding towards a building opposite. It had a black-and-white speckled marble facade, with a wide doorway of tinted glass and gold lettering cut into the marble pillars that flanked it. It looked serious, solid and respectable.

'We make B-movies.'

I wondered that anyone should actually set out to make a B-movie, because I thought B-movies were just not good enough A-movies. But I was too polite to say so.

'What about you, girls, what do you do?'

'Oh, we're dancers,' I said quickly.

'Oh yeah? What sort of dancing?'

'Jazz, contemporary. We do cruise ships, that kind of thing.' We lied all the time about what we did.

'Well, since you're in the business, do you want to come and take a look at what we do?'

On the other side of the tinted glass doors we took a lift down to a large windowless basement. A metal-framed couch with red cushions ran the entire length of one wall. The room was filled with lots of technical equipment, and a massive screen.

Saf and I sat on the edge of the couch, and the Terry Wogan guy, who was called Jim, sat down too.

A picture appeared on the screen in front of us. The red-haired guy waved the remote control. 'Watch this!'

Jim said, 'Yeah, this is great, see what you think.'

On the screen, a half-dressed and highly distressed woman was trying to get away from a man with a chainsaw. She sweated and panicked, running from room to room in a big house, slamming doors. The chainsaw man relentlessly sawed through each door and advanced on her again.

Finally she was cornered in a small kitchen, sobbing as she scrabbled to get away from the chainsaw, which the man was using to cut her clothes and skin. Her long limbs smacked against the kitchen units and we saw her breasts and buttocks as her clothing tore.

I became aware of being watched. The two guys were gazing at Saf and me rather than watching the screen. Eyes glazed, and mouths slightly open, they looked like they were watching us strip.

Saf was leaning forward, her face registering shock at the action on the screen. I moved in my seat, pretending to yawn and contriving to nudge her hard at the same time.

Saf looked at me, and I tapped my watch.

The guy with the remote control flicked the screen off. 'What do you think?' he said.

'Yeah, did you like it?' said Jim.

'Yeah, yeah,' I murmured. 'Got to go. Promised to meet a friend at six.'

I left feeling like I'd been coerced into watching someone wank.

A lot of the jobs we did were favours for friends, or friends of friends, and I tended to forget that earning money was the objective.

There was a promotion for a new optician where I walked up and down Oxford Street in a mini-dress, holding a giant pair of spectacles. I starred as a scantily clad 'snake woman' in a music video for some unknown band and paraded around boxing rings in my swimsuit, holding a card announcing the number of each round.

That first year at the Pageant, the time went fast. In May 1988 Saf and I went to Auntie's to celebrate our first year at work. We drank champagne and tried to count the one-night stands I'd had since she met me. There were more than fifty.

'Sex is addictive,' I said.

Saf laughed. 'You're a sad case, Harri!'

But I wanted her to understand – the intensity of it, that there was nothing else that made me feel so good. 'It's about joy,' I told her abruptly and rather inadequately.

'Oh yeah, the Joy of Sex,' she said.

'It's about love then.'

'Jeez! It's about *sex!* Anyway, one-night stands are for losers.'

'If two losers make love, maybe that's a kind of winning.'

Saf shook her head. 'You need a serious man.'

Eight months later I was still alternating between lonely nights and one-night stands. Then I found Andy.

It was at the opening of a new nightclub in Beckenham, where I almost took part in a wet T-shirt contest. There were six girls from the Pageant including Saf and me. One of the girls at work, Olga, was a friend of the proprietor, and she'd persuaded us to go along. There was no money involved, but we were promised an evening of free drinks.

A wet T-shirt contest was not my scene at all, but I thought the evening would be fun once we got that out of the way. It wasn't, at first. The locals at the club resented our presence there. Some lads started shouting,

'These model girls have been paid to be here!' It wasn't fair on the local girls entering the competition, they said.

I was dreading the competition anyway: wet T-shirt competitions were all about big tits so I felt at a disadvantage. Now it appeared the crowd were hostile, I wanted to do it even less. But Olga begged me not to back out, and reassured us that her friend intended to make a local girl the winner.

I stood up to go to the platform. But as I made my way round the tables, one of a group of heckling lads got up and shouted, 'Let's see ya then!' and he chucked his lager down my front.

Olga came with me to the loos to clean up, and when I got back to sit with the other girls, Saf whispered in my ear, 'You've got an admirer.' She gestured at a bloke sitting on the other side of the table.

'Hi Harri, I'm Andy. I thought you would've won, if you'd have got up there.'

'No, mine are too small,' I said, used by now to directly stating the facts of my appearance.

'Babe, you never see big tits when people want things to look really beautiful. Statues and figurines and all that stuff always look like you. You're the lady on the front of the Roller, that's what you are!'

'Roller?'

'Rolls Royce.'

Andy was an Eastender and, being a Midlander, I was charmed by his cockney accent. He offered to buy me a drink, free drinks for Pageant girls having stopped abruptly at the end of the contest, which thankfully had finished whilst I was still in the loo.

He bought the drinks and sat down again. 'I see you know Marbles?' He was indicating Saf, who grinned.

'As in "lost them",' she said. 'I was trying to explain how the moon affects us.'

Andy looked at me and made a face. 'Barking,' he said. But I could see that it was okay, Saf seemed to like being teased.

Andy was lovely-looking. He had black hair and blue eyes, and an easy, flirtatious style. When he smiled his teeth were crooked and a bit black in places, but somehow this only seemed to add to his attractiveness. He knew how to talk to women and he talked to us all, but he made it clear it was me he was interested in. He quickly nicknamed me 'Spanish', and every now and then he'd just stare into my eyes, as if we were the only ones there.

I felt so hot, I was surprised my clothes didn't just melt off.

At the end of the evening he said, 'You could do anything you wanted with me,' and I took him home to bed.

Soho, London 1989

'Wilt thou not mix for this little maiden that wonderful draught which will give her the strength of twelve men, and thus enable her to overcome the Snow Queen?'

'The strength of twelve men!' repeated the wise woman. 'That would be of much use to be sure!'

A ndy didn't know what I did for a living until the morning after the wet T-shirt contest. It was Saturday and he asked me to go to his gig that evening. I said I couldn't.

'I'll be working until midnight,' I told him. I was sorting through the debris of our clothes for something to wear while I went to make coffee. Andy stretched out on the bed. 'Doing what?'

'At the Pageant.'

'Babe, I don't know what you're talking about.'

'I thought you knew where I worked?'

'Right, well I don't.'

'Okay – I work at Vince Veroni's Pageant of Venus, in Soho.'

He looked blank.

'I'm an erotic dancer.'

He sat up and laughed. 'Right! Right! I thought it was too good to be true. Me with a model!'

'You think it's a strip club, don't you?'

'Sounds a bit like it, babe.'

'Look, I'll get you some tickets. You can come and see it. It's not what you think. We have proper dances to do. It's all choreographed, and on stage and everything. It's a proper show.'

'How come everyone at the nightclub thought you were models?'

'I think that was Olga's friend, Bernie, the owner. He must've told people that.'

'You didn't correct them?'

'No, because of how everyone thinks! You saw what they were like – how d'you think they'd have been if they thought we were –'

'Strippers.'

We looked at each other, registering that word. It was a word no girl at the Pageant ever used: we were erotic dancers, show-girls, artistes, even Veroni's girls, but never *strippers*. There were a couple of beats, then Andy said, 'See what you mean, babe. See what you mean.'

I'd put on his boxer shorts, but hadn't found a top yet, and his eyes lingered on my body.

'C'm'ere,' he said finally, catching hold of me, and pulling me back down on the bed.

Andy played guitar and sang in a band called Blue Fish. Two or three nights a week he'd have gigs, which I didn't see unless I took time off work. But we got into a routine of meeting after-wards and going for a drink together, then back to my place.

I had a new flat. It was on the eleventh floor of an uninspiring concrete block, at the New Cross end of the Old Kent Road. There were four blocks close together, all named after beautiful places in the Lake District. Mine was 'Borrowdale'. After the Roger incident everyone knew I wanted to move and when this council flat came up for one of the girls at the Pageant and she didn't want it, she sold the keys to me instead. The council thought my name was Jacqueline Simms, which was a bit awkward – I had to be Jacqueline for my neighbours too, just in case – but it was bigger, and seemed safer, than the bedsit I used to live in.

My flat was close to the band's rehearsal studios. Andy and I would arrive back there in the early hours of the morning and sleep until midday. Then I'd make brunch and when we'd eaten, Andy would leave to go and rehearse.

I shopped for food and cooked. I ate more too. Andy loved sausages and I'd buy all different kinds. I was happy and grateful to have him with me, and I went to great lengths to please him.

Occasionally, if we both had a night off, we went out to eat. I took Andy to Delilah's once, but Delilah virtually ignored him, for reasons best known to himself.

Andy showed me a photo of his Mum and Dad's place in Virginia Water. His dad had come into an inheritance in his fifties and moved the family out of their East End terraced house into a mock mansion with a swimming pool. We went there once, but they were out. Andy was very proud of it though and we peered in through the security gates at the luxurious-looking garden. I assumed Andy got money from his dad, because he always seemed to have some, despite earning next to nothing with the band. He was on the dole too, but that would hardly account for it.

The night Andy came to see the show, I'd offered to get tickets for him and his friends. But he came alone.

I was so worried about what he'd think, I drank most of my usual quart of rum before the first curtain went up. I didn't know where he was sitting, and I couldn't see him. He was just out there somewhere, with all the punters.

After the show he said, 'Yeah, it was good. I liked it.'

It was clear he didn't want to talk about it anymore, and the only time he brought the subject up voluntarily was when an article about Tracey Veroni appeared in the papers. It was head-lined 'BOOB JOB FOR PORN HEIRESS':

It seems that Tracey Veroni, heiress to the massive Vince Veroni porn empire, is fed up with looking at breasts, even her own. Yesterday an unknown source alleged that Ms Veroni was in recovery, having had reductive breast surgery at The Rowlar, an exclusive cosmetic surgery clinic in London.

'Is this true?' Andy asked me.

'I think so,' I said. It made sense; Tracey had been off work for a while. There were rumours.

'Why'd she do it?' Andy asked.

'Maybe she wants to be a Rolls Royce.'

'Did you talk to her about it?'

'No! Tracey Veroni doesn't talk to us about stuff like that!'

Later on I tried to imagine what it would be like to be Tracey. I didn't think I'd like it. In some ways she was a celebrity: the papers wrote about her, people knew who she was. But, like me, I don't suppose many people would have wanted to swap places with her. And I think she walked around knowing that lots of people – maybe the majority of people – judged her low and dirty, because her money was dirty, because it, and she, came from a world of porn.

I could see why her life might be easier with small tits.

A couple of weeks before my twenty-sixth birthday, I went with Saf on one of her night-hunts.

The venue was Waterloo station. The weather was cold and wet. I stood with Saf under an ancient canopy, where buses stopped and dirty rain fell into black puddles. The smell of diesel was so strong the rain seemed ready-mixed with it.

We made our way round the filthy back end of a stationary night bus, and I looked up to see a passenger sitting in the yellow light inside, looking snug and secure.

Saf was heading for a railway bridge opposite the station and I hurried after her, soaking my new leather boots in a deep puddle.

The bus droned off down the main road behind us, leaving the night lonelier as we reached the first railway arch where Saf came to a halt. She flicked on her torch, pointing its beam into the pitch black recess.

There was something pale in a corner at the back – a woman in a dirty white coat with a hood. It looked like a dressing gown.

There was a noise, a rattle like something being shaken. Then the torchlight found her face, and she screamed.

Saf turned back, and I clung to her arm.

When we were out from under the archway, I looked back. The darkness had swallowed the woman up. The rattling had stopped too.

Saf walked on to the next arch, and I kept pace with her. But I wanted to leave. 'Saf!' I whispered.

She shone her torch into the second arch.

'Saf!'

She jumped up and down on the spot, a finger over her mouth. 'Shhh! Look there! There!' she said.

I caught a glimpse of someone retreating into the darkness. I wanted to run, but Saf moved forwards.

'Hello, hello?' she said, making me feel even more panicky. There was no reply.

She flicked off the torch, and I immediately envisaged someone creeping up behind me. Then she moved further forward into the blankness. I moved with her, still clinging to her arm. There was a whiff of alcohol and urine.

Saf spoke again, 'Hello? Can I talk to you?' she said.

We were about halfway in and I couldn't see more than an inch in front of my nose. This was crazy.

I fished in the deep pockets of my waterproof jacket, looking for the small torch I'd brought.

Saf stepped forward again just as I switched it on.

In front of her, not two feet from her face, was another face.

This time I screamed and ran, pulling Saf with me. I didn't stop running until I got back to the station entrance.

'What the fuck did you do that for?' Saf shouted as soon as we came to a halt.

'Because you're dangerous. "Have a look," you said. "See where they are." Not start making introductions to some alky in the pitch dark!'

'We were so close, and you bloody ruined it!'

'Ruined what? Did you actually think you were going to have a conversation?'

''Course I bloody did! That's how you start a conversation, isn't it? Saying "hello" and stuff. Or do you think all homeless people are sub-normal?'

'I think some of them are.'

When we'd calmed down a bit we went for coffee at the All Night Café off Piccadilly. Saf carried on about how she'd seen that tramp before, how he was unlikely to be violent because he didn't have the body language. 'You can't go running away from people like that. It's like begging for something bad to happen. It's bad karma, Harri.'

If anyone was begging for something bad to happen, she was, I thought. But she was dreaming aloud again by then, about her dad, and how all would be right with the world when she found him, so I didn't say anything.

Saf got a black cab to take her home, and I walked into Soho to get a mini-cab.

There was a queue at the mini-cab place, so I sat down to wait on a plastic chair that needed a wash and glanced at the unshaven profile of the man sitting on my right. He needed a wash too.

I was still thinking about Saf. Now that I'd experienced the reality of what she did on her own night after night, I was really concerned for her. I imagined her on her own, trying to introduce herself to strange, filthy, wandering men, and I shivered. 'My father . . .' she kept on saying, 'my father is out there waiting for me.'

'Wee lassie?'

I turned to my left. The man who'd spoken had lots of wild, curly grey hair. He nodded toward his lap. 'D'you know what that is?' he said. Crawling slowly up his exposed forearm was a black and orange spider, as big as his hand. He chuckled, evidently tickled pink by his own audacity or my reaction, I couldn't tell which.

'It's a tarantula! She's a beauty, she is. Would y'like her on you?'

The cab office was full, the operators behind glass at the end, the dealers leaning on the counter, and the line of people sitting in the plastic chairs. Everyone watching me and the man and the spider.

'Okay,' I said.

The unshaven man on my right muttered something and walked out. The dealers laughed. The man with the spider put his forearm next to my arm and shoved the spider over with his other hand. I was glad I'd kept my mac on.

'Is it poisonous?' I asked him, as the spider moved up my arm.

'D'you no' ken tarantulas? She's deadly.'

'I know.' The spider had reached my elbow. 'But I thought maybe you'd had the poison taken out.'

The spider started climbing my upper arm. Surprisingly I could feel its grip, gentle but definite, through my coat.

'Och no! She's poisonous! But she's alright. She likes you!'

It was okay, I reasoned with myself. If this idiot wasn't frightened of it, it couldn't be that dangerous.

The spider reached my shoulder.

'Has she got a name?' I knew I wouldn't be able to cope with it on my face.

Just then one of the controllers rapped on the glass, 'Yours!'

Spiderman's mini-cab had pulled up on the pavement outside and he wasn't going to hang around; there were too many people waiting. He plucked the tarantula from my shoulder and dropped it in a shoebox.

'See ya, hen!' he said and vanished outside.

That night I dreamed of spiders. One in particular, its body balloon-full of some malignant fluid, waited quietly under a pile of decaying leaves for Saf.

Soho, London 1989

She saw Kay, she recognised him . . .

On my birthday I got a phone call that pushed worries about Saf to the back of my mind.

For birthdays at the Pageant we brought cream cakes to work – except Lynn and Elaine who brought LSD. I'd bought a Black Forest gâteau from a patisserie on Old Compton Street, but when I got to work I realised I'd forgotten to bring a knife. So I nipped out to Delilah's to borrow one.

When I got back, the payphone was ringing. I picked it up, and someone said, 'Hello. May I speak to Arabella Cordon, please?'

I didn't recognise the voice, or maybe some part of me did, because my stomach lurched.

'Who's speaking?'

'Edward Cordon. I'm her brother.'

'Teddy? It's me.'

'Right. I . . . er . . . It must be a bit of a surprise to hear from me.'

I didn't say anything.

'I got your number from Linda. I'm calling about Mum. You might want to sit down or something. It's not good news. I mean, it might be a bit of a shock.'

I'd been drinking and was on a bit of a high. Now I was sinking fast, like a brick in water.

'What is it?'

'Well . . . look, is there anyone else there with you?'

'There's loads of people. I'm at work. What's the matter?'

'Mum was diagnosed with cancer a week ago. It was at a very

late stage.' He paused to let his news sink in. 'She only survived a week after they told her. She died yesterday.'

I didn't know what I felt. Maybe anger more than anything. I wanted to ask why she hadn't wanted to see me when she knew she was dying, but I didn't trust my voice.

After a long silence Teddy said, 'Are you there? Arabella, are you okay?'

'Yes.'

'Dad thought you might want to come to the funeral. It's on Friday.'

I felt incapable of replying.

Teddy said, 'I think she would have wanted to see you, there just wasn't any time. Arabella?'

Time, I thought, time! And it was this easy to get in touch, in the end. Just pick the phone up, and speak to each other.

'Arabella, do you want to phone me back?' It was so odd to hear this stranger-brother of mine, talking to me now, as if the years of silence had never taken place.

'Okay, yes, I'll call back,' I said.

'Will you take down the number?' There was a pencil on a string next to the phone and I used it to scribble on the wall.

I put the phone down, wandered into the dressing room and sat down, still holding the knife.

Lynn said, 'Are we eating this cake, or just looking at it?' She took the knife from me. I could hear Olga's solo finishing, two acts to go before mine, so I went to see Sean, our stage manager.

'I just got a phone call. My Mum's died. I'm not going on.'

'Okay,' he nodded. 'Are you alright?'

'Yes.' I left him to sort out the change in the running order.

I started putting my clothes on. Saf walked in, and I told her what had happened. It was difficult to concentrate and taking off my stage make-up seemed a huge effort.

Soon everyone knew, and they were all speaking in hushed voices and asking if I wanted anything.

Once I'd removed my make-up and put on my daytime face,

I realised that I had to call Teddy back before I left because I had no phone at home.

I knew I'd go to the funeral. I'd known it since he said it. Why do we feel compelled to do things for dead people that we might never have done had they been alive? But if my living mother had wanted to see me, I would have gone. I knew that in my heart, though it was hard to admit it, even to myself.

I guessed that the request had come through Teddy, but from Dad. Dad would have asked Teddy to contact me, because he thought it was the right thing to do. He was observing protocol. I was Eileen's daughter, I should be there, and that was that. He would probably ignore me.

I felt angry with Teddy. He could have phoned me anytime over the years.

But then I could have phoned him, I suppose.

I called him back.

'I'll come to the funeral.' I had to swallow my pride to say it. I would go, but only because I couldn't not go. If I opted out now, I'd be opting out for good. Part of me wanted to reject them as they'd rejected me, to show them I didn't need them, that I had my own life now. But I knew Mum would have said that I was cutting off my nose to spite my face.

Family. My family? I was everything to do with them, and nothing. I had thought the link severed long ago. Now I found I was still attached.

Nottinghamshire 1989

'Gerda, my dear little Gerda, where hast thou been all this time? And where have I been?'

I took a taxi from the train station in Nottingham to Woodstowe church. Teddy had said he'd try and meet me there before the service.

I sat in the back of the taxi and looked out of the window. The driver tried to talk to me, but I told him brusquely that I was going to a funeral and he left me alone after that to listen to his radio. We had to go twenty miles out of the city and into the countryside.

Nottinghamshire countryside was tea-caddy cosy, beautiful on a small scale, like the world of Peter Rabbit – all green slopes and hawthorn hedges, winding lanes and kissing gates, cattle grids and water splashes. Somewhere inside I felt a massive loyalty to it and once, when an article in the paper called it 'unremarkable', I had felt personally insulted.

I pressed my face against the window, remembering the smell of wood and ditchwater, the feel of wet grass and the smooth white insides of conker shells.

Up past Cuttingford and down into Bagley's Basin, along the gully, and past the start of Salt Hill footpath. The patterns of the little brown lanes and the shapes of the hills were exactly the same as when I was little.

Teddy had tried to give me directions on the phone, and I'd stopped him. It made me feel like an outsider. I wanted to yell, 'I was brought up there! It's where I came from!'

As we drove through Broomdene, the last village before

179

Woodstowe, I started to look carefully at people in the street, in case there was someone I knew from schooldays. But we reached the church without me recognising anyone and the driver fetched my roll bag out of the boot.

Teddy wasn't there. Nobody was. I heaved my bag onto my shoulder and walked into the graveyard.

I was wearing a black fake fur I'd got in a Harrods sale and underneath, a black dress with black court shoes. Worried about how I would be judged I'd tried for sophisticated and dignified. But I'd forgotten about my old army surplus bag, and now I felt it gave me away, like a signpost that said, 'Good for nothing really'.

Woodstowe graveyard was full so no one was buried here anymore. Although the service for mum was here, she would be cremated at Tiley Green, with a gathering at Woodstowe village hall afterwards. The gravestones were all in a crowd, a close-knit community set among hillocks of earth, covered in coarse tufty grass which grew long close to the stones. Some of them had sunk down on one side, like old people with bad hips. Others had fallen over altogether. When I trod on one I hadn't seen I apologised in my head to the person underneath.

I like graveyards. Old stones with writing inspire a respect that pots of ashes just can't compete with. Ashes can be thrown out over the sea, to lend some sense of mystery and grandeur to the occasion of death. But no matter how grand the ceremony, as soon as it is over the body vanishes.

Gravestones, on the other hand, are always there, even for strangers who might re-interpret engraved messages and spin tales of their own concerning the dead.

I wandered around reading the inscriptions. The older ones were stoic and biblical: 'Thy Will Be Done 1890'; Alfred Ernest Baker 'Who Went Forward 1925'; Beatrice Louisa Edwards 'Looking for that Great Hope and the Glorious Appearing of the One True Father'.

I read that one over several times, my stomach contracting. Further on there were others more like greetings cards. One was addressed to 'Mother' and read 'Since you can no longer stay / To cheer us with your love / We hope to meet again one day / In yon bright world above.' It was like something written by a child, accidentally cheerful, innocent of the terrible finality of death.

There were mothers and fathers, husbands and wives, sons and daughters. 'Lily Swan, my beautiful wife, forever living in my heart'; 'In memory of a dear son James; your life is beautiful memory, your absence silent grief.' As a child I had been frightened of graveyards. Now I wondered why, when there was so much love here. 'Jenny Bennett, Only goodnight darling, never farewell.'

I didn't realise I was crying until I heard Teddy shout: 'Arabella!'

He seemed too big. He was tall, well over six feet, and his hands and feet were massive. I realised I'd been nursing a picture in my mind of Teddy, aged fourteen and a half, the age he was when I left home.

He strode towards me, and put out his hand. His body language, the way he bent forwards from the waist, was my father's.

I shook hands with him awkwardly. It felt odd; not least because I couldn't remember the last time I shook hands with anyone. But also because he was my brother. Did real brothers and sisters shake hands? I thought not.

'Sorry I'm late,' he said. 'Dad and Lucy are about two minutes behind me. Shall I bung your bag in the boot of my car?'

The way he spoke seemed too chummy. I didn't know what I expected, but I didn't want him to pretend to be my friend, like nothing had ever been wrong between us. But I couldn't think of any other way to behave. So I went with him to put my bag in his car.

There were other people arriving now, moving towards us in twos and threes, making their way from their cars to the church. I didn't recognise anybody, but Teddy greeted people as we hurried past them to the car park. 'Hi! Hello!' He held his hand high with a flat palm, a favourite gesture of Dad's.

★

Dad and Lucy pulled up as we reached the car park. I saw Dad's face through the windscreen at the moment he caught sight of me.

His face muscles worked to find the appropriate expression. It looked for a second as if he might smile, but in the end his cheeks were too stiff, his mouth set too tight.

He ended up with a sort of surprised grimace. And maybe I was doing the same.

Dad and Lucy got out of the car. I wouldn't have recognised her away from his side, and again I realised that my mental picture was inaccurate. Over the years I had imagined Lucy as demure, pretty in a restrained way, and ultra polite, like a child from the last century. I suppose it was the only sort of child I could imagine living with my father.

Now my first impression was of a typical teenager, looking down, shuffling and chewing gum. She wore a pair of grey, scruffy-looking trousers, the likes of which Dad would never have allowed when I was a child.

Dad stood slightly in front of Lucy, and I looked straight into his eyes. Eyes like slits for firing arrows from, eyes as opaque and green as the surface of a pond in winter. It was impossible to read anything in them except a kind of cold neutrality.

'Arabella.' He nodded. Then he put his head down, and walked on.

It was as if he'd slammed a door in my face. I felt the roaring anger and hurt of childhood rise up, my body tensing, my face flaming red. My feelings were so strong they frightened me and I fought to overcome them.

It was what I had feared, and expected. But it hurt all the same.

Teddy put a hand on my shoulder, and I jumped.

'He doesn't know what to say to you.' We both watched Dad going into church with Lucy. He was smaller and greyer than he had been when I last saw him.

'Come on. Let's go in,' Teddy said. 'She was his wife, but she was our mum.'

So I stood in the family pew with Teddy, Dad and Lucy, feeling very different from them, and from everybody else.

It was a short service. Lucy started crying as the priest began his address and continued all the way through. Afterwards, people filed out quickly, making their way back to their cars for the drive to the crematorium.

The family was chauffeur-driven. Dad and I sat at opposite ends of the back seat, as far apart as possible, but still too close for comfort. We turned our heads away from each other, staring out at the cold dull day from our separate windows.

Teddy sat between us, Lucy in a pull-down seat opposite him. Teddy did his best to make conversation, asking about my journey from London, talking to Dad of a neighbour who'd been at the funeral and was also a widower.

But the dark, sharp obstacles of the past were right there, threatening to crash through the red glass of the day's stifled emotions.

In the end Teddy gave up and for an excruciating ten minutes the silence of my childhood came back.

The crematorium was an ugly, angular building, all rendered beige with dark brown window frames. I didn't want to go in. Instead I sat in the tiny garden outside at the back. It had concrete paths and huge flower beds with nothing in them but rosebushes, all quite bare.

I thought about Mum's body burning, with all the illnesses and hurts ever inflicted on it. She had been beautiful when she was young; a beauty that deteriorated as I grew up. I hadn't lost the guilt, remembering Dad's refrain, *you're making your mother ill.*

I wondered if he blamed me now for her death? Or was I exonerated by time and distance?

Would Dad take her ashes home? And if he did, where would he put them? There would be no gravestone for the rest of us to visit, so even if I wanted to come back and put flowers by her grave, I wouldn't be able to. Maybe I wouldn't be coming back. I hung my head. I'd assumed that Mum dying would change something.

When people started coming out of the crematorium, I wished I too could disappear in a puff of smoke. Although some of the mourners glanced my way, no one approached. Instead they moved slowly towards the car park, a solemn procession, feigning aimlessness — as if to have shown purpose would be disrespectful to the dead.

Then Teddy appeared, taller than everybody else and looking for something. When he caught sight of me, he came striding over. He moved quickly, which made him appear less pretentious, more his own man, a breath of fresh air. 'Are you coming to the village hall?' he said.

'I don't know. I thought maybe I'd go back.' We had planned on the phone, however, that I would stay the night at Teddy's.

He said, 'It seems such a waste of time. I don't know why you came in the first place if that's the way you feel.'

'Why did you ask me?'

Teddy was silent, so I gave him the answer. 'Because Dad thought it was the right thing to do.'

Teddy fixed me with a glare I remembered his six-year-old self having. 'If that's what you think,' he said, 'why did you come?'

'Because I thought something might change.'

'And you think you've given it time to?'

'What? You think there's going to be some amazing about-face at Woodstowe village hall? I've been universally ignored since I arrived, in case you hadn't noticed.'

'Well, you've led a pretty radical life. Are you saying you can't take the consequences?'

'What do you mean "radical"?'

'Your job — the men's mag — just because people live in a village doesn't mean to say they don't know what's going on.'

I was shocked. It had never occurred to me that my family, or people in the village, might know about the men's mag. I hadn't mentioned it to Linda. Nor she to me.

'You don't know me!' I told Teddy. 'You don't know the first thing about me. So don't presume to judge me.'

'I don't,' Teddy said.

There was a pause. Dad came out of the crematorium with Lucy. I could see now that his body was bent over a little. He looked old and vulnerable. It made me think of the night Mum disappeared and he came to my room, convinced I might know where to find her. *I do love your mum, you know.*

Teddy spoke. 'He's going straight back to the house.'

'He's not going to be at the hall?'

'No, he says he's tired, and Lucy's had enough. Look, I'd like to talk to you. But I have to be at the hall. If you'd stay at my place tonight, we could talk then.'

Teddy surprised me. He certainly hadn't learned his communication skills from his father. I felt proud for a moment about how well he'd grown up, my baby brother, and I wanted to reclaim him.

Nottinghamshire 1989

He was busied among the sharp icy fragments, laying and joining them together in every possible way, just as people do with what are called Chinese puzzles.

Woodstowe village hall, the site of my childhood kamikaze jump, also brought back memories of bring-and-buy sales, barn dances and fancy-dress parties. Now that the village school had closed, the hall was used mostly as a day centre for the elderly. It smelled of boiled cabbage.

There were heavy dark clouds outside now, and somebody had switched on the hall's fluorescent strip-lighting. Teddy asked me to serve vol-au-vents and sandwiches, and I was grateful for something to do. Some of the mourners, including Auntie Irene and Uncle Donald, were distinctly cool with me. I sweated inside my stiff dress, constantly aware of the sideways glances I was getting; feeling like I didn't belong in the village, or in the family.

I offered the tray of pastries to a plump woman in her late fifties. She was holding a small dog, a snuffly Pekinese type with a red collar round its neck. 'So you're Arabella?' she said, as the dog scrabbled towards the vol-au-vents. She pulled it back.

'Yes, hello,' I replied politely, and we shook hands.

'My name's Sheila. I knew your Mum a long time ago, before she had you.'

'Before?'

'Yes, we met when we were working for the same firm. We were clerks for Jessops in Nottingham and then at the Labour Exchange. I lost touch with her after she moved here.'

'Did you know my real dad then?' I spoke quietly. I didn't want anyone to overhear. It was a bit frightening to talk openly with family nearby. The subject of John Dodd had been taboo for so long.

'I met him a couple of times,' Sheila said.

My heart beat fast. 'What was he like?'

'He seemed nice enough. I don't remember him very well, it's so long ago.'

'But he looked like me?'

'He did, dear, yes. It put me in mind of him again when I saw you.'

'Do you know why he left Mum? Was it because she was pregnant?'

'Oh, no, at least I don't think so. They were having problems before that.'

'What problems?'

'Oh, you know, just the kind of problems we all have, getting along with each other.'

'Oh.'

'I know they were very much in love at one stage, but they were very young, and it takes a lot to make it last.' She adjusted a tiny bell on the dog's collar. 'It was your father that named you though – did you know that?'

'Really? How do you know?' I was full of fast-swimming feelings that I couldn't stop to identify. The news that my real father gave me my name made me feel like someone had just stroked my hair.

'Eileen said he liked the name Arabella. I think she thought if she called you that . . .' Sheila looked down at the dog. Smoothing its hair back between its ears, she said, 'She was heartbroken actually. She used to sing a song, you wouldn't know it, I suppose . . .'

'What song?'

Sheila sang her reply. '*Wise men say only fools rush in . . .*' I recognised the song as an old Elvis number. Maybe there'd even been a few cover versions. She had a strong clear voice and a few people turned to stare at her. She sang a whole verse, stopping to outstare the starers at the end so they all turned away.

'It was Top of the Pops in those days,' she said. 'Your Mum sang it all the time she was waiting for your father to come back.'

'To come back from where?'

'Didn't she tell you anything about your dad, dear?'

'No, not much, she didn't like talking about him.'

'Yes, well, some cuts run deep.'

'But where did my dad go? Why was she waiting for him?'

'He went off on a boat doing something – working, you know. It might have been France . . . somewhere . . . I don't remember now. They left their relationship sort of open-ended. Oh, he knew she was pregnant, but she'd said, and I don't know what possessed her, that he should take this job on the boat and he didn't have to come back to her. She thought he would though, for the baby as much as for her. After you were born and she called you Arabella, I knew she was still hoping.'

'Where was I born?'

'I'm sorry, I can't remember, dear. Your mum went away. But I remember it was a difficult time for her. The birth and that. There was an awful midwife, and when your mother cried out – I'll never forget her telling me this – when she cried out, as women do in the pain of labour, the midwife said, "What do you think you are – a farmyard animal?" It was difficult for your mum to take that, and then all the stigma. It wasn't easy to be a single parent in those days, a lot of people condemned you.'

'What about my dad – John Dodd? Did she get in touch with him after I was born?'

'She always called him Jed, and, no, she didn't, dear. I don't know if she knew where to find him.'

'Jed?'

'Yes. John Emmanuel Dodd, she used his initials. I think all his friends did.'

'I didn't know. Was he foreign, then? Or his parents?'

'I never thought of that. He spoke English like you and me, I'm pretty sure he was from the Midlands.'

'Did he talk about his family at all?'

'Oh, I wouldn't know about them. I only met him twice, and only very briefly then – I hardly spoke to him, dear.'

'And where did Mum go? Where was I before I came here? To my stepdad's house, I mean.'

'Well, I can't believe she didn't tell you these things, but you were looked after by your grandma.'

'My grandma?'

'Yes, your mum went out to work, you see. She was having a terrible time. You were a tiny baby and she was still living with her parents. Her dad was awful to her. You'd cry, her dad would shout and she had to fetch you out of the house, even if it was the middle of the night. She'd arrive at work looking like death warmed up. No wonder she had trouble bonding with you at the start. We can say that nowadays, can't we? "Trouble bonding" – I think it's quite a common problem. And it didn't help she wasn't with you for most of the day. Then of course she got the new job – with your stepdad, and that was better.'

'Did she come to stay with you once? When I was small, after she moved here?' I was thinking of the time Mum left for two days. I still didn't know where she'd gone.

'She did, dear, yes – I remember it well because we hadn't seen each other for a very long time when she turned up that day.'

'Did she want to leave Duncan then?'

'Well, she may have done for a short time, but God knows, we all have those moments.' She gathered the dog up closer to her, and continued in a different tone, as if she was afraid she'd said too much. 'Anyway, I'm sure you know more about their relationship than I do. We lost touch after she got the job with your stepdad, except for that one time, when I don't think she had anywhere else to go. Listen, dear, I'm going to have to go now, but you can always ring me again if you think of something else. Your brother's got my number.'

'Do you mind if I ask you one more thing? It's just that once Mum said John Dodd, Jed, was a liar and a thief. Do you know why she would have said that?'

'No . . . I don't remember her telling me anything like that. But your mother could be a very private person.' Sheila sighed. 'All I can say is there's a fine line between love and hate, and your mum had a lot to deal with after Jed had gone. I think she thought he was one sort of person, and when he didn't come back, she decided he was another.'

'Do you know where he might be now? If I wanted to look for him, I mean?'

'No, no, I wouldn't have any idea, not now. It's such a long time ago, you see.' She paused. 'But it's been nice to meet you at last. I didn't want to go without having seen you. Now I'd better go and thank that brother of yours.' She stretched her red-painted lips, showing her teeth, and moved off muttering to her dog.

Jed, I thought. And *Emmanuel*, a long, foreign-sounding name, like mine. Had Mum tried to make him sound plainer to me on purpose?

A memory of Mum came unbidden to my mind. Wearing the red jersey, she came towards me. I'd done something wrong, pulled up weeds instead of flowers, wet the bed again, answered back. She shook me, holding me by the wrists with her tired hands. She shook and shook, until I thought my head would fall off.

Mum had often shaken me when she was angry. But was she softer once? Full of love? And why did she let Jed go? Did she think she'd stand more chance of keeping him that way – by offering him his freedom? My head was spinning. I went to sit in the loo, to be on my own.

Sheila had confirmed much of what I had guessed already. But guessing and having things confirmed were different. I had a picture now of my mother in labour, and of the awful midwife. Mum had been so young. I wondered if her mother had been there for her. She was an only child, and her parents had died when she was twenty-six, so I never knew them.

But the biggest thing for me was my name. I felt comforted

by the thought that my real father had said it, once. But did this mean he knew I was a girl? That he wanted a girl? Or did he have a favourite boy's name too? When did Mum stop hoping he'd come back? And when did she start hating him? When did she start hating me?

'Alright in there?'

Someone was outside the door. I must have been in there longer than I thought.

'Fine, thanks,' I replied cheerily and flushed the toilet.

A few more people introduced themselves to me: second cousins, great aunts and uncles. Dad had a brother who lived abroad, and a sister, Ginny, that he detested, but Teddy and I hardly knew them. Mum and Dad had never been keen on family get-togethers.

A couple of whom I had no recollection said they were very old friends of Mum and Dad. People didn't seem to want to get into a conversation with me so much as to simply declare their opinions. Stating their relationship to me first appeared to make them feel justified in doing this.

From one of my mother's aunts I heard how hard Mum had worked, how proud she had been, that she'd loved me and never wanted me to go. 'She could never understand why you left,' the aunt said, in an accusing tone.

An ex-neighbour pressed my elbow. 'Look after your father, he's a good man.' And someone's smirking teenager kept murmuring something I couldn't quite catch every time I went past him, so I just smiled. It was only after he and his parents had said their goodbyes that he turned up the volume. 'Where's your boots?' he sniggered over his shoulder as they left. He could only have been referring to the men's magazine.

An old man raised his glass to me and said, 'Live and let live,' before quaffing his sherry. And Dad's sister Ginny gave me a lecture on how it was time to return home to the fold. 'You're a lovely-looking girl, and you've been off and lived your own life in your own way. I don't agree with everything you've done, but I believe in forgive and forget.'

I started to really see red then, but luckily Teddy – who must have had a sixth sense, or perhaps just knew Ginny better than I did – came up to ask if I'd stack the dishwasher.

I stayed busy in the kitchen for the remaining time, just lifting my head briefly to say goodbye until they'd all gone.

Teddy locked up and dropped off the keys to the hall with someone in the village, while I waited in the car. He drove us to his place, a flat over a shop in Tiley Green, where I changed into a sweatshirt and trousers. Then we walked to a pub.

We talked about the funeral, Teddy reminding me of the names of people we'd seen that afternoon. I told him I'd spoken to Sheila, but he couldn't remember who she was. 'She had a dog,' I said.

'Oh yes, I noticed that,' said Teddy. I knew what he would say next, so I said it with him. 'Little yappy dog.' That's what Dad would have called it.

Teddy smiled, 'She was an old biddy, wasn't she? I was going through an ancient address book of Mum's and she was in there. What did she say to you?'

'She was talking about Mum and when she had me. And she knew my real father.'

'Did she? Do you think about him then?'

'Sometimes.'

'He sounded a bit of a con-artist from what Mum said.'

'Yes, well, she had a bit of a prejudiced view of things.'

'Yeah – as you would if you were left holding the baby.' Teddy's loyalty lay with Mum of course, he had no reason to question her version of the truth.

'Yes, as you would,' I agreed with him because it was true in a simple sense, and I didn't want to argue. I asked him for Sheila's number and Teddy said I could have the whole address book if I wanted.

'I rang everyone in it,' he said, 'but the others had all moved on.'

We looked at each other. 'You're not thinking of looking for your real dad are you?' Teddy said.

'I don't know.'

It felt like dangerous ground so I changed the subject, and we talked about old school friends: who had married, what they were doing for a living, which house they'd bought. It was comfortable in the pub where there was a blazing fire and I felt better in the soft clothes I'd changed into. Teddy suggested we eat there and by the time we got back to his place he felt like a friend.

I was surprised when the conversation turned accusatory. The subject was my leaving home.

'Why did you leave like that?' Teddy asked.

'Like what?'

'Suddenly! Never saying anything to anybody. What was so bad you couldn't stay and sort it out?'

'You don't know what Dad said to me, do you?' All this time I just assumed he knew, but how would he have known unless Dad had told him?

'You don't just leave home because of something someone says to you! People have rows all the time, especially families. Then they make friends again. You have no idea the trouble you caused. Because they never understood it. I don't understand it! It was like you died, for God's sake! Why?'

I told him about Dad's ultimatum. It stopped him for a moment, but he only said, 'They didn't mean it.'

'If they didn't mean it, then why didn't they stop me, or get in touch later on? They did a pretty good job of sticking to their guns, for people who didn't mean it! I've been gone ten years!'

'I just don't think you had to go, that's all.'

'Oh, thank you, Teddy! Great, I'm really glad to know I needn't have gone through half the crap I went through! Were you there when Dad said what he said? No! You don't know how it was because you weren't there! Do you really think I would have gone through what I've gone through, if I didn't have to?'

'What about what we went through?'

'You didn't go through anything.'

'I dealt with the aftermath.'

'You were a kid.'

'Yes. A kid who lost his sister.'

I swallowed. 'I didn't create that situation. I wasn't happy about going. I was told to go. I was made to go.'

'They both loved you.'

'Well, they've had a funny way of showing it then. Do you treat people you love like that?'

Teddy looked at me. 'Do you?' he said with Dad's eyes.

'You think I started all this! I was a child!'

'And what about now?'

'What are you talking about?'

'What about now? Are you a child or a grown-up?'

'You don't think I've had to grow up pretty quick? It's been quite an education, I assure you! In fact it still is. Not all of us are Daddy's boy, everything taken care of, nice flat, nice job, management accountant!'

We went in circles for a while, but by one o'clock we had mellowed sufficiently to realise we quite liked each other. We talked about Dad, and what he would do now, with our mother no longer there, and Lucy leaving soon to study in York.

Teddy was keen for me to make friends with Dad.

'Just think of the things he did do, as opposed to the things he didn't.'

'Right, okay. Well, he did throw me out of home . . .'

'Oh, look, don't start on that again. At least you escaped.'

'Escaped what?'

'Well – being an accountant for a start.'

'But I thought you wanted to be an accountant?'

'No, I never have.'

'So why are you doing everything you're doing then? You've been studying your whole life! And you're good at it! There's loads of money in it, what more could you want?'

'Well, how's this: I'm not interested in the money, I'm no good at it, and I never have been. I did it to please Dad. I've failed more than half my exams so far.'

'You've failed them! Does Dad know?'

'No. He doesn't know I've got the sack either.'

On the train on the way back to London I closed my eyes. Teddy had said he would write. I was very tired, and my brain in its sleepy state was chanting, *got a brother, got a brother, got a brother* and then, *lost my mother, lost my mother, lost my mother*. Even so, I had a sense that something good would come now, that my relationship with Teddy would grow, and that it would be good for both of us.

I fell asleep until the train stopped at Leicester. When I woke up I watched a man playing a game with his daughter. The girl was about two or three, and the game was 'catch the bear'. Her father had a tiny bear's head that fitted over the end of his thumb. It was very simple, made of brown felt with black felt eyes, nose and mouth, but the expression on its face was somehow comic. The father clenched his hand underneath it to make the body, and the bear bobbed about comically along the edge of the table, in front of the little girl who tried to catch it. The little bear hummed and talked to itself, seemingly oblivious to its predator, but it would just happen to go for a jog or jump over to look out of the window as the little girl made a grab for it. She laughed when she missed.

The bear sang and the girl pounced. The singing voice became very high as the bear sprang up into the air above her head, then remained there peering down at her. She turned her face to look up at it, then giggled as it dived suddenly, disappearing under the table. When it emerged it had a hanky over its head. She exploded with laughter. She pulled the hanky off and the bear burrowed into her ribcage, making her laugh even more.

I laughed at the bear's antics too and I examined the little girl's father when he wasn't looking. He held her so carefully, so lovingly.

After the bear game he read her a story and I was transfixed by the way he stroked her head, kissed the soft hair at her temples. I fell in love with him several times before he got off the train at Clapham Junction.

I wondered what it would be like to have a dad like that, whether I would feel connected to things.

Soho, London 1989

He often formed whole words, but there was one word he could never succeed in forming – it was Eternity.

A ndy met me at Waterloo.
'Spanish!' he shouted, as soon as he saw me. He wrapped his arms round me, and lifted me in the air.

That was when I began to imagine he might be there to return to always. I felt I was really sorting my life out, building relationships that would anchor me to a bright new world. After all, hadn't my brother seen me onto the train at Nottingham? Now my lover was here to meet me.

We were excited to see each other and we headed straight back to my flat, where we jumped into bed.

Several hours later we were still there, and we chatted until I had to get up for work. Andy's music wasn't going well. Blue Fish had plenty of gigs, but they weren't well paid. Andy had drummed up some enthusiasm for the band from major producers, and then watched it disintegrate before they'd got so much as a sniff of a record deal. He told me he was looking into other ideas to make money for a national tour now.

At work I told Saf about the funeral, about seeing Dad, and about Teddy.

Saf had been looking for her father in a cardboard city at Vauxhall. She'd had no luck, Vauxhall was too far out, she said. She was planning a second assault on London's parks.

She consulted a chart to see what the moon would be doing for the next quarter and noted down the auspicious dates. She used her rune stones too. We had to ask them a question with a yes–or–no answer. Saf's question was, 'Will I find my Dad this year?' The stones answered 'yes' and that cheered her up.

'You have a go,' she said.

'What'll I ask?'

'You have to ask something important. Ask something about Andy.' So, like a schoolgirl, I asked, 'Will I get married to Andy?'

The stones gave an immediate 'no' and Saf said quickly, 'You'll probably just live together instead.'

'It doesn't matter to me, I don't believe in them anyway.'

Saf struck a match and lit a cigarette. Waving the match out, she said, 'Okay, another game. You have to imagine some kind of water, right? You have to draw it.' She proffered a little book of hers with a flowery cover and a pen hooked onto it.

I took it from her, but dithered. 'What sort of water?'

'That's what you have to decide – stream, river, lake, sea, rain – whatever you like. Think of it, then draw it.'

I drew quickly then pushed the open book over to Saf. 'Stormy sea?' she said, looking at me to check. I nodded and she smiled. 'Passionate tempestuous relationship.'

'And how do you work that out?'

'Water – it's a metaphor for love. Didn't you know?'

'According to who?'

'Jeez, I don't know, psychologists I suppose. There's loads of quiz-type things you can do.'

'I nearly drew rain. Is rain good?'

'Mmmm. It depends if it soaks you right through or not,' Saf said throatily.

A couple of weeks went by, during which I waited for a letter from Teddy. Each day I got an overwhelming feeling of disappointment after the post had been. At the end of the second week, I phoned him. But his answer-phone was on. I would have felt vulnerable leaving a message, so I didn't.

I talked instead to Andy, who said, 'He's a geezer, isn't he? He's not gonna just call for a chat. When he's got something to say, he'll give you a bell, babe.'

I was lucky to get even that much out of Andy. His excitement at seeing me again had dwindled quickly. He explained how much 'business' he had, arranging gigs, networking and marketing to promote Blue Fish. He needed a good night's sleep, he said, and he couldn't be doing with me walking in from work at one in the morning.

So he stayed at his place most of the time. We met sometimes after his gigs. But he'd be drinking and the other band members were there, so I couldn't talk to him properly.

Mostly I saw him on Tuesdays, after I finished at the Pageant, when he'd be waiting in bed at my flat, and on Sunday evenings after he finished rehearsing. It was feeling less like a relationship and more like an occasional bonk.

A month went by without my having heard from Teddy, and Delilah, perhaps prompted by my long face, invited me to lunch.

It was the third time I'd been to Delilah's, and Saf, who'd never been there said, 'You'd better make sure you wear a tiara.' She said Delilah liked me because I had a posh accent and dressed up for him. 'Or you could buy some Jackie Onassis sunglasses and a headscarf,' she teased.

But Delilah treated me like something precious, and I liked having a reason to dress up.

When I told Andy I was going to Delilah's, he said, 'What do you want to go to lunch with that gender-bender for?' It wasn't like him to say such a yobbish thing. He apologised quickly and said he hadn't meant it, it was just one of those stupid remarks. I thought perhaps he was jealous, but then it wasn't as if we could have been together that Saturday anyway, as he was rehearsing.

The day I went to Delilah's I received a parcel. Not from Teddy, but from Dad.

Inside the parcel I found a photo and a flag. The flag was of a kind for sale in souvenir shops everywhere: a small red pennant, made out of cheap material, with a print of Che Guevara on it. The photo was of a lad of about eighteen, sitting on a wall near a waterfall. His head was covered in luxuriant black curls of hair.

I looked and looked at the photo, the first one I had ever seen of my real dad. It said nothing on the back of it, but I was in no doubt. He was a male version of me. Not just his hair, but the jut of his jaw, his lips, his teeth, his eyes.

He was slim and confident-looking, someone who expected things to go his way, or perhaps wasn't too bothered whether they did or not. I wondered what he looked like now, in his forties. Would I recognise him if I passed him in the street?

I picked up the flag. Was it his or Mum's? Maybe she bought it because she thought it looked like him. It did a bit, but it seemed odd she'd kept something so unimportant. Maybe it was all she had to keep. Except for me. I could see now that I must have been a constant reminder of her heartbreak and his betrayal.

Also in the parcel was a note from Dad, the first direct communication I'd had from him in ten years, not counting the 'hello' at the funeral.

Dear Arabella,

I think your Mum would want you to have these. They are the only things she kept concerning your father. I hope all is well.

Best wishes,

Dad

Before I left for Delilah's, I put the photo of my real dad in a transparent pocket in my purse, next to one of Andy and me. Then, as an afterthought, I folded Dad's note, and stuffed it in behind.

★

Delilah wore a blue satin dress with a Japanese neckline and one of his trademark turban-style hats. He had a tailor who made clothes especially for him, and he designed most of them himself. Today he was also wearing low-heeled sandals and I noticed he'd painted his toenails turquoise.

After a feast of whitebait, homemade cannelloni, and rum-filled bombe, I showed him the photo of Jed.

'He look very like you,' Delilah said, and we spent a few minutes finding the similarities.

'Your mother took this picture?' he asked me. I didn't know, it seemed likely.

'How do you feel about your mother's death?'.

'I don't feel anything.'

'You don't feel anything?'

I searched my insides again for feelings concerning my mother. 'I lost her a long time ago,' I said.

We looked at the photo again – the sunny day, the smiling young man, the waterfall. Delilah said it was a lover's picture, and I imagined my mother taking it, what hopes she must have had.

Memory rose then, like a wave in my chest: my mother singing '*Treat me nice, treat me good . . .*' I had liked it when she sang, and when she stopped I would beg her to continue. Sometimes my pleas for an encore had made her laugh. I'd liked that too. How old had I been? Three? Four?

I told Delilah about Sheila and the other song Mum used to sing.

'Do you think your mother was loved?' Delilah asked me.

I considered this for a second before I answered. 'Yes, but not in the way she wanted.'

Delilah traced his fingers slowly along a seam in the fabric of his chair. 'And if someone loves us, not in the way we want – is this really love?'

I thought of Dad's words again. *I do love your mum, you know.* 'The person offering it might think so.'

'And the person receiving it?' Delilah said.

203

'Might think it's as good as it gets,' I replied.

A silence fell between us. It wasn't uncomfortable. I sat and thought about Andy, how he was nothing like my stepdad, in spite of what people say about girls falling for their fathers. And I was nothing like Mum, I thought. Nor would I ever be.

I wanted to tell Delilah I was thinking of getting married to Andy, but Delilah had taken a dislike to him without ever having really spoken to him. Every time I mentioned Andy's name Delilah found a way to turn the conversation in a different direction.

So I talked about marriage generally instead.

'Have you ever wanted to get married?' I asked.

'I like my own company.'

'What about lovers?'

'Sex is over-promoted by the media.' Delilah said that he was inclined to agree with Boy George, who had stated a preference for a nice cup of tea. He got up smiling, and fetched tea on a tray.

'What are you doing for Christmas?' he asked.

'Spending some time with Andy, I hope. I haven't seen much of him lately. I'm going to meet his mum and dad this year.'

I told Delilah about Teddy too, and how I'd hoped to see more of him.

Delilah's own half-brother Antonio was due to arrive in London just before Christmas, and Delilah talked me through the itinerary he had planned for his visit. He had decided not only where they should go, but what they would eat each day.

I looked at the menus he'd prepared and asked him if he took after his mother.

'Maybe,' he laughed.

'What's Antonio like?' I said.

'He is a typical man. A strong man. Made in Italy.'

'What does he think of you being a transvestite?'

'He doesn't know,' Delilah said, 'I take a little holiday from the restaurant, the cabaret. He will see the galleries, what he wants . . .'

204

I was shocked. 'But what about being true to yourself? Being who you really are and all that?'

'There are many different versions of the truth. Some of them not good for Antonio.'

'How do you know? You haven't given him a chance!'

'He is from a different culture. A different way of life, a traditional way of life.'

'But he doesn't really know you!'

'He knows the part of me I am prepared to show him.'

'Because you're scared of losing him,' I said. It sounded more aggressive than I'd meant it too.

'I am scared of losing him, yes. And my sense of myself is not so small that I think he won't lose something also, if our relationship is no more.'

Delilah got up.

'Now you can excuse. I have to wash the dishes, and to repair my green dress for the show.' He chased me to the door and wouldn't hear of any help with the washing-up.

All the dreary way to work, it rained. I sat on the top deck of a droning double-decker bus, staring at piles of fag-ends and brown cack on the floor.

The bus conductor said, 'Cheer up! It might never happen!' and I hated him for it. But he didn't know that, and instead he took my silence as an invitation to chat. He nodded at a building blackened by fire.

'Poll-tax riots did that. Nobody's going to pay poll tax. Not a cat in hell's chance. You going to pay it?'

It was everybody's favourite question. The correct answer was 'no' and I shook my head. He looked at me, weighing up my level of interest, and I sunk into my coat until the collar swallowed my neck.

He wandered off murmuring, 'Thatcher – that's a woman from hell!'

Hating the prime minister was the national pastime. People

didn't comment on the weather anymore, those passing-the-time-of-day remarks. Instead it was, 'That Thatcher woman, I can't stand her, can you?'

And the prime minister was 'Thatcher' now, all the time, for everyone. At first she was called Maggie, or Mrs T, but I think those names proved too feminine or too affectionate for her.

It was a funny thing about names, I thought, how being called something else changed the feel of things. It was Sophia who'd first called me Harri, when I started the telegrams, and I liked it. It sounded tougher than Arabella, and it made me feel tougher; like a boy.

But when Delilah called me Arabella, his accent curled around the word, like someone writing it up all big and fancy, in ink. It sounded all woman, my name, when Delilah said it, and something in me responded to that too.

There were two sides to me definitely, two sides to Delilah, maybe two sides to us all.

I thought of discussing this idea with Andy, but when I saw him he was too busy watching *Spitting Image* on TV.

I perched on the edge of his chair and watched the grotesque Thatcher puppet, standing in a boxing ring, kitted out just like a boxer in boxing gloves and a purple and gold robe.

I would never have chosen to watch the programme because I found the characters so ugly, but Andy was passionate about it.

We watched as the Geoffrey Howe character climbed timidly into the boxing ring. 'Cup of tea anybody?' he said and Maggie clouted him, knocking him out.

Andy roared with laughter.

When it ended, Andy pulled me onto his lap and started playing with my nipples. I enjoyed the sensation of having my nipples gently plucked and twisted, but Andy didn't like having his own touched at all. In fact, he was quite paranoid about it. I think he believed that he might like it, and if he did, this would somehow throw his sexuality into question.

So he probably wouldn't have liked my two-sides-to-us-all ideas either.

Each evening before work I bought my usual quarter-bottle of rum. The bloke in the off licence fetched it down from the shelf when he saw me coming.

Now I was considering getting two bottles.

I was miserable over my upset with Delilah, but it was more than that – my misery had put me in touch with a depression I was feeling about lots of things.

What I had seen as a budding relationship with Teddy had caused a surge in brother fantasies – fantasies in which Teddy and I talked a lot and held hands, helping each other towards a brighter future, Waltons style. I was terribly disappointed it hadn't worked out that way. And Teddy's silence had left me feeling alarmed at my capacity to inspire rejection from my family when my intention was just the opposite.

Andy and I never seemed to talk in the way I wanted. I was worried too, that he might reject me, grateful for the times he said, 'Love ya, babe', even if it wasn't the same as 'I love you'.

We never went out anywhere together anymore. If I asked him about it he pointed out that we were both always working. He worked during the day as well as at night now, and Sunday night was the only night I had off from the Pageant. Even then Andy was rehearsing until seven or eight o'clock. What he said made sense, but I kept thinking how much more we had seen of each other at the beginning. It would be good to spend some time together at Christmas.

Until then, I felt I was always just killing time until I saw him. Weekdays weren't too bad. I slept until two or three in the afternoon, then got ready for work. I'd spin the time out, having a bath and dressing, making tea and smoking too many cigarettes, before catching the bus to town about five o'clock.

But work was depressing me too. At first I had thought I'd have lots of girlfriends at the Pageant, but there was only really Saf, and she was tied up with Simon and her search for her dad. I never felt on the same wavelength as any of the others, though it wasn't for lack of trying. The hours made it difficult to meet new people, and if I did meet anyone I'd have to tell them where I worked, which always led to me being judged and feeling inferior.

Weekends on my own I tried to think of things to do. A couple of times I went up to Greenwich Market to see Sophia, but I felt like I was in the way. She asked me to go clubbing, but I didn't go to clubs on my own anymore because I didn't think Andy would like it.

Then, the week before Christmas, I rowed with Andy. The argument was about condoms, which he still insisted on using, even though I was on the pill. He cited the safe-sex campaign and said that everyone should use them, but I'd always been faithful to Andy, and I saw the condoms he insisted on using as barriers to trust and intimacy.

In the end, I said I wouldn't sleep with him if he was going to use one.

'Fuck you then,' he said.

'No, don't fuck me, that's the point.'

'Babe — sort yourself out!'

'I am sorted. I just want you to trust me.'

'It's not about trust! It's about fucking AIDS!'

'I haven't got AIDS.'

'Know that for sure, do ya?'

'I don't need to. But you obviously do. Have I got to have an AIDS test? Would that satisfy you? Well, I'm not going to!'

'Do what the fuck you want!'

He walked out of my flat, and I stood in the open doorway, watching him stab the lift button. When the lift came he stepped into it, and then turned. 'If you don't wanna fuck me, baby, fuck off.' The doors closed before I could make my own parting shot.

That night I cut my arms again. Just a little bit, to ease the pressure inside.

Soho, London 1989

He looked at the fragments, and thought and thought till his head ached. He sat so still and so stiff that one might have fancied that he too was frozen.

I felt very small, too small to phone Teddy, although I thought of it a lot.

I might have gone to make up with Delilah, but Delilah's was closed now for Antonio's visit and I didn't want to turn up at his flat uninvited while his brother was there.

Through Saf I was offered a modelling job for a guy who was making a video to demonstrate his stage make-up skills. It was a one-off and didn't pay anything, but it gave me something to do. I was to be body-painted and then filmed standing on a scaffold.

I wore a flesh coloured G-string and had to keep very still while Eric, Saf's friend, painted a map of the world on my face and body.

It was strangely erotic watching Eric concentrate on the canvas of my skin, feeling the delicate movements of his paintbrush on my stomach, thighs and breasts, where he created countries and oceans.

We were at a remote place with no running water. It was nearer work than home, so afterwards I got a lift and then took the tube, still covered in paint, to the Pageant for a shower.

I raced out of the shower dripping wet to fetch the towel I'd left behind in the dressing room and ran smack into Tracey Veroni, almost sending her flying.

In the short time I'd worked at Veroni's Tracey had become more and more withdrawn. More often than not she looked like she was on something. The days of her puppet shows, if there had ever been more than one, were decidedly over. The woman I collided with now was switched into self-destruct mode.

She was in the habit of carrying a black briefcase which came open, and all her stuff flew out of it. I braced myself for her attack, but all she said was a barely audible, 'For fuck's sake!' She started picking it all up.

I grabbed my towel, fastened it around me, then came back and bent to help her. I couldn't help noticing at least four glossy brochures for cosmetic surgery placed among her stuff.

I glanced at her, crouched on the floor next to me, slowly picking up pieces of paper. She moved with a visible effort like the air around her was heavy, like it was water.

She must be stuffed full of drugs, I thought. Maybe that was why she wasn't shouting.

Her face was tanned and very lined. She was thirty-two but she looked ten years older.

When everything was picked up I said sorry again and went straight back into the dressing room. I got dressed then wanted to get something to eat, but I hadn't heard the door from the corridor to the stairs shutting, nor Tracey's footsteps on the tiled floor or mounting the steps to the stage. She had to move one way or the other, and either way she'd make a noise. I hadn't heard anything, so she was still there, just outside the dressing-room door. I didn't want to run into her again, in case she got angry with me. So I waited.

It was a good five minutes before she moved. Five minutes during which I could imagine her motionless, like a fragile robot frantically trying to re-programme itself, to remember where it was she'd been going before I bumped into her.

Time stretched ahead and around with very little to mark the days. Once I went for a walk in a park in New Cross. But a bloke with a can of Tennants and a Rottweiler followed me everywhere leering and talking, until I got fed up and went home. Maybe I'd have more luck if I went uptown, Hyde Park or Holland Park or something.

I thought about it, but I never went, because I was finding it more and more difficult to go anywhere at all on my own. Going to work was alright because I was into the routine of it, but anywhere else I felt too conspicuous.

In the space of a week I became so paranoid that even going food shopping, or for a walk to the call box frequently presented too much of an ordeal and I'd end up staying in and going hungry. I would normally have eaten at Delilah's at least three times a week. Now I bought fast food instead.

So far as I could I avoided people, hiding from eyes that seemed to probe my skin in the Pageant dressing rooms, eating chips or pizza in the quiet dark before anyone else got to work.

Christmas was coming, and occasionally I panicked because I had nothing planned. But my head was mostly too full up to think about it much.

I caught myself saying words out loud every now and then, and it was like hearing snatches of someone else's conversation, except I knew it was really my conversation because sometimes there were names: Martin, Teddy, Delilah, Dad.

I looked at my watch all the time without understanding what time it was.

My thoughts were so clamorous and impossible to decipher that several times I physically seized up. I had to go and lie down in the middle of getting dressed, or I found myself weighted in a chair in the sitting room, hours after I'd decided to go to bed.

The Pageant was closed Christmas Day and Boxing Day and I was glad it wasn't longer. Saf had booked a holiday to visit Simon's parents in Leeds and she left three days before Christmas. With me it hardly registered.

On Christmas Day I slept and watched TV. I ate some chocolate I'd bought for myself and I opened a present from Saf. It wasn't the worst day I'd had.

But Boxing Day there was still just me and it was quiet and

scary, like time had become elastic, or somehow rearranged itself so that I might spend the rest of my life alone in my flat.

Neither Dad nor Teddy had sent a Christmas card. I took Dad's note out of my purse and re-read it:

Dear Arabella,

I think your Mum would want you to have these. They are the only things she kept concerning your father. I hope all is well.

Best wishes,

Dad

Suddenly it was obvious. This was another cut off. I noted the use of the word *your*, as in *your* mother and *your* father; it seemed to me that Dad was saying, take them, or everything that remains of them, and have a good life on your own.

Now Mum was gone, there was nothing to link me to Dad. I wasn't a blood relation, and given our long estrangement, and our extraordinary capacity to infuriate one another, it seemed unlikely he would be in touch again. So this was a farewell note, a signing off. Another thought occurred to me: what if Dad had something to do with Teddy not calling?

After the holidays everybody at the Pageant seemed as subdued as I was. Saf told me how Simon's parents had spent the whole of Christmas watching TV and ignoring everyone else. Some of the girls asked how my Christmas was, and I mumbled that it was okay. I was there and not there, heavy with my thoughts.

Three days after Christmas Dad's card arrived. But I didn't feel any real sense of relief. I was waiting for something else, but what it was I couldn't have said.

★

One morning the rattle of the letterbox woke me earlier than usual and I got out of bed to fetch the post. Returning with a single envelope, an electricity bill, I sat on the bed and cried. It wasn't from Teddy, it wasn't a way out, but it seemed clear I had to find one.

After a couple of hours of tea and cigarettes, and having made numerous changes of clothes in my anxiety to be properly dressed for going outside, I went shakily into New Cross to see my GP.

My GP was a gentle Indian man who asked about my family. I told him instead about Andy, about Saf and Delilah. Having mentioned Delilah I then had to explain that he was a 'he'. The doctor became very concerned. He warned me to stay away from gay men and he gave me a leaflet about AIDS. What about my parents? he asked. Couldn't they help? I found I couldn't speak for crying, and he prescribed Valium.

Taking the pills frightened me. I collected the prescription but I didn't take any. I just kept them in a kitchen cupboard, for emergencies. I continued to cut my arms, telling myself I was just blood-letting. It did make me feel a bit better, like I was getting the poison out.

Then Andy phoned and asked me to lunch.

It was a whole month since our condom row, and I'd almost given up on him. He wanted to know if I would have lunch with him on Friday, in a French restaurant in Covent Garden. I knew the one he meant, and it was posh, very posh. He'd got something special to ask me, he said.

It was like he had waved a magic wand; I was suddenly ecstatic. I was bright and joyful again. In the three days before Friday I prepared like a bride. I had my hair cut, my eyebrows shaped and went for a facial. I bought a new outfit too, a red dress from Selfridges that cost a bomb.

All my earlier confidence had returned and I took the dress into work on Thursday night to show Saf and the others. I pranced around modelling it while everyone said how fantastic it looked and I told them what had become a magic mantra, that I was going out to a French restaurant because Andy *wanted to ask me something*.

Everyone said good luck and told me they'd keep the champagne on ice for me. Saf gave me a big hug. 'Come back with a rock,' she said.

My excitement about what Andy would say to me – I positively, utterly and completely knew what he would say – made it difficult to sleep that night. I had to keep reminding myself that I had set the alarm for half past eight, an early call for me, and how knackered I'd be if I didn't get my beauty sleep.

I spent the whole of Friday morning getting ready, bathing, shaving my legs, rubbing moisturiser into my skin and styling my hair. My hand shook applying my make-up, and every now and then I stopped for a cigarette to calm down.

Then I was ready, and I knew I looked great in my red dress, red shoes, red lipstick.

But I also knew I didn't look right for the neighbourhood outside my flat. I stood in the dark hallway gathering courage until a voice in my head said, 'Done up like a Christmas tree,' and I hurried back to the bathroom with diarrhoea.

In the end, I put on an old black mac to cover me until I reached the West End. When I got there I'd carry it.

Walking into the restaurant, the mac over my arm, I didn't need a mirror. Three middle-aged men at the bar visibly pulled their stomachs in as I entered, and Andy, who was sitting waiting, actually stood up when he saw me. 'Spanish, you look amazing! Out of this world, babe!'

He grinned his old grin, and I saw the black teeth and knew that I loved him. He hadn't dressed up of course, dressed down if anything. But I knew that the wearing of his Stiff Little Fingers T-shirt and favourite jeans indicated a special occasion.

I had a Scotch and American while he had a beer, and we looked at the menu. Then he ordered wine and said, 'You must have spent ages getting ready,' which took the edge off his earlier compliment a bit. 'I hope you'll think it was worth it,' he added.

'I'm sure I will,' I said, taking his uncharacteristic nervousness as a good sign, and feeling brave as the whisky eased all the joints of my body.

I ordered snails to start. I'd never eaten them before, and it suited my mood to try something new. Andy followed suit; he'd eaten them before, he said. But when they came they were still in their shells, and he hadn't had them served like that the last time. There was a torturous-looking tool on each plate, presumably for extraction. Andy and I raised our eyebrows at each other.

I picked up my snail tool optimistically, and inspected it. 'It looks like an eyelash curler.'

'Babe – it's a good idea! You curl your eyelashes with it, and while everyone's distracted, I'll stamp on your snail shells!'

We laughed a lot because it was one of those posh places where you feel like you're not supposed to.

We talked about my work, and his, and we made an effort to entertain each other. I told Andy about climbing scaffolding half-naked and covered in paint, then travelling by tube with my hair backcombed like a loon, and my face orange with a map of Argentina.

Andy told me about the national tour he was organising for Blue Fish. He'd come up against a woman in Devon who wouldn't book them into a venue, because she was against animals in captivity – even if they were only fish.

Andy had tried in vain to explain that Blue Fish was only a name, but she didn't listen. She absolutely couldn't take a booking for a show with fish in it, she said, alive or dead. Andy reported that she had also said, 'I don't care how big your aquarium is either,' and we fell about.

After the meal and the wine, we sat and looked at each other in silence for a minute. I think we were both thinking about the future.

'This thing I want to ask you,' he said.

'Before that.'

'What?'

'Did you miss me?'

'Spanish, I always miss you,' he stubbed out his cigarette. 'What I want to ask you, it's an idea for making money.'

My heart sank. I looked down at the tablecloth, which was grainy and white. There was an oily tomato stain where my plate had been.

'You see,' he continued, 'I've met a whole load of Japanese businessmen, and there's more where they came from . . . Japan! It's full of 'em!' He laughed.

I composed myself, trying hard to listen. I had no idea where this was going.

'Anyway, the thing is that Japanese businessmen like English girls. I mean they're keen, really keen, to meet them. And I know someone else who'd be prepared to hire out the top floor of his building, very central and luxurious. You know, upmarket, babe.'

I looked around the restaurant, noticing for the first time that the customers were mostly business people and tourists.

'I thought you could talk to some of the Pageant girls, and you could all come and meet these guys. I'd introduce you,' Andy said.

'What for?'

'Well, just "party on", you know. Massages and stuff.'

As the meaning of Andy's words became clear I was gripped by sudden hard cold – as if I'd been water, flowing along one minute, turned to ice in the next.

Andy's formula for instant ice was simple: create an expectation, then confront it at its climax with something opposite. *Prostitute* was the opposite of *bride* alright.

I threw the remainder of my wine in his face, and walked out.

I could do frozen, frozen was easy. But it wasn't being strong. It was just a physical reaction, an automatic response. And it was just the surface. Underneath I was still weak and pathetic. Ice was a temporary state.

When I imagined ice melting I thought of geography lessons in school, where we drew huge ice caps dissolving and watched a TV programme in which meltwater hurtled down mountainsides, creating waterfalls and rapids. As it slowed down there would be a river, meandering to the sea.

But it depends where you are: ice can just as easily be the sort that gets trampled on city streets and ends its days as grey slush on a grey pavement. Eventually slush turns back to water, dirty water which runs down a gutter to a drain, where it disappears into darkness.

Slush was the rest of that afternoon and early evening. Slush was crawling into bed from the bottom end of it, red shoes and all. Crumpled up, not crying, but moaning and rocking. Slush was the inevitability of breathing, of having to go to the toilet, of stepping out of the hated whore-red dress, the shoes without any magic in them. Slush blurred the edges of everything, so I no longer knew if that grey cold was me, or the world, or both.

I went to work, in the end, in search of human warmth, some comfort.

At the Pageant I managed to croak a sad 'no' to enquiries about the existence of an engagement ring. I got undressed, applied my stage make-up, and put on my gold harness for the parade. But the effort of keeping words and tears packed tight inside made me stumble.

So I excused myself with illness and sat down underneath the bench where Saf was doing her make-up. Someone had smashed a glass and left it there, and I was cold dirty water by then, only thinking of disappearing.

PART TWO

Soho, London 1990

'But canst thou not give something to little Gerda whereby she may overcome all these evil influences?'

'I can give her no power so great as that which she already possesses. Seest thou not how strong she is? Seest thou not that both men and animals must serve her – a poor girl wandering barefoot through the world?'

When I come to, I'm on a stretcher in an ambulance and Saf is sitting next to me looking anxious. We arrive at Charing Cross hospital, and the ambulance man asks me how I feel. 'Okay,' I say because anything else seems too complicated, and he helps me into a wheelchair. Saf talks to people on my behalf, and eventually pushes me slowly along pristine, bright corridors, to the X-ray department. Nurses do their duties concerning me without speaking or smiling. Perhaps they are unsympathetic to self-mutilation? Or perhaps they know where I was picked up from and have categorised me already as a stripper, a slut. Either way, I feel like a wanker, caught in the beam of the spotlight.

Once I have been processed through X-rays and stitches, I am given a prescription for Valium and told to go home. Outside the hospital Saf and I share her last cigarette.

'What're you gonna do?' she asks.

'I don't know.'

'You can come back to my place if you want. But Simon's there.'

'I know. Thanks. It's okay, I'll go back to mine.'

'I'd come with you, but . . .'

221

'No, no. It's okay.'

'It's just the cats, and Simon . . .'

'I know. It's okay.'

When I used to sign on there was always a box for dependents. I would look at it out of the corner of my eye, some part of me imagining those who were dependent on the one who drew the dole.

'Dependency' registered with me then as it does now, like a dirty word. It's bad enough signing on. Dependency on another individual is the absolute pits.

Of course any of the girls at work will offer each other comfort, of a sort. But we all have our own tightropes to walk, and we can't afford to follow each other too far.

A mini-cab pulls up, and Saf goes to ask him if he'll take me to New Cross.

The cab stops at the kerbside next to the grey shopping precinct beneath the flats, and I pay the driver. It's sleeting outside, long, cold needles of it and I half run the short distance to the lift, aware of wanting to be dead whilst not wanting to be cold and wet.

Underneath the tower block the air smells foul, but the lift is working and I step inside and push the button for the eleventh floor. Sprayed onto the steel interior near the emergency button is some graffiti that's been there since I moved in. It just says 'I'd give my soul for a pair of Nike trainers.' I always wish the writer had left an address. I'd have bought the trainers and delivered them just to see his face. But the kids in this area don't expect a response.

I'm exhausted, and once in my room I go straight to my bed, where I immediately fall asleep.

When I wake up it's eleven on Saturday morning and I don't have any cigarettes. I don't want to go outside, but my craving for a fag is overwhelming, and drives me finally to the shops downstairs.

Back in the flat I make tea and sit on one of the mustard-coloured chairs in the sitting room, smoking. When you're sitting down all you can see is sky out of these windows. Today the sky is dirty white with clouds so dense I can't even see where the sun might be.

Sometime during the afternoon it starts to hail, and this disturbance moves me out of my chair and into the bedroom, where I take the necklace Andy gave me for my birthday out of my bedside table. I leave my flat and throw it down the rubbish chute near the lifts.

Back in my flat I'm very cold, so I start running a bath. When it's half full I remember the photo, a picture of Andy and me beaming, outside the wrought-iron gates at his parents' house. He really wanted to show me that house. I thought he wanted me to meet his parents too. Now I feel sure he knew they were out. Crying, I take the photo out of my purse. Then I burn it on a plate in the kitchen.

I switch on the TV, and the news blasts at me too loudly. *The waxwork image of Prime Minister Margaret Thatcher was voted most popular attraction at Madame Tussauds in London . . .* I press the spongy volume control on the remote with my thumb to turn it down, but it's not working properly, so I kneel in front of the set trying to find the right knob. *Critics of the Prime Minister were quick to point out that she also came second in a vote for the 'Hate and Fear' section of exhibits. Finally in Shropshire . . .* To my relief the voice fades out and I flick through the channels with no sound. But my attention is no longer on the screen. The story about Thatcher has made me think of Dad again.

'Come on – get up! You should be enjoying some fresh air!' Dad says.

Curled into the scooped-out armchair in the kitchen next to the Aga, I am reading *The Mystery of the Missing Man*.

He continues. 'It's a lovely day out there.'

'Dad, I'm reading.'

'Arabella, I won't have you sitting around all day long. Get up NOW!'

Dad had this list called 'British Behaviours' he'd taken from an article in the paper. A Conservative MP, who was also a fan of *The Good Life* on TV (as was Dad), argued that the qualities exhibited by Felicity Kendall and Richard Briers in the programme were natural to Conservatives and essential to entrepreneurs. On the list were: *Independent*, *Self-sufficient*, *Driven*, *Right-minded*, *Persistent* and *Adventurous*. Dad liked it because it was a description of him. He loved Thatcher, because he thought she'd put the Great back in Great Britain. 'She gets things done,' he said. 'That's what we need at work – a bit more war-room mentality.'

Dad had a habit of picking up phrases, from the *Daily Telegraph* usually, and using them over and over again. When Thatcher started shaking up nationalised industry, all we heard about for ages was *cosy complacency* and how it had to go. Perhaps that's why I always had to be ousted from the armchair.

Dad fancied Maggie as well; that was part of his obsession with her. He always went for blondes. I remember watching TV when she was on the campaign trail in 1979, the year Dad threw me out. She was doing a 'walkabout' on a farm and holding a calf in her arms while she talked to a journalist. Dad was watching her face and hanging on to her every word.

All I could see was how close she came to strangling the calf. I think her husband stopped her. He said something to her out of the corner of his mouth, which looked like, 'You're strangling that bloody calf,' and she dropped it.

Sleeping, smoking, making tea and toast and watching TV see me through to Sunday. On Sunday afternoon I spend ages getting ready for a short walk into New Cross. I shop at the mini-market and buy chips from the Chinese takeaway. Then I call Teddy from a call box, gripping the phone between my head and shoulder so I can unwrap the chips a bit and ease a few out. His answerphone message has 'Here Comes the Sun' as background music.

'Hello. This is Teddy Cordon. If you want me please leave a message. No one else lives here. So if you don't want me you must have the wrong number. Bye.'

I put the phone down. It's months since the funeral and I have no idea where Teddy is. The only person I know who might know is Dad.

On Monday afternoon I go back to work for a rehearsal. I'm late but Tracey doesn't say anything. Everyone's already moving around the stage to the tune of 'Material Girl' and there's no time to talk. I drag my gold ra-ra skirt and frilly collar on over my clothes to match the others, and we line up in the usual formation.

We're rehearsing changes to the parade because of Katie, a new girl who's totally unfit, but really stunning. Tracey's changing the parade especially for her, because she can't do the same moves as everyone else. Katie sits on a chair centre stage, and Tracey directs her through some on-the-spot poses which they've already rehearsed. On the fourth pose the rest of us set off around the stage, making the same crosses and turns we've done all year. The other changes are also minimal, and when we take a break a few of the girls grumble about having to come in. Tracey overhears Jill complaining and just says, 'You can go now, Jill.'

Of course Jill says she's sorry straight away. She'll lose her bonus if she leaves. Tracey doesn't force her to go, but she makes her change into full costume. 'Full costume' consists of the neck frill and harness, and the ra-ra skirt which is removed halfway through the act. So Tracey's instruction means that poor Jill has to bare her bits all afternoon, while the rest of us are fully clothed.

When the rehearsal finishes most people head off quickly to avoid Tracey in this mood, but some of the girls stop to ask me how I am.

'I'm okay now, thanks,' I tell them.

They don't really seem to want to talk about it any more than I do, but there's a curious kind of acceptance, as if I've been away with nothing more than flu. Liz says, 'Did you have stitches?' And because for some unknown reason we are in the habit of showing each other any scars, I peel back the flesh-coloured plaster I have used to replace the hospital dressing. Liz peers at my wound. 'How many?'

'I don't know,' I say, suddenly worn out by the attention.

'You cut the wrong way,' she tells me. 'You have to cut along your arm, not across, if you really want to inflict damage.' She squeezes my shoulder and adds, 'You'll be fine,' then heads backstage.

As I am sticking the plaster back down on my wrist Tracey appears beside me. She looks at my wrist with her dark, spaced-out look and then says, 'I didn't think you lot had any feelings. You must be the original tart with a heart!'

She doesn't seem to expect a response, as she strides to the edge of stage right, jumps off and heads out through the swing doors towards the foyer.

Her remark is completely nonsensical to me, but I can't shake it off. I go backstage to hang up my costume and Saf is the only one left in our dressing room.

'Tracey Veroni just called me a tart with a heart,' I tell her.

'She didn't! What did you say?'

'I'm stunned. I didn't say anything, and she just walked off. She said she didn't think any of us had any feelings – isn't that mad?'

'She is mad. She was taught by her dad,' says Saf. 'He's a madman – and she's a seriously sad woman.'

'Tart with a heart, though? It sounds like a line from the *Sun!*'

'Think porn mags. She used to write the copy for them.' The phone rings in the corridor and Saf runs to get it. I stop for a moment in the empty dressing room – wondering whether to wait for her – but I feel too vulnerable, and I need to prove that I'm not. I hang up my costume, and pick up my bag.

I stop by the phone on my way out, where Saf is chatting to Simon.

'I'm going to eat,' I mime.

She puts a hand over the receiver. 'Delilah wants to see you.'

Delilah seldom dresses as a woman for daytime. In the café he wears black trousers, starched white shirts with heart-shaped silver buttons he sews on himself, and colourful silk scarves. I haven't seen him since the row about his brother, but he comes straight over and embraces me as if nothing had happened.

'*Ciao*, Arabella,' he says. I look in his eyes; I see he doesn't know about me slitting my wrist, and I'm glad. 'How was Christmas with Antonio?' I ask him.

'It was very good,' he says, but he can't stop to talk straight-away because he's got customers. Instead he steers me to a seat with his usual kindness and care, taking my coat as though I were someone important.

When I finish my meal he comes to offer me one of his coloured Sobranie cigarettes. I take a breath to speak, but he holds up his hand.

'Every one a different colour,' he says, and I meet his eyes which are soft on me.

He scolds me then for not 'making the most' of my hair. 'If you put it up, you will look like Joan Collins as Cleopatra, or down with a few curl, like the woman on the cover of *Vogue* magazine – did you see? You can be so beautiful! You would be out on the pavement and people will think they see an angel! But you have to take care – a little, of yourself.'

I guess we're friends again.

Soho, London 1990

Meanwhile the cold was so intense that she could see her own breath, which, as it escaped her mouth, ascended into the air like vapour.

A failed suicide attempt is a cry for help. But my effort seems to have gone mostly unnoticed. So you have problems too, the world seems to say, and everything carries on as before.

It is 1990: more than a decade since Dad ordered me to leave home. But for me, in many ways, not much has changed. I want the same things, to understand where I come from, and to belong somewhere. But my dreams are of being respectable now, of becoming a wife and mother, or of wearing a suit to work in an office somewhere.

A psychiatric appointment comes through the post; the hospital has referred me. I am apprehensive, but I have high hopes. I think maybe they can fix me.

I arrive by bus on the appointed day outside an ancient stone building, an old presbytery that now houses the psychiatric unit. I walk through an iron gate in a high hedge. There is a huge arched doorway, with a heavy oak door that I close behind me; the other side is in a kind of twilight.

I stand still while my eyes adjust to the semi-darkness. I am in a large room with a high ceiling and a flagstone floor. It is lit only by the daylight coming through small windows high up in the walls. Lots of wooden benches, like pews, are set in parallel lines. At the far end there is a stone counter that looks more appropriate for the laying out of bodies than for administrative purposes. Nevertheless, there is a woman behind it, responsible for greeting patients.

I check in and sit down in the middle of a pew. Almost at the end of it, on my right, is a middle-aged black woman who shuffles further to her right when I sit. She clings to the carved end of the seat and hunches her body away from me.

A little to my left is a white man whose age is difficult to judge, because his face, although very lined, wears the surprised innocent expression of a young boy.

A droning sound draws my attention to a man with bare feet, walking round and round the perimeter of the room. He is talking to himself in a voice that hums down his nose. He shakes his head to get the sound out, as if it were a bee flown up his nostril.

On the pew opposite is a young woman with darting eyes and a facial tic.

Whilst I have seen people like this on the streets of London, the impression is more forceful among so many. And it's a shock to realise I'm part of this group. My immediate impulse on taking in my companions is to make for the door. But it's an instinct immediately subdued by the teachings of childhood. 'Do as you're told' is the phrase inculcated in me with regard to institutions, and I feel compelled to keep my appointment.

A woman on the other side of the room makes a sudden whooping noise and I stand up in spite of myself. But at the same moment my name is called by the receptionist and I am directed upstairs.

The stairs begin in the corner of the room, climbing the wall at one end. They make a right angle at the corner, climbing another short stage and then there's a landing. The landing runs three quarters of the way around the room, about a third of the way up between wall and ceiling. On the left at the start of the landing is a door of dark wood. A white card, with 'Mr M. L. Lamply' typed on it sits in a black metal frame attached to the door. I knock and a male voice calls me in.

I expect the usual friendly and bland bedside manner adopted by the majority of GPs. But this is more like a visit to the police to account for a series of petty crimes. It's a short interview, in which I am asked for a brief explanation of my current situation, and other points of fact, all based on my understanding of the present.

'Will you attempt to take your own life again?'

'No, I don't think so.'

'Are you taking any medication?'

(I tell him about the Valium in the cupboard. That I am on the pill.)

'Do you live with anyone?'

'No.'

'Who do you see on a daily basis?'

(Saf, the others at work, Delilah. I used to have a boyfriend.)

'Do you suffer from any illness, or do you suspect that you have an illness?'

I mention the agoraphobia, a little less acute following my wrist-slashing episode, also that I am lonely.

'Loneliness is not an illness,' Mr Lamply replies. 'You seem reasonably intelligent. Have you any idea why you're in this situation?'

'No. Well . . .'

'Do you have any family? Where are they living?'

'In Nottinghamshire. But I don't really see them. My father . . .'

'I'm not interested in that at the moment. Are you promiscuous?'

(Not recently, but sometimes.)

'Are you prepared to attend fortnightly appointments here?'

'Yes.'

Dismissed.

I walk out of his office and back down the ancient staircase from where I can see the sad, tattered people in the room below. Whether moving or sitting still, their body language indicates abnormality. They have not taken up the socially civilised positions that adults adopt in relation to each other and their surroundings: no sitting back observing, no reading the newspaper, no chatting to another patient. Instead they are sealed off in separate worlds.

I reach the bottom of the stairs and tug at the heavy door to open it, letting the daylight in. Even as I open the door, I know I'll never come back. I may not know where I belong, but I don't belong here. I prefer to be alone, I prefer my own help to this. It's a choice that lifts me; it gives me a little power back.

I march back to my flat, where I stick the Che Guevara flag on the inside of my wardrobe door. Then I move it to the wall next to my bed. I look and look at it, as if it might provide a clue to my continuing existence. Or suddenly speak, and tell me what to do next.

One morning I get a letter from India. It's from Teddy.

Dear Arabella,

It occurs to me that you may be waiting for this, or trying to ring me at Tiley Green. I'm sorry I'm not around. I had a bit of a crisis after you left. Maybe it was Mum dying. I had to change my life somehow. I've spent the last three months in India, doing yoga. I'm now a Siromani! (It's a title awarded by the Sivananda World Yoga Organisation.) I can teach yoga. No more accountancy! You can't imagine how good that sounds! I haven't told Dad yet. I'll do it man to man when I get back.

I arrive in the UK on the fifth of February and I'm going to take a bit of a break, to prepare for my change in lifestyle. I would like to meet up with you.

I'll call you when I get there.

Love,

Teddy

I'm glad to have the letter, glad for him about the yoga, but it doesn't seem real. I can't imagine seeing Teddy again now – not here in my flat, not in Soho.

Even if he does come to visit, it seems unlikely to me that our lives will ever relate in any meaningful way. He will probably want to visit the Tower of London or Buckingham Palace. Then he'll go home, and send me a card every Christmas.

But it's better than nothing, this letter from my brother, and I put it away carefully.

Towards the end of January, I see Delilah in the street outside work. He's pacing up and down.

'Delilah! Hi!' I shout and walk towards him.

He turns and grabs my hands. His grip is tight and urgent. 'Arabella!' he says and looks down at my hands. He turns my hands over so my palms are upwards. I get what he's looking for then; but my coat sleeves are long. He lets go of my right hand and moves to take hold of my left sleeve. But I snatch my hands away. He backs off like he's surprised himself, and I look daggers at him.

'Saf told me,' he says.

'Well, she shouldn't have!'

'She thought I was knowing. She thought you have told me! Why you didn't tell me?'

I didn't know it but the words were already waiting at the back of my mouth. They shot out when I opened it. 'Because you don't like that sort of thing! Sordid stuff! Suicide! Not very stylish, is it? You think you know me, but you don't! And it's because you don't want to know me!' I realise I'm shouting, and people on the street are looking at us. The men who always stand on the corner have started to pull at their shirt cuffs and lift their legs, like they're limbering up for something.

Delilah looks like I've hit him.

'It's not that I didn't want to tell you,' I say more quietly.

He looks down, then up again. 'Will you come now and speak with me? I close the café.'

233

'I can't, I've got to go to work.'

'Afterwards then.'

'Okay.'

Later in the locked café Delilah hands me a hot chocolate. Then he says, 'So you think you can't tell me these sordid things? But if I have made myself such a saint, it is a joke. And style for me is about making the real more big, making it the centre, not covering it up.'

'It's just . . . all the women you like, they're all so . . .' I take in the pictures on the wall with a sweep of my hand, realising as I do that there's at least Marilyn and Judy Garland who were really screwed up.

'Crazy?' says Delilah, and we both laugh.

'It's not really to do with you,' I say. 'It's to do with me. I'm ashamed. And it's over now anyway. There didn't seem much point you knowing about it.'

'Except if it makes you feel better.'

I start to cry, and he puts his arms round me.

After a few minutes I blow my nose on some kitchen roll, and I tell him about Andy and his proposition, about the cutting and the agoraphobia, the visit to the psychiatrist.

Afterwards I feel more peaceful than I have for ages and he gives me a lift back to my flat.

We're only at work to drop our bags, but Saf sits down on her dressing-room chair and lights up. She looks upset.

'Did you see your man?' I ask, referring to the St James Park tramp.

'Yeah, I did. I saw his bloody dick as well.'

'What?'

'Yeah – a flasher, he flashed at me.'

Saf brings her feet up onto her chair and hugs her knees. She blows out a stream of smoke. 'It wasn't the thing itself, right? I mean, flashing, I can deal with that. It's just that I was there thinking . . . thinking that he might be my dad! Jeez!' She looks up at me. 'Well I guess it doesn't rule him out, does it?'

'How did it happen?' I say.

'Well, I was there about an hour, right, sitting behind a bush . . .'

'Saf, you're a headcase!'

'Yeah, right. When he finally poled over, he went straight to the fence – that's where he was before, like he was looking for something. Anyway I watched him for about fifteen minutes, right. You know I was gonna wait till he left again and follow him? Anyway, I got fed up, it was cold, man, and I thought he was probably gonna kip down there. So I thought if I was ever gonna talk to him I might as well go for it . . .'

'Oh Saf!'

'He was under a streetlight then, anyway. He didn't look like he could've moved very fast, and I thought, fuck – I could always run. I mean, if it really looked like something bad was going down.' She takes another drag on her cigarette, then stubs it out in the ashtray.

'I came out from behind the bush and stamped my feet a bit. I wanted him to look round before I got too close, you know? I didn't want to make him jump – hah!' She pauses, pushing little piles of ash into each corner of a blue star-shaped ashtray. 'He didn't turn round,' she says finally. 'He was huddled over doing something. I moved in closer. Not realising, right? And that was when he did it. It's bloody pathetic, but I was really shocked.'

'It is not pathetic! You're on your own with . . .'

But Saf isn't listening. She's fallen on the floor. She's thrashing around. She flings her arm out and the back of her hand hits the metal base of her chair. I rush to move the chair out of the way and get kicked in the shin. Her legs are going like she's running a race. I grab some coats off the back of the door and put them on top of her. I have to get astride her to do it.

I'm trying to hold them round her, to hold her in one place. I am thinking 'epileptic' and I'm sure that I should put something in her mouth to prevent her biting her tongue.

But I haven't got anything to put in her mouth. We're in

the middle of the floor and there's nothing within reach. I could use clothing but I'm scared of choking or suffocating her. I don't think she's breathing properly anyway. Her face is going blue. I haven't got hold of her arms and she keeps whacking me. I shout for help. But I don't think anyone can hear me.

Then, as suddenly as it began, it's over and she just lies still.

'Saf? Saf?'

She's still breathing and her eyes are open. But she doesn't seem to see me.

'Saf, I'm going to get help. I'll come straight back.' Then I run to front of house where they call an ambulance.

The show will go on.

Later that evening I'm trying to tell people about Saf's fit, but there's a mad atmosphere. A notice next to the hastily rearranged running order says that management have hired an 'Assistant Choreographer'.

Our stage manager has also announced that the new employee is in the audience tonight, so everyone that goes on stage is trying to spot him or her.

Tracey Veroni's away again, rumoured to be having a nose job this time. The girls in my dressing room are reading a new story about her in the paper. She's battling for custody of her daughter with an ex-husband who accuses her of being a drug addict.

I didn't even know Tracey had a daughter, but then it occurs to me that the children's drawings I saw in Vince's office before I came to work here must have belonged to her. I squirm to think of Vince as a grandpa.

I imagine Tracey in hospital, trying to put right what she thinks is wrong with her. I wonder if she would be having a nose job if she hadn't been born into the sex industry, if she didn't have Vince for a father.

I suppose Vince Veroni can't be held to blame for all of

Tracey's troubles though. She could have gone off and lived her own life. But a different life would have meant leaving him, and the only time I've ever seen her look happy is clinging on to his arm.

However much I should have liked to be close to my own father, I don't envy her. Who'd want to be close to slimy Vince Veroni? I'm sure Saf's dad is better than that. I'm sure my real dad is.

When it's time for my solo, I stand in the wings. Over the top of our stage manager's bald head, I can see Elaine on the monitor performing 'The Milkmaid'. She's lying on a bale of straw, and as the music gets faster she simulates a frenzied exaggerated wank in time to it. A lot of the solos end like that.

I'm watching, but I'm not thinking about Elaine, I'm thinking about Saf. She's at the hospital with Simon, and they say she'll be okay.

The cloakroom lady at front of house said, 'Thank God you didn't put anything in her mouth, she would've choked and died.'

I'd like to be with Saf, or at least talk to someone about what happened. Instead, I'm going on stage in a minute.

Elaine comes off stage in a flurry of dry ice, and I follow the stage hands as they push my prop, a space rocket with lots of flashing lights, onto centre stage.

The stage hands run off, and I get into position astride the rocket.

The music starts and the curtain rises.

I step off the rocket and stride around the stage, dancing my striptease to an obscure rock number called 'Planet Love'. I've performed this solo so many times, I don't need to think about the moves.

Step, kick, turn, bend. What if the flasher was Saf's dad? *Mount, slide, stretch, roll.* He could be anyone. *Stand, slow, suit off.* So could my father. What if he came to see the show? *Wiggle, turn, wiggle, smooth.* I peer out at the faces. *Mount, slide, stretch, roll.* The music builds to a climax. *Kick, rock, kick, down.* Dry ice pours from the wings as I simulate sex with the rocket. *Hold!*

I'd never know, I think, as the lights go down.

A week later there's just me and three Italian guys waiting for the night bus. I'm feeling very relaxed, on account of having drunk almost a quart of rum, so when they start up – 'Hey baby! *Ciao bella!*' – I just smile and say '*ciao*' back.

On the bus I sit upstairs to smoke, and the Italians join me. One sits beside me, the other two behind. They ask questions.

'You English, baby? Where are you going, baby? Where you living?'

I answer some, and ask some. Then, as we join the Old Kent Road, the guy next to me starts whispering in my ear. He wants to know if I will take him back to my place for coffee. Just him and me, not the others.

I say no, but when we come to their stop and the others get off the bus, he stays with me. His friends shout to him from the pavement outside, laughing and gesturing, talking quickly in Italian, but he ignores them. He will walk me to my door, he says, he will make sure I get home safe.

'But how will you get home?' I ask him.

'I will walk,' he says.

It is rather nice to be escorted home by a dark, handsome stranger. He asks me where I've been and I say I've seen a girl-friend for a drink. He has been to a bar with his friends, he says. They make things out of leather to sell, he tells me, and he shows me a leather bracelet he is wearing. His accent is beautiful. It reminds me of Delilah's.

When we reach my door I invite him in and make some coffee. I sit on the sofa and he lounges in my armchair, rolling a joint. He lights the joint and takes several long tokes, then passes it to me.

Most people I know smoke dope and I usually refuse the stuff, but it's easier to say no in a crowd. I take it from the Italian now, to keep him company. His name is Georgio and he calls me Bella.

Very soon, feeling fuzzy and a little sick from the joint on top of the alcohol, I am in bed with him.

I hardly notice the sex, and then he's getting up, putting his clothes back on.

'No – stay,' I tell him.

But he says his friends will wonder where he is. He has to go now, immediately.

I curl up tight in the foetal position, eyes open, looking into the dark.

The following week, feeling as if I'm taking control of my life, I start to look for my real dad, John Emmanuel Dodd.

I'm missing Saf too. She's off work now, and I suppose I think that if I find my dad, it might just make up in some way for her not finding hers.

I start with my birth certificate. The birth certificate I've never seen. Go to Somerset House, the girls at work say, and the name makes me think of cornfields and sunshine.

On the bus I sit at the front on the top deck, watching the traffic below and feeling apart from everything. I wonder why I didn't look for my birth certificate before. What if my mother's not my mother, for Christ's sake? I have never thought about this before – maybe that's why I didn't bother looking.

But I remember now, I did think about it once; I have a sudden picture of an afternoon at Julie's house. A shiny day full of colour and candles: Julie's birthday party. We played Pin the Tail on the Donkey and dressing-up. Julie's mum pressed an extra piece of cake into my hand as I left and she said, 'You're a lovely girl.' On the way home I fantasised about how Julie's mum might turn out to be my mum, and everything else was just an awful mistake. Like the story of the little princess, who lived right next door to her father's friend for a long time before she was found.

At Somerset House I'm surprised by how many people there are. It's full of people looking earnestly into the pages of huge old books. The books lie open in rows on long wooden lecterns and they are brown and ancient-looking, like magic books.

At the information desk a kind grey-haired woman explains that I have to look for the correct reference, which I will then need to take to a desk at the back of the room. She shows me how to start looking and I am soon leafing through the ancient pages.

I find my own reference quite quickly, and go to the back of the room where a man disappears for a moment, then returns and hands me a sheet of paper:

CERTIFIED COPY OF AN ENTRY OF BIRTH

WHEN AND WHERE BORN: 25th September 1963, Framley
    Maternity Hospital, Tuxford
NAME, IF ANY: Arabella
SEX: Girl
NAME AND SURNAME OF FATHER: —
NAME, SURNAME, AND MAIDEN NAME OF MOTHER: Eileen Bishop,
    a clerk of 78 Acacia Road, Bingham, Notts.
OCCUPATION OF FATHER: —
SIGNATURE, DESCRIPTION AND RESIDENCE OF INFORMANT:
    E Bishop, Mother, 78 Acacia Road
WHEN REGISTERED: 10th October 1963
SIGNATURE OF REGISTRAR: *B. J. Harris*

There's a handwritten note to one side: *Adopted. B. J. Harris, Registrar*. But there's just a slash across the pink box where my father's name should be. The same for occupation.

Well, it looks like Mum told the truth about something, I think. She was my mother. But she hadn't put my father's name down. She must have started to hate him already, at the time of registering my birth. Perhaps my birth was the turning point, a point at which love became hate – the pain of labour turning long-term grief into something suddenly tangible, something acute and physical. Something red and raw and ripping.

Mum must have felt the unfairness of being a woman, in addition to being left; the vulnerability of her position as an unmarried mother. In the 1960s some women had been committed to mental hospitals for having sex before marriage, I read somewhere. And the baby – me – was tangible proof of sin. *A lot of people condemned you,* Sheila had said.

In the absence of my father's name I examine the slash of ink which sits in place of it. To me it looks angry, like someone striking my father out forever. But maybe I'm just imagining it. The handwriting's all printed and I can't tell if it's my mother's or not. Maybe Mum didn't fill the form in herself, maybe she just answered the questions of some official whose job it was to record it all, someone not even curious, someone disapproving.

The absence of my father's name also has a practical implication. It means I can't go to one of the organisations set up to help adopted children trace their natural parents.

I go instead to the post office where I get a copy of the Sheffield area telephone directory. Back at my flat I highlight all the Sheffield Dodds, then I take a page of them to the phone box.

'Hello. May I speak to John Dodd please?' My stomach is hollow. I feel like I'm committing a crime.

Incredibly, the first person to answer the phone goes off to get John Dodd, without even asking my name first.

My nervousness builds while I'm waiting, and I almost put the phone down. But then I decide I'll just listen, I can just listen if I want.

'Hello? Who wants me?' It's a young lad and I put the phone down.

What would I have said if he'd sounded the right age? 'Were you once the boyfriend of Eileen Reed?' What if he didn't remember her? Or I could say, 'Do you, as far as you know, have any illegitimate children?'

I try to think of something less likely to scare him off. I can't think of anything, but I carry on anyway. 'Hello. May I speak to

John Dodd please?' The hollow is still there in my stomach. But there's no John Dodd at that number.

The next three are wrong numbers too, so I change my approach a bit.

'Hello. I'm looking for my father. I've never met him, but his name is John Emmanuel Dodd, and he was from Sheffield. Do you have anyone in the family with that name?'

Some wish me luck, some are disinterested, others suspicious. After eight calls I stop, worn out. I'll try again another day.

Soho, London 1990

Two miles hence is the Snow Queen's garden . . .

Teddy calls me at work to say they're coming.

'Arabella, it's Teddy! I'm back!' he says.

'Hi.' I can't help being a bit cool with him. I'm still hurt about the way he vanished.

'I want to come and see you. Is that okay?'

'Yeah, great.'

'The thing is, Lucy's got a dance competition in London on the nineteenth of this month. It's this contemporary dance she does. She won the regional heat, and the final's in London somewhere. Apparently she stands a good chance of winning the whole thing. Anyway, Dad's coming with her, just to see she gets there okay and give her a bit of support. But I think I might do the journey with them, because Dad can probably use some support himself these days. He's been a bit fragile since Mum died, and he hasn't been to London for years. I thought we could come and visit you at the same time.'

I don't ask about the 'we', just arrange to meet him at St Pancras.

I see them before they see me. The straggle of them, on the platform. Lucy's awkward adolescence, my Dad looking more like her grandpa than her father, and Teddy, lean and tanned, like a visitor from another country. Obviously a family – what else would bring such a disparate group together? – obviously incomplete.

When they see me, Dad and Lucy turn and look at Teddy, who greets me with his arms open and his head on one side, 'Arabella!' He gives me a hug.

When he releases me I move back a pace, and find myself staring at Dad. He stares straight back. 'Hello Arabella,' he says after a beat, and nods deeply, which seems to me to be about the right level of gesture for now anyway.

Lucy half smiles. 'Hi,' she murmurs. She looks down at her feet.

We're standing together, a little island amidst a river of people, marooned, in spite of the strong current moving along the platform in the direction of the exits. Dad says, 'Where do we go from here?' I can see two meanings for that, but I know he's talking about the journey across London.

'We have to get the tube,' I say.

'We need to go to South Kensington. South Kensington, SW7!' Dad shouts, at the same time as a late train announcement comes over the PA system.

He doesn't say it to me exactly, just into the air.

He seems to have aged, even since the funeral. I can see that old-person type of anxiety in him.

'Yes. We have to get the tube,' I say again. 'All of us do. It's over there.' I point and we start walking, Teddy next to me, Dad just behind us with Lucy close by his side. We walk onto the main concourse, where I look up at the clock. Eleven o'clock. I count the hours they'll be here, something I've already done several times this morning.

Teddy said they'd be leaving about four o'clock. That's five hours from now. The responsibility for entertaining them until then makes me feel panicked. But then I remember that Dad and Lucy won't be with us for long. I'm relieved about this and angry at the same time, because Dad hasn't really come to see me. In this situation, I'm incidental.

I'm jealous of Lucy. Not only has she got her real dad, but she's going to be a real dancer, not a dodgy one like me. I make myself look at her properly, to see what's good about her. I see her nervousness, the way she's jiggling change in her pockets and looking up at us now and then, trusting us to get her to where she needs to go. Her shoulder-length hair shines like an advert for shampoo and she moves her head quickly, wrinkling her nose at things, bright-eyed and curious like a little mouse.

Whereas Lucy's head appears to swivel a hundred and eighty degrees every few minutes, in an attempt to take everything in, Dad is determined to ignore his surroundings. The sea of people around is too much and the crowd's too alternative for him, I can see that.

I watch him as he catches sight of two women with short spiky haircuts, one pink, and one pillar-box red. He looks away quickly, as if hairstyles are a disease that might be contagious.

I can see it's irritating to him that he doesn't know where he's going, and he has to rely on me. As we near the tube station entrance, he strides out ahead. He turns his head back at the top of the steps, 'Down here?'

'Yes,' I say, and he sets off again, blinkering himself against shaven heads, piercings, tattoos, as if it's the only way to stay safe and survive.

In the tube station I direct them to the ticket machine and show them how to use it. Then I find a map and we all stand round.

'We're here,' I say, and show them where the Piccadilly line is and how it takes them all the way there. They have a little map that shows them how to get to the dance venue from the tube.

'Break a leg, Lucy,' I tell her, and explain how it's said instead of good luck. I wish I'd brought her a mascot or something, but I didn't think of it earlier.

Teddy says, 'How do they get to your place?'

'My place? I didn't know they were coming to my place.'

'Yeah, afterwards. That's alright with you, isn't it?'

'Yes, yes, of course it is,' I assure him. 'But I'm a long way from SW7. Might it be easier to meet up in town?'

Dad turns his head sharply. 'Surely we can catch a cab?'

'Well, they don't always want to come south of the river. But the dance place might call a mini-cab for you.'

'Okay,' Dad says. 'We'll ask them. Give me your address and telephone number.'

'I'm not on the phone,' I say, thinking that most dads would know that. I write down my address anyway and hand it to him, along with my *A to Z*.

Teddy kisses Lucy.

Dad's already a few feet away from us. He raises his hand in a wave and walks off, taking long definite strides. Lucy has to trot to catch up with him.

'I hope he doesn't lose her,' I say to Teddy. 'You'd think he'd hold her hand or something.'

'Oh, I should think she's used to it. He's always been like that, hasn't he?'

'I thought he'd be different with her.'

'Would you feel better or worse if he was holding on to her?'

'Oh, I don't know,' I say. Then I think, *definitely worse*.

We get the tube to Elephant and Castle, and Teddy says, 'He's the same with me, too, you know.'

'Does it bother you?'

'Yes, of course it does. I always wanted him to cuddle me. Even now sometimes I just want to throw my arms round him and give him a big hug.'

'But you don't.'

'I didn't before, but now I've started. That's something the yoga's done for me. When I came back from India, I asked him to meet me at the airport. The first thing I did was hug him. I wanted to, so I did.'

'What did Dad do?'

'Oh, he stood bolt upright, with his arms by his sides as usual. When I let him go he had a good look round to see who was watching. But what I've realised is, we shouldn't let his inability to show affection prevent us from demonstrating ours.'

I don't know if I've got any affection left for Dad, and I don't think I could ever find the amount required to hug the inflexible line of his body.

Teddy talks on about what he learned in India. Love cures everything is the main message, but then Teddy's secure in Dad's love, even if he doesn't openly demonstrate his affections.

Help! I want to say to Teddy, *I'm hanging on by a thread*, but I just listen and let his warm voice soothe me.

Back at my flat I ask Teddy how Dad took the news of his defection from accountancy.

'Resigned, I think. I thought he'd blow a fuse. But I'm twenty-four years old. I think he knows there's nothing else he can do. He's not in charge of me now.'

We talk about Teddy's plans to travel the UK a bit, visiting a whole network of yoga people, or 'yogis' as he calls them.

Teddy asks about my job, and I tell him I've had enough of it. He thinks I should leave straightaway if it's not what I want.

'And do what?' I ask him. 'I went to the agencies about an office job when I was with Martin. They don't want to know unless you can type and do shorthand. And what else would I do? Work in a shop? Go back to dental nursing? I'd earn way less money than I do now, and be mind-numbingly bored.'

Teddy's brought a photo album with him. He put it together himself from photos kept in suitcases in the loft at Mum and Dad's. Or just Dad's, as I suppose it is now.

The photos are old; they were in the loft for years, stuffed into their original paper wallets. Mum always said she wanted them in albums, but never found the time to do it.

'I'm slowly sorting through them,' Teddy says. 'It took ages to find the people among the machinery. Do you know, more than fifty per cent of these photos are cars, bikes, or engines?'

'I'm not surprised.' I remember a couple of times we looked at photos when I was a child. Dad would show no interest at all as long as the photos were of people, then suddenly leap up and crane over your shoulder when you came across one of an Aston Martin.

The material world is the one he understands. He knows the

history of every mechanical object he has ever taken a picture of, so seeing a photograph will always spark off a monologue: 'Oh that was Joseph Treacy's car. It was written off, but he rebuilt it. It's a beauty now, goes like one-oh. He's raced it five times at Donington . . .'

Perhaps for Dad, the meaning of life is held somehow within pieces of information like this. Or he just feels comfortable with practical projects.

Teddy says, 'I spoke to Dad on the phone while I was away. One time in three months – and he spent the entire phone call talking about the Triumph he's working on. The problem he had with the gears!'

I laugh, imagining Teddy hanging onto the phone in India, while Dad talks about bike bits from a million miles away.

'But you're mechanically minded,' I tell Teddy. 'You must have some interest in what he talks about.'

'Yes, I do. But there's a time and a place. He should say how he feels sometimes.'

'Maybe he's expressing his emotions through his engine stories,' I say, thinking of Delilah's mother, expressing affection through food.

'Or it's a way to avoid expressing them,' Teddy says.

The album Teddy's put together is mostly pictures of us as children, and a few of Mum and Dad. There's Teddy and me on the steam engine, in our black engine drivers' caps. Teddy with a new bike one Christmas. Me on an orange spacehopper.

I find one of Mum sitting in a deckchair in a swimsuit and another where she's been surprised doing the washing up. She doesn't look too pleased about it.

There are only two photos of Dad, probably taken by Mum. In one, he's standing next to his old red Jag.

I took the other with a Christmas-present camera, and it's strangely angled. Dad's carrying a plate of party food across the sitting room. He's wearing a stripy shirt, and his arms look white and thin. When I look at it I find myself remembering how rough those arms could be.

Teddy points to a photo of me and him, in which I have deliberately closed my eyes. 'We used to think it made us invisible. D'you remember?'

'I remember,' I tell him, and I think how I am much more invisible now.

I wonder about all the photos taken after I left home. The ones without me in them. If there are any, Teddy hasn't brought them.

In the photos he brought we look new and bright, like flowers. But when I search for smiles they're in short supply.

Mum took most of the photos of us. We'd wipe our hands and faces first, then she'd arrange us, and we stood to attention in the instructed pose. It was like a record she had to keep, as if someone might ask her to offer up a report later.

Teddy likes them though.

'Look at your hair!' he says more than once, and about his bike, 'I loved that bike. I've still got it in the garage at home. I suppose I'll give it to my kids when they come along. Or yours.'

'Do you think you'll have children then?'

'Sometime, yes. Not now. I'll need a wife first. Or a girlfriend at least! What about you?'

'I don't want any.'

'What about men? Are you seeing anyone?'

I think of my one-night stand of the other night; of Andy and his proposition.

'No,' I say, and carry on pretending to be respectable.

About three o'clock, Dad arrives with Lucy. He looks out of place in my block of flats, like the elderly rich gentleman who comes to rescue the little princess from her hovel. Except the little princess is obviously Lucy. She looks much more relaxed now. It went okay is all she will say – she won't find out the results of the competition straightaway – but she seems happy.

Dad crosses my sitting room in about three strides, coming

smack up against the window, like a large bird unused to small cages. I can see him searching for something to say.

'You're quite high up here,' is what he manages in the end, looking out of the window, having already cast an eye over the sparse furnishings, the blank walls. I look with him and wonder belatedly why I haven't made more of a home for myself.

We all stand looking out of the window, except Lucy who goes to sit on the sofa. There's silence until Dad says, out of the blue, 'You know I did a green-lane run a few weeks ago, and I bumped into Geoff Sanders. Do you remember him, Arabella? Super chap. He used to supply bits for Norton's.'

I don't know if I remember Geoff Sanders or not. 'Yes,' I say for the sake of Dad's story, and he continues.

'He had a stall at those trials we went to in Derbyshire when you were little. Anyway, the bike he was riding was a Silk he found rusting in some old lady's garage. She let him take it for scrap! And he's really cracked on with it. He's won some prize now, for restoring classic bikes. He had to come to London to the prize-giving ceremony.'

He stops expectantly, and I understand that 'London' was his justification for speaking, his link to me.

I rack my brains for a response, but nothing comes and he tries again. 'Isn't it marvellous, that some people will go to so much trouble to get things working again?'

It sounds like something Thatcher would come out with, and I imagine Dad and his cronies doing the rounds of the village garden parties, under the slogan 'GETTING BRITAIN WORKING AGAIN (CLASSIC BIKES SECTION)'. Teddy and I murmur our agreement, and then I say, 'Would you like a cup of tea?'

Dad looks down, disappointedly I think, before he answers, 'Yes please, Arabella.'

In the kitchen I make tea and I take deep breaths. When I come back Lucy says, 'Have you lived here a long time?'

'Nearly two years.'

'Oh.'

Dad picks up where she left off, 'Did you have to furnish it yourself or . . . ?'

'Yes. Why?' I say, a bit too sharply. From talking to Teddy I know that Mum and Dad gave him a lot of the furniture for his place, and I feel resentful.

'Oh, I thought maybe the council . . .'

'The council's Conservative, they don't give help, only hassle,' I say. In fact I have no idea whether the council is Conservative or not, I just want to have a go at Dad.

Teddy steps in, 'You've got some interesting shops up the road – old fireplaces. I wouldn't mind having a poke around in there next time I come.' It's the kind of thing that interests Dad, of course, and we all talk about old fireplaces for a while, how beautiful some of the tiles are, that you can get them sandblasted to clean the layers of old paint off.

A conversation about the weather accompanies some final tea-drinking, then Dad looks at his watch, 'Well, I suppose we'd better make a move,' he says, and I see them out.

'I don't know what you want to do about your mother's things,' Dad says at the door. 'I haven't . . . er . . . I've just left them for the time being. Would you like to come and look through? There might be something you want.'

I don't reply straightaway because I'm thinking too many things at once; thoughts that jump and sink, and wrap themselves around one another. Dad says, 'Well, you can let me know.'

'Yes, okay, I will.'

Teddy pecks my cheek. I kiss him and Lucy. Dad's already at the lift.

'Goodbye, Arabella,' he says, and they all step into the lift, which smells especially terribly of piss for their visit.

Teddy presses the button, but the doors don't move. So we stand staring at each other, them inside, me outside.

Just as it becomes unsettling, the doors close. At the same time Dad says something that sounds like, 'Call me if I can help with anything.'

They disappear, and I go back into my flat, waiting by the window to watch them cross the road. But they must have walked around the base of the block and crossed the road from a point behind it, because I don't see them.

Soho, London 1990

The cold grew intense, the vapour more dense, and at length it
took the form of little bright angels, which, as they touched the
earth, became larger and more distinct.

The following Saturday, I'm up earlier than I have been in a
long time. I'm going to help Delilah who has promised to
decorate an old woman's kitchen as part of a local charity project.

I find it difficult to get up so early, but once I'm outside I see
that mornings can be beautiful. Although the sky is white with
cloud, there are less people about and the air smells like it's been
replaced overnight.

Delilah's wearing yellow overalls that fit him exactly. On his
head is a wide-brimmed green canvas hat, with a large, orange
silk pansy attached to it.

'I will paint the ceiling,' he says, tapping the hat. Before we
leave he puts on an orange scarf and silver puffa jacket.

He takes me into the basement storeroom at his block of flats
where there are tools and materials for decorating and cleaning.
We load cans of paint, brushes, rollers, masking tape, sandpaper, a
plane and dustsheets into a wheelbarrow, which I push. Delilah
carries a large stepladder, and we make our way to the old lady's
house which isn't far away.

It's a council flat on the ground floor of a long two-storey
block. We go through a small wooden gate with peeling maroon-
coloured paint and stand on a concrete path next to a tiny litter-
strewn garden to knock on the front door. I can see faces peering
from windows, and a group of raggedy-looking small children
stand across the road, watching.

I look at the unrelieved grey of our surroundings. Even the children are wearing dull colours. Then I look at Delilah. He looks like he's from another planet, or a children's TV programme.

An overweight woman of about sixty answers the door and Delilah says, 'Mrs Watson! How are you today?'

Mrs Watson looks at us like we're something the cat left on the doorstep. She grunts, 'Not too bad,' then turns back into her flat.

She walks slowly, dragging one leg, and we follow her through a hallway and into the kitchen.

It's a small room, made smaller by the presence of several airers hung with clothes. There's a low fridge with pans piled on top of it, and the stainless steel sink is full of dishes. Mrs Watson says she's waiting for a plumber to come and fix the washing machine.

'If he comes you'll have to clear out!' she tells us, like she's doing us a favour having us there. 'There's more important things than paint,' she adds, as she goes out of the room.

She's so much the opposite of the grateful little old lady I had expected, that it makes me laugh. Delilah goes after her to see if we can move the airers full of clothes into another room, and we start on our job.

I cover everything with dustsheets and put masking tape around the door and windows. Delilah starts stripping wallpaper. It's hot and after a while he pulls down the top of his overalls, tying the sleeves around his waist. Underneath he's wearing a vest top.

It's strange to see Delilah doing something requiring so much physical effort and I keep looking at his arms. I don't think I've ever seen his bare arms before. His dresses and shirts usually have long sleeves.

He has lightly tanned skin, and remarkably large biceps. This is surprising to me as biceps are, to my mind anyway, such a masculine thing.

About midday we're painting the woodwork, when Mrs Watson comes in. She stands watching us for a few minutes, then she says, 'If my old Dad could see this mess, he'd turn in his grave.'

I was anticipating a compliment, and I stifle the urge to laugh as she comes nearer to where I am. She peers at the magnolia paint.

'Was your dad a decorator?' I say when I've got my laughter under control.

'He was. He was a decorator, and a plumber, and all else. He had to be. He couldn't afford to pay for it, so he did it himself. And became expert in the process. Expert!'

She leaves the room, and I look at Delilah, who's laughing.

'I can't believe she's not even a bit grateful!' I say.

'She is. But she only knows to say what she knows,' says Delilah. 'She won't be in this afternoon,' he adds. 'I will bring music.'

We go back to Delilah's for lunch at one o' clock. Delilah insists on making Kir Royale as an apperitif, and there is a companionable silence as I sit drinking it, an extension of the morning's teamwork.

I watch as Delilah smoothes the palm of his hand over the surface of a large wooden breadboard. He's brought bread from the local delicatessen. It's a soft brown loaf and he handles it carefully, taking it from its sheath of floury paper, as gently as if it were an egg. He lays it on the breadboard, and I see it dip under the knife.

I've worked up an appetite and I begin to salivate as he spreads butter on the slices and unwraps glistening pieces of pink salmon.

I bite into my sandwich and feel all the contrasting textures in my mouth, the soft bread and its crust, slippery fish and creamy butter. We eat the whole loaf between us. Then I wash up, with some geranium aromatherapy washing-up liquid a friend of Delilah's brought back from the States, and we head back to Mrs Watson's.

The tape Delilah's brought is all classical music. I don't listen to that normally, so I'm surprised by how much fun we have.

Very quickly we're painting to music, hopping and leaping across to the paint-can to refresh our brushes. I let the music dictate up and down strokes, or great sweeps of paint, and I wait for quiet fiddly bits to do the edges and corners.

Delilah is doing the same, marching and tip-toes, ballet and mime, his whole body following his arm, or his arm acts independently in a piece that strikes him as more slapstick.

I'm surprised and excited by the music's great crashes, followed by periods when the instruments are so quiet I can hardly hear them. I exaggerate my surprise to entertain Delilah, jumping into action as each tumultuous crash sounds through me. He laughs and uses his voice like an instrument to accompany the music.

The music is loud and we're so concentrated on the strange form of paint-dance-singing we have evolved, that we don't notice Mrs Watson come back in.

'I thought you were going to fix my door?' she says, and we both spring up, as to another cymbal crashing.

'I will do it now,' says Delilah, and I rush to turn the music down.

At the end of the day, the room looks clean and neat painted in magnolia, with a brilliant white door and window frames. The door is fixed, and we've even done the washing up.

Delilah asks Mrs Watson in to take a look.

She stands in the doorway for a moment, then walks to the right-hand wall. There's a tiny bubble of paint which she pops with the tip of her finger.

She moves back into the centre of the room. 'Well, I suppose it's better than a poke in the eye with a sharp stick,' she says.

Outside in the street I clutch Delilah. We're weary, and we've been on the brink of serious laughter all afternoon. Now we laugh until the tears run down our faces.

Back at the basement store, I hang on to all the tools while Delilah fishes for the key in his pocket. He pushes the door, it sticks, and he pushes harder. Then it pops open suddenly, taking him with it.

He trips over a bucket just inside the door and falls. I'm up too close behind, my arms full of tools. I trip over a long-handled roller I'm carrying, trip again on his feet, and fall right on top of him.

We put our arms up to protect us from the shower of decorating equipment, and when the last thing has fallen Delilah says, '*Mamma mia!*'

We start laughing. Then we stop laughing and start kissing.

Saf's back. She's kissing everyone, and handing out plastic bubbles of the kind you shake to see the glitter fly up. They've got surfing scenes in them. She's handed in her notice, and she'll be leaving in a month's time to go and live in Cornwall, she says.

Our solos are both down to appear in the second half, so after the parade we've got a long break. We put our clothes back on and go out to a café on Old Compton Street.

Saf looks well. She hasn't experienced any more fits, and though the hospital has said they will keep an eye on her, the specialist has told her it could just have been a one-off. Her plan is to go to university and I'm stunned. University is something other people do, people with connections and career plans, money and family.

But Saf seems to have it all sorted. She's booked up for Sociology and Spanish, and I pick her brains. How will she live without being paid? How did she find out about it? How did she get in? Saf says she's going to get a grant and she'll be working in a bar, weekends and evenings.

'What about looking for your dad?' I ask her.

'I've given up.'

'That doesn't sound like you!'

She just looks at me, so I say, 'I've been looking for my real dad.'

'Is that what you really want?' she says.

'Yes! Why? I don't understand you! One minute you're all for me looking for my dad. And the next you've completely changed your mind!'

'Right. But I had a good reason to change my mind.' She lights a cigarette, takes a drag and continues. 'That fit I had, right? It was to do with remembering something, man. I remembered . . . I remembered my dad . . . abusing me and stuff.'

'Oh Saf! I'm really sorry.'

'It's okay, I'm cool. Shit happens.'

'I'm sorry it happened to you.'

'Yeah, well.'

'Is Simon helping?'

She looks into space, then seems to click back into gear, 'Yeah, he's a dude. I think he's always known there was something wrong. I've got a habit of going off sex right in the middle of things, I just stop right? He's always been cool about it. No pressure. Now I'm Mrs Frigid, and he's exactly the same. Jeez, I get more frustrated with me than he does.'

'I'm sure it'll get better in time.'

'Yeah, that's what Simon says. It's just right now it's a bit raw, you know?'

'Have you talked to your mum about it? Does she know?'

'I don't know what she knows. Knew. I mean I talked to her about it, a bit. She says,' – and Saf puts on a pathetic whining voice – '"I told you not to go after him".'

'Are you saying she knew about the abuse?'

'I don't know. It's one of those things I've got to sort.'

There's silence between us for a minute.

'Maybe your dad left to protect you from himself,' I say.

'Yeah, maybe,' she gets up. We pay and walk out.

From the wings, I watch Saf performing Miss United Kingdom. The monitor shows a girl in grainy black-and-white, doing high kicks and cartwheels to brass-band music, the picture of youthful energy and good health. Then the music changes, which is the cue to strip off, and she looks like she's really smiling as she flings the various parts of her costume to the back of the stage.

She takes up her final position on her side on the floor. Facing the audience she slides the sceptre back and forth along the line of her legs, then through them.

The music changes again, rather abruptly this time, signalling the end of her act. *Rule Brittania, Britannia rules the waves. Britons never never never shall be slaves.* It's just the music, no words. I remember Saf telling me how she creased up laughing the first time she heard it in rehearsal. Only I know that to the tune of 'Rule Brittania', and through a grinning mask of gritted teeth, she sings, '*Up yours, you suckers. You'll never get to fuck us! Haah haah hah-hah hah-hah hah-hah haah haah haaaah!*'

Regardless of Saf's experience, I carry on looking for my dad. It makes me feel I'm going somewhere and going somewhere has to be better than going nowhere. Also it's the first thing I've decided to do for myself in a long while, so it seems important to see it through. No U-turns.

I've started making the calls from work. I feel more comfortable at the Pageant than in the call box at New Cross. There's often a lock on the payphone at work when I get there, and I have to fetch a key from the box office. But no one seems to object to me being there out of work hours.

I go in the backstage entrance and check the phone, which is in a corridor on the way through to the dressing rooms. If the lock is on I dump my bag in my dressing room and continue on through the backstage area, across the stage and into the auditorium, then down the stairs to the foyer, and the box office.

One day, as I come into the backstage area on my way to fetch the key, Tracey Veroni's there, peeking through the curtains at someone in the auditorium. She doesn't see me and I stop for a minute in the backstage gloom, watching her watching somebody.

I go back the way I came in, through the stage door and outside to get to the box office. But I am curious to see what Tracey's looking at, so once I've got the key I go on up the stairs and into the auditorium.

My eyes scan the seats. I can't see anyone at first, then I spot Vince Veroni sitting in an aisle seat, half a dozen rows back. He's staring at the stage, making a steeple of his hands. I wonder if he knows his daughter is there, hiding behind the curtain.

'Hi,' I say, with a quick wave of my hand, as I go to climb onto the stage. Vince looks up, but he doesn't say anything. I suddenly feel like I'm trespassing. What will I say if he asks me why I'm here in the middle of the afternoon? But he doesn't.

Tracey isn't behind the curtain anymore. She must have moved when she saw me coming. I assume she's already left, via the back stage door, so I get a fright when I walk into my dressing room and she's there.

She's as thin as ever, and she's taken to wearing baggy T-shirts again. Before you could see the swell of her breasts underneath, but now there are just folds, so her chest looks kind of caved in. She's got dark circles under her eyes. Where her long, straight nose gave her a proud patrician look, the new button nose sits centre-face like a reluctant impostor, too insignificant to measure up to her brooding eyes and wide generous mouth.

She's leafing slowly through the costumes on the rail. She turns her head carefully when she sees me.

'Hi,' I say. I pick up my bag and rifle through it to look for my purse.

'Hi,' says Tracey, and stops all pretence of being involved in something else to watch me.

I feel very self-conscious and I'm worrying that I don't want to leave my bag in here with her. What if she goes through it? I don't know why I'm bothered, as I haven't got anything important in it.

I'm going to have to leave it anyway, as dropping my bag off is the only excuse I've got for having come into work. I don't want to say I came to use the phone in case there's an objection. Maybe Tracey will leave before I do.

'I was really sorry to read about your custody battle,' I say. 'I hope it's going okay for you now.'

She stares at me, and I'm anxious I've overstepped the mark. Our relationship is only employer–employee. We never talk about personal things. I try to make it clearer, that I'm on her side.

'I mean, I hope you'll be able to keep your daughter with you.'

'I will,' Tracey says.

Having found my purse, and pulled the drawstring fastening on my bag shut, I hang it over the back of a chair. Now I no longer have any excuse to stay in the dressing room.

'See you then,' I say and head for the door.

But she says, 'Do you want to come for a coffee?'

'Yeah, okay.' I act casual, but I feel really nervous. Her behaviour is so unpredictable it's scary. And this is unheard of as far as I know, coffee with Tracey Veroni.

I follow her downstairs and out of the backstage door. She takes me into the White Horse on Rupert Street, where she orders two coffees. We sit down in a dark corner and the first thing she says is, 'Don't stay too long.'

I think she's talking about being in the pub. 'No, I won't,' I say, hoping it's the right answer.

'Because it gets to you, this business, and it does your head in. You know that.' It's a statement, not a question.

I nod, and she says, 'How's your wrist?'

'Okay,' I hold it up for inspection, but she doesn't look.

'You need something else,' she says. 'You've got to have something else to keep you going.'

For a moment I think she's going to offer me some of whatever she's on. But she doesn't. She just stares at me without blinking, like she's weighing me up for some purpose known only to her. It's unnerving.

I show her the photo of my real dad in my purse, for something to talk about.

'This is my dad,' I say. 'But we've never met.'

She looks at the photo and says, 'My dad's the best dad in the world.' She laughs. Then she drinks her espresso down quickly. 'I'll pay for these.' She puts money on the table. '*Ciao*,' and she leaves.

I go back to work and check there's no one there before I make my phone calls.

'Hello. May I speak to John Dodd, please?'

'There's no one of that name here.'

'Hello. May I speak to John Dodd, please?'

'Wrong number, love.'

'Hello. May I speak to John Dodd, please?'

'You've got the wrong number.'

Soho / Nottinghamshire 1990

Her power is greater than ours; it proceeds from her heart, from her being a loving and innocent child. If this power which she already possesses cannot give her access to the Snow Queen's palace, and enable her to free Kay's eye and heart from the glass fragment, we can do nothing for her!

T he second note from Dad comes a week after his visit to my flat. It's a card with a picture of Berkeley Square on it, and inside he's written:

Dear Arabella,

It was lovely to see you last week. You will be pleased to know that Lucy came third in her dancing competition. Let me know when you want to come and sort through your mother's things. I believe Teddy is having a party soon, so perhaps that will be a good time for you.

Best wishes,

Dad

'It was lovely to see you last week' is the line that interests me most. I read it over a few times before closing the card.

Looking again at the picture on the front, I realise it's the same one that appears on one of six place mats we had when I was a child. They were all London scenes. The Houses of Parliament, St Paul's and Leicester Square were some of the others. I used to stare at them for long periods of time when Dad insisted I eat whatever it was I didn't want.

I prop the card up on top of the radio. The picture is made up entirely of different shades of blue.

After staring at it for a while, I pick it up and fold it back on itself. Then I prop it up inside out. Now I can't see the picture, just Dad's writing.

I move backwards and forwards for a bit, seeing how close I need to get to read the first sentence. 'It was lovely to see you . . .'

The day after Dad's note arrives, I receive Teddy's party invitation. The party is in three weeks' time, at the pub near his flat. There's a note with it that just says:

I'm celebrating a new lease of life! Hope you can come. You can stop at my place, or the pub, or Dad's.

Love,

Teddy

P.S. Fine if you want to bring a guest.

A guest. I think of Delilah. I haven't seen him for two days. Not since we kissed. I've been thinking about him the whole time though, in the back of my mind.

I remember the way it felt to kiss him. If he was a 'normal' guy, I think to myself, I wouldn't be avoiding him now. But then Delilah knows where I work, and he hasn't come to seek me out either.

Our kiss was wonderful, and completely spontaneous. I don't think either of us was expecting it, and we were both shocked by it. It was gentle, and ferocious. Our lips and bodies just came together, without any thought to it. I could feel the part where we started thinking and stopped kissing.

'Wow! That was a surprise!' I said.

Then Delilah stood up and started brushing his clothes off, which made me feel like *I* was getting the brush-off somehow.

I got up and took both his hands in mine. 'Delilah,' I said, a request for him to look at me.

So he looked at me. 'I enjoy being with you today.' His voice was sad and quiet.

'I enjoyed being with you too.' I tried to push all my happiness of the moment before into my voice. But the way he'd spoken had already affected me, and the words came out falsely bright.

We stacked the tools away without saying another word, then Delilah locked the door. He didn't say anything about going back to his place, so I said, 'I'm filthy, I'd better get to work and shower or something.'

'Okay, see you,' he said.

It was as if he decided kissing me had been a mistake.

If I'm honest, I have my own doubts too. Taking a transvestite lover was never what I had in mind, so far as I have anything in mind. And what would it say about me? I picture myself holding hands with Delilah, his six-foot-three-inch frame (six-feet-nine in heels) clad from head to toe in gold lurex, and I wonder if I would ever dare go public with such a relationship. It certainly wouldn't improve things with Dad.

In the end though, the love, if that's what it is, the wanting, at any rate, isn't a rational thing. It's a need, a pull. So I go to see Delilah, without any idea of what I'm going to say.

He's in the restaurant. I see him through the window before he sees me, his confident graceful movements as he welcomes a group of four, and gets them seated.

When I walk in, he steps forward without saying anything. He cups my elbows in the palms of his hands, so the whole lengths of our forearms are in contact. I grip his upper arms then, just above the elbow; where I can feel the swell of his biceps begin.

When I look into his face, I can see things I haven't seen there before. I think maybe it's the part of him that is Franco. In his eyes I see his concern for me.

'Can you come to Islington after work?' he says.

At his place, he makes coffee with cream and Tia Maria. We avoid the big issues for a while. He wants to know what my flat is like so I describe it, and end up talking to him about the Che Guevara flag that belonged to my real dad, the latest phone calls to try and find him. Somehow I get onto the subject of rejection.

'I felt rejected in the basement,' I say.

'I know. I'm sorry. But I want you to have some time to think.'

'About what?'

'About being involved with an old transvestite.'

'You're not that old,' I say, ignoring the transvestite bit.

Delilah says, 'How do you think he will be like, your father, if you find him?'

'Just a bloke, I suppose. Probably married. Maybe with kids. I might have brothers and sisters I don't know about! And he definitely looks like me – maybe a similar character. God knows I'm not like anyone else in my family!' I pause. 'You could kiss me again now if you wanted to.'

But Delilah's going somewhere and he hasn't got there yet.

'What kind of character is yours?'

'Stupid. Confused.'

'You are not these things. Well, maybe the last, but not the first.'

'You make me confused.'

'I? Because I am transvestite?'

'No, because I don't know what you want.'

'It should be what you want is important.'

'That's easy, I want you to kiss me again. I want you to want me.'

'I want you,' he says, and I move towards him, but he holds me at arm's length.

'Answer me a question first,' he says. 'If your father is a transvestite, what will you think?'

266

'My real father?' I say, as the alternative and impossible image – my stepfather in a dress – sails across my mind.

'Yes, the one you look for.'

'I don't know. I'd be surprised. Curious.'

'You would not care if he was?'

'Well, he'd be very different from my picture of him, but I suppose I'd adjust to it, I'd have to.'

'And your picture of me?'

'I don't know. You're just Delilah.'

'But I am also Franco.'

'Yes.'

'So this is okay with you?' he asks me.

I look at his beautiful face and I say, 'Yes,' because right now it is, very okay. He lets me move into him then, wrapping his big arms all the way around me. He kisses the top of my head and I say, 'I'm not a baby.'

He tilts my chin up towards him and smiles. 'No, you're not,' he says and he puts his lips on mine.

There's a jolt like before, and I push against him.

Slowly, deliberately, he undoes my blouse and removes it. He takes off my bra and runs his hands over my breasts until I'm weak, and we're sinking down onto the floor.

'*Mia cara,*' he says, surveying the whole stretched-out length of me before putting his mouth to one of my nipples.

I can feel the hard lump of him against me, and I moan and arch up toward him. He removes my jeans, and very gently kisses the pink hood of my clitoris. Then he takes his own clothes off quickly.

His body is all male and magnificent, like the glimpse I had of his arm when we were painting.

As he enters me I look into his eyes and concentrate hard on it being him. *Delilah Franco*, I say to myself, and look and look, because I don't want to fantasise.

Then he's moving in me, slowly, not too much.

'I love you,' he says. 'I . . .'

'I know,' I tell him. 'Me too.' We ride high and supreme for a moment, like surfers on the crest of the same wave, collapsing into each other as it breaks, then gradually becoming aware of our surroundings again, the texture of the carpet.

At Teddy's party, Dad is in the centre of the room. I can see straightaway that he's enjoying himself. He's standing with a group of younger men, Teddy's friends: accounting, not yoga, from the look of them. He's rosy-cheeked with a little too much wine, and he's in the middle of another of his mechanical anecdotes.

This one's about a steam engine. 'Smoke box', 'reversing rod', 'driving pin', 'clack box' – he relishes the words, taking pride in naming correctly every working part of the engine he's describing. Now he imitates the sound she makes, chuffing hard to get up a hill. And he makes the noises of other things, a British motorbike (makes a better sound than a Japanese one), a threshing machine.

As I head past the group to get to the bar, he's explaining how to fix something, holding some imaginary lever in his left hand, pointing with his right. It's funny, and the young men laugh and ask questions.

I remember how Dad's hands seemed like giant's hands to me, as a child. I was always fascinated by the gentle way he handled things made of metal and wood. Once I found a broken bracelet and went to him with it. If it had been a modern thing I'd not have stood a chance, but it was old, silver, delicate and ornate. It fastened with a hinge and pin, but the hinge had gone out of alignment, and the pin was missing. I'd not expected him to bother with it much, after all it was only pretty, not a working model, a girl's thing. But he examined it carefully, seemed almost to caress it. He was a perfectionist and mending it took time, time during which I basked in the attention the bracelet was getting, as if it were me.

I get my drink and cross the room again. Dad is laughing now. He slaps his thigh – he only ever does that when he's had a few.

His eyes sparkle and I can see everything he is, was, and could have been, so I feel sorry and proud, and happy and sad, all at the same time.

A thought comes then, dispersing all other thoughts, like a magnet pushing away a pile of iron filings: *I wish you were my dad.* When I think this something breaks in me, some barrier holding things back. *I wish you were my dad.*

The thought repeats and grows, leaving my defences wide open. Tears fill my eyes as I fight to escape it, to remain in control, looking wildly around for distraction, grabbing other thoughts and thinking nonsense quickly.

I get through without crying, but that night in bed I howl into the pillows. I sob and cry until there is snot everywhere, and I'm too busy with the business of crying to go and fetch a hanky.

I wish you were my dad. I allow myself to think it over and over, and for the first time I allow myself to feel it – the loss of him. That he was dazzling, funny and energetic, he was who I wanted to be, and to be with, then suddenly he wasn't mine.

I stop crying when my thoughts turn from the past to the present. *I wish you were my dad, you obstinate, unaffectionate son of a bitch!* I say to myself. *I wish you were my dad, you opinionated old snob! You racist! You hypocrite!*

I reach one hand out of bed to fish for the bedside light switch. I find it and the light comes on, illuminating a yellow shade on a mahogany effect stand. The bedroom is above the pub where Teddy and I ate last time I came, and it has recently been redecorated. Teddy's flat was full to bursting when I arrived, with all the people he's putting up, and their luggage. He would've found a space for me, but it seemed simpler to stay here.

I fetch toilet paper from the bathroom and blow my nose, looking around for a switch to regulate the heat which is uncomfortably high for sleeping. I can't see one and I climb back into bed.

I think of calling Delilah, but it's late. Delilah didn't come along this time, because he thought it was too soon, that things would go better for me alone. In the future though, Dad may have to deal with my transvestite lover. If Dad stays in touch with me – if I stay in touch with him. I can't imagine Dad and Delilah together, or if I can then I don't imagine Dad would have a great deal to say.

Does Dad love me? Did Mum love me? These questions, still there, still unanswered, are central to my life.

Delilah says we can only know if someone loves us or not by their actions. He says, 'Love is a verb, not a noun; love is a doing word.' When I apply that to my relationship with him, it makes a lot of sense. He listens to me, entertains me, encourages, supports and protects me. Applied to Mum or Dad it starts to look a bit more complicated. Can I believe that feeding and clothing a child is love?

I reach out and switch off the light.

Is it love I feel for Dad? Whatever it is, it's involuntary. Unconditional? That makes it sound like a lot of compromise on my part. And I think there will always be a line beyond which I can't go. If Dad refuses Delilah for instance. I don't think I'd be able to carry on seeing him, Dad that is, not Delilah. I don't suppose that would stop me from loving Dad; although if love is a doing word, then it would, because I wouldn't be doing it anymore.

Unless I prayed for Dad or something – would that count as love?

The more I think about what love is, the further I get from any useful kind of definition. Is that because love is unreasonable? But I have a need to think it through, a need to protect myself.

When Teddy and I get to Dad's in the morning, he's fixing the gate. He straightens up to greet us, oil can in hand, as though it were the most normal thing in the world to see me there.

'I'm a bit oily,' he says instead of kissing me.

The garden has changed. There are lots more plants, two big tubs of them by the gate. A small tree, that must have been even smaller when I left, leans prettily over the gatepost.

I stare at the velvety moss on the wall with its texture like skin, remembering.

Teddy turns to me, 'I'll pick you up in a couple of hours,' he says.

'My train's at 12.55,' I tell him.

'Yeah, I know. I'll get you there.'

Then he's gone, and Dad says, 'The door's open if you want to go in. I've put all Eileen's things in her old workroom'.

'Okay,' I say.

'See you later, then. Plenty of time.'

Mum's clothes are piled on the sofa in her workroom. Utilitarian clothes. Still and heavy in navy and brown, they smell of nothing in particular; but they underline her absence like an empty chair.

In the middle of a pile of woollen fabrics in sober shades, I spot some pink cotton. I pull it out, just because it's brighter than the rest. It's a summer dress, a sleeveless shift. But I don't remember it, and it's difficult to visualise the Mum I knew wearing it.

A collection of little boxes catches my eye, on top of a chest of drawers. I open a box with a rose pattern on it, but there's nothing inside. I shake the others one by one. Nothing there either.

I crouch in front of a cupboard by the window, where I find school reports for me and Teddy, and a sampler I made once in needlework class. The sampler says 'Mum' on it, in a variety of purple and orange stitching. I sit on the floor with it in my hands. It seems to come from a time before: when Mum was Mum and Dad was Dad, when I never questioned whether I was loved or not.

Did Mum and Dad stop loving me? Did they ever love me?

At sixteen I was certain their love had stopped. I built my life accordingly.

But who knows what they felt? Perhaps Dad thought I didn't want him. After all, I wasn't really his. And I could never seem to communicate how much he mattered to me. I tried to do it by jumping off a building; I knew nothing of the value of softer virtues.

I think about the seemingly un-crossable line that has separated me from my parents for all these years. And about other lines, lines I've known people draw, lines I've known people cross.

My real father crossed a line when he left my Mum, my stepfather crossed another when he rejected me. Sharon's teacher crossed a line when he seduced me, and I crossed a line by being unfaithful to Martin. I crossed another when I took my clothes off for money. Then there was that line I chose not to cross at the psychiatric hospital.

From my list I could assume crossing lines was a bad thing. I could add Delilah crossing the line between male and female, and see that as a bad thing too. But maybe not, because all these crossings, the ones I thought about before Delilah's, they were all crossings away from people. In all of these instances people were drawing lines; lines to separate themselves from other people. At first I think taking my clothes off is an exception, until I see it as a step away from myself.

Sharon's teacher looks like an exception too, but then I see he's not; because his action wasn't the crossing of a line to come towards me. It was the drawing of a line between him and me so he could do what he wanted.

Tracey Veroni has drawn a similar line, between herself and the women who work for porn mags or in the Pageant. Tarts don't have hearts, I realise, because feelings are reserved for women on Tracey's side of the line. Did her father teach her that? And did my suicide attempt shake her faith a bit? I wonder what she'll teach her daughter? If she's around to teach her anything.

Delilah's case is different because he's not drawing the line, he's destroying it, bringing two things closer together.

And finally there's the line that Mum has crossed, from life to death, reuniting me with Teddy, shaking the line between me and Dad.

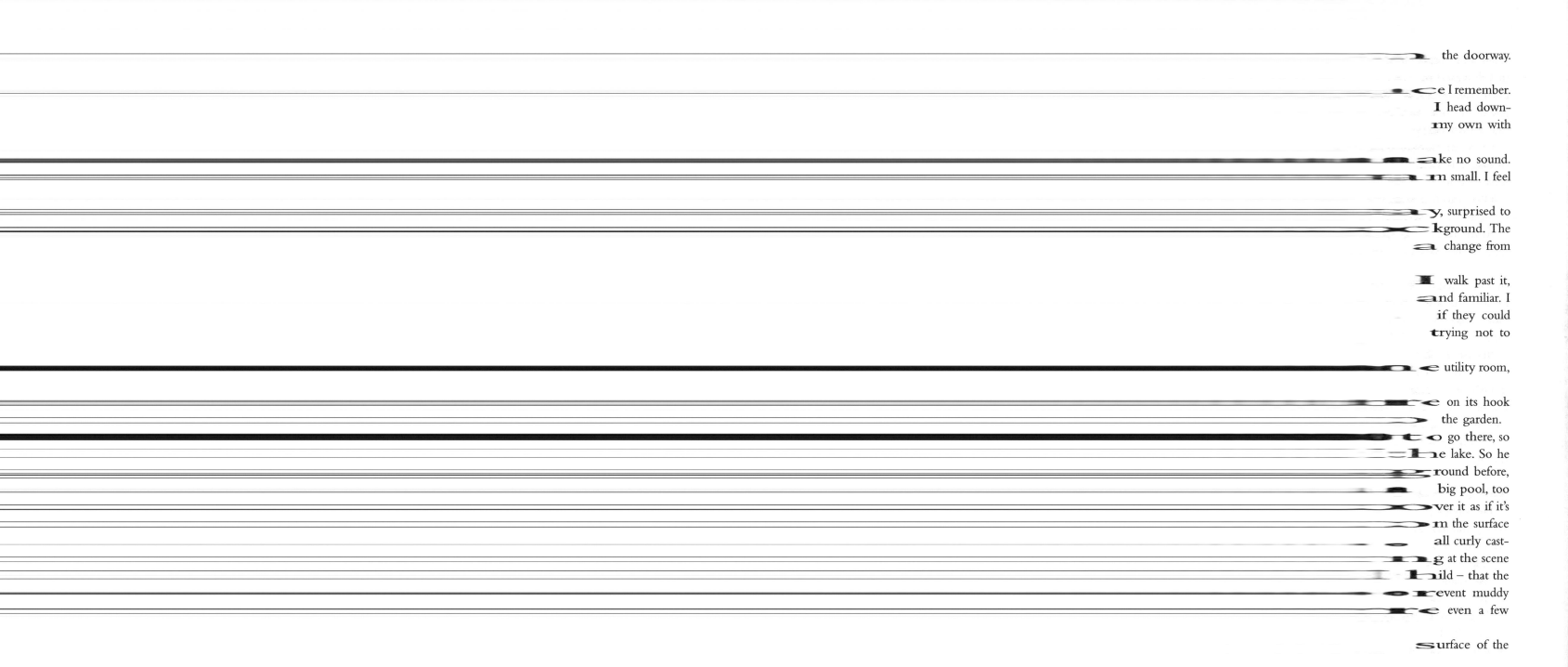

the doorway.

e I remember.
I head down-
my own with

ake no sound.
m small. I feel

y, surprised to
kground. The
a change from

walk past it,
and familiar. I
if they could
trying not to

utility room,

on its hook
the garden.
go there, so
e lake. So he
round before,
big pool, too
ver it as if it's
m the surface
all curly cast-
g at the scene
ild – that the
event muddy
even a few

surface of the

I stare at the velvety moss on the wall with its
skin, remembering.

Teddy turns to me, 'I'll pick you up in a couple
says.

'My train's at 12.55,' I tell him.

'Yeah, I know. I'll get you there.'

Then he's gone, and Dad says, 'The door's open
to go in. I've put all Eileen's things in her old wor

'Okay,' I say.

'See you later, then. Plenty of time.'

Mum's clothes are piled on the sofa in her workroo
clothes. Still and heavy in navy and brown, they sm
in particular; but they underline her absence like an

In the middle of a pile of woollen fabrics in so
spot some pink cotton. I pull it out, just because it's
the rest. It's a summer dress, a sleeveless shift. But I do
it, and it's difficult to visualise the Mum I knew w

A collection of little boxes catches my eye, on t
of drawers. I open a box with a rose pattern on
nothing inside. I shake the others one by one. N
either.

I crouch in front of a cupboard by the window,
school reports for me and Teddy, and a sampler I
needlework class. The sampler says 'Mum' on it, in
purple and orange stitching. I sit on the floor with it
It seems to come from a time before: when Mum w
Dad was Dad, when I never questioned whether I
not.

Did Mum and Dad stop loving me? Did they e

At sixteen I was certain their love had stopped. I
accordingly.

But who knows what they felt? Perhaps Dad tho
want him. After all, I wasn't really his. And I coul
to communicate how much he mattered to me. I t

I look up, thinking I see my father's shadow in the doorway.
'Dad?'

But the house is quiet, sunk into the absolute silence I remember.

I don't want to sort through any more stuff, so I head downstairs, even though I'm a little afraid of being on my own with
Dad.

On the stairs the carpet's thick, and my feet make no sound.
I have the impression that the house is big, and I am small. I feel
like a trespasser, one who risks being shot at.

I pause nevertheless, in the centre of the hallway, surprised to
see new curtains, a flower print on a white background. The
whole room looks different because of them, like a change from
winter to summer.

But the still-bolted back door glares at me as I walk past it,
and the old wooden coat hooks loom too large and familiar. I
skirt around them, scared of getting close. It's as if they could
hook me up, crochet me back into a past I'm trying not to
remember.

I walk straight through the empty kitchen into the utility room,
looking for Dad.

The sight of the old gong startles me, still there on its hook
by the door, as I grab my coat and hurry out into the garden.

Dad will be in his workshop but I don't want to go there, so
I wander up to the orchard, gasping when I see the lake. So he
finally dug it out! Where there was only swampy ground before,
a bit of a dip with no visible water, there's now a big pool, too
big to be called a pond. The trees bend elegantly over it as if it's
always been there and a couple of birds take off from the surface
as I approach. There's a bench by the water's edge, all curly cast-
iron with a wooden seat and I sit down on it, smiling at the scene
in front of me. I couldn't have imagined this as a child – that the
patch of bog we always had to step around to prevent muddy
shoes could become this magical space. There are even a few
tattered-looking bulrushes.

A gust of wind sends ripples across the glossy surface of the water and I look back at the house where bare trees are reflected in a downstairs window. It's a big place for one man on his own, but I don't think Dad will ever sell it. I try to imagine him in a retirement bungalow and fail. He'd rather be dead, I think, than live anywhere else.

I wonder when the lake was dug out. Can things be changed so easily? Is it only me who remembers the past so vividly, who feels so marked by it?

I'll never talk to Dad about my childhood now, I know. We'd be bound to disagree, and what's the point?

At my feet are a few pieces of broken red roof-tile. I pick them up and throw them into the lake.

In a little while Dad comes walking up the field. He waves when he sees me and when he gets within speaking distance he says, 'Sorry you've been waiting; I thought it might take you a long time.'

'It's okay,' I say, 'I was looking at the lake. It's fantastic.'

'Yes,' says Dad and he looks at it too. 'We've had plenty of moorhens; it'd be nice to get a couple of swans on it.' We've run out of words again, so we both stare at the water. The wind blows and the seconds tick by.

I fiddle with my coat buttons. 'Teddy'll be here soon to pick me up.'

'Yes,' Dad says. 'Would you like a cup of tea, while you're waiting?' Then he adds, 'Or a glass of sherry perhaps?'

He smiles, and I find myself smiling back, the offer of the sherry and the smile somehow putting me on a more equal footing with him, no longer the child.

'Okay, sherry,' I say. 'Thanks.'

'We could have it out here if you like.'

'Yes, that'd be nice.'

'Right. Stay there!'

He wheels round and marches off, like he's starting some sort of military manoeuvre. I think how strange and pleasant it is,

by jumping off a building; I knew nothing of the value of softer virtues.

I think about the seemingly un-crossable line that has separated me from my parents for all these years. And about other lines, lines I've known people draw, lines I've known people cross.

My real father crossed a line when he left my Mum, my stepfather crossed another when he rejected me. Sharon's teacher crossed a line when he seduced me, and I crossed a line by being unfaithful to Martin. I crossed another when I took my clothes off for money. Then there was that line I chose not to cross at the psychiatric hospital.

From my list I could assume crossing lines was a bad thing. I could add Delilah crossing the line between male and female, and see that as a bad thing too. But maybe not, because all these crossings, the ones I thought about before Delilah's, they were all crossings away from people. In all of these instances people were drawing lines; lines to separate themselves from other people. At first I think taking my clothes off is an exception, until I see it as a step away from myself.

Sharon's teacher looks like an exception too, but then I see he's not; because his action wasn't the crossing of a line to come towards me. It was the drawing of a line between him and me so he could do what he wanted.

Tracey Veroni has drawn a similar line, between herself and the women who work for porn mags or in the Pageant. Tarts don't have hearts, I realise, because feelings are reserved for women on Tracey's side of the line. Did her father teach her that? And did my suicide attempt shake her faith a bit? I wonder what she'll teach her daughter? If she's around to teach her anything.

Delilah's case is different because he's not drawing the line, he's destroying it, bringing two things closer together.

And finally there's the line that Mum has crossed, from life to death, reuniting me with Teddy, shaking the line between me and Dad.

I look up, thinking I see my father's shadow in the doorway. 'Dad?'

But the house is quiet, sunk into the absolute silence I remember.

I don't want to sort through any more stuff, so I head downstairs, even though I'm a little afraid of being on my own with Dad.

On the stairs the carpet's thick, and my feet make no sound. I have the impression that the house is big, and I am small. I feel like a trespasser, one who risks being shot at.

I pause nevertheless, in the centre of the hallway, surprised to see new curtains, a flower print on a white background. The whole room looks different because of them, like a change from winter to summer.

But the still-bolted back door glares at me as I walk past it, and the old wooden coat hooks loom too large and familiar. I skirt around them, scared of getting close. It's as if they could hook me up, crochet me back into a past I'm trying not to remember.

I walk straight through the empty kitchen into the utility room, looking for Dad.

The sight of the old gong startles me, still there on its hook by the door, as I grab my coat and hurry out into the garden.

Dad will be in his workshop but I don't want to go there, so I wander up to the orchard, gasping when I see the lake. So he finally dug it out! Where there was only swampy ground before, a bit of a dip with no visible water, there's now a big pool, too big to be called a pond. The trees bend elegantly over it as if it's always been there and a couple of birds take off from the surface as I approach. There's a bench by the water's edge, all curly cast-iron with a wooden seat and I sit down on it, smiling at the scene in front of me. I couldn't have imagined this as a child – that the patch of bog we always had to step around to prevent muddy shoes could become this magical space. There are even a few tattered-looking bulrushes.

A gust of wind sends ripples across the glossy surface of the water and I look back at the house where bare trees are reflected in a downstairs window. It's a big place for one man on his own, but I don't think Dad will ever sell it. I try to imagine him in a retirement bungalow and fail. He'd rather be dead, I think, than live anywhere else.

I wonder when the lake was dug out. Can things be changed so easily? Is it only me who remembers the past so vividly, who feels so marked by it?

I'll never talk to Dad about my childhood now, I know. We'd be bound to disagree, and what's the point?

At my feet are a few pieces of broken red roof-tile. I pick them up and throw them into the lake.

In a little while Dad comes walking up the field. He waves when he sees me and when he gets within speaking distance he says, 'Sorry you've been waiting; I thought it might take you a long time.'

'It's okay,' I say, 'I was looking at the lake. It's fantastic.'

'Yes,' says Dad and he looks at it too. 'We've had plenty of moorhens; it'd be nice to get a couple of swans on it.' We've run out of words again, so we both stare at the water. The wind blows and the seconds tick by.

I fiddle with my coat buttons. 'Teddy'll be here soon to pick me up.'

'Yes,' Dad says. 'Would you like a cup of tea, while you're waiting?' Then he adds, 'Or a glass of sherry perhaps?'

He smiles, and I find myself smiling back, the offer of the sherry and the smile somehow putting me on a more equal footing with him, no longer the child.

'Okay, sherry,' I say. 'Thanks.'

'We could have it out here if you like.'

'Yes, that'd be nice.'

'Right. Stay there!'

He wheels round and marches off, like he's starting some sort of military manoeuvre. I think how strange and pleasant it is, having my Dad smile and wait on me. He comes back with two small glasses of sherry and hands one to me.

'Rule Britannia!' he says, and I almost choke, my mind springing back with '*Up yours, you suckers! You'll . . .*'

But I don't say anything, just watch him holding the fragile stalk of the glass in his big dirty hand. His little finger is in the air. Funny, he didn't toast Thatcher like he used to. But even he must realise she's on her way out.

Teddy's car pulls up then. Teddy smiles when he sees us standing together, and Dad calls, 'Hello! Would you like a glass of sherry?'

'No, thanks,' Teddy says, 'Alcohol isn't part of the yogi lifestyle.'

Dad ignores this and turns to me. 'Did you find anything you wanted to keep?'

'No. I don't want anything,' I say. 'Thanks.'

We walk to Teddy's car. 'Well, bye then.'

'Bye,' says Dad. He inclines his head, just ever so slightly, and I kiss his leathery cheek.

Author's Note

I am deeply thankful to my husband, Chris Dunscombe, who supported and encouraged me throughout the process of writing this book.

I would also like to thank the following people for reading and commenting at various stages: Nic Smith, Nancy Swing, Victoria Rothwell and Damien Noll.

Thanks also to Ann Alexander, Ann Kelley and Maurice Smelt in Cornwall for a timely injection of enthusiasm; Elizabeth Woodgate, former reader in residence in Hampshire, for putting me in touch with a whole new world; Caroline Pilbeam, operational manager at St Richards hospital in Chichester, and Anna Dunscombe for medical information; Guy Tillyard for doing his best; the Arvon Foundation and all the writers and tutors I met at Moniack Mhor and Totleigh Barton, but especially Edward Hower and Andrew Greig.

Thanks to Rose Atfield, Tim Crook and Richard Shannon too for support and encouragement way back when; to Karen Lewis for always holding such a high opinion of me; to Lumineuse for so much fun when the going was tough; to Sarah Ream at Polygon for her guidance and to the Dundee City of Discovery Campaign.